The Lost Treasure

The Paladin Princess Series Book 3

Also by Samaire Wynne:

Mad World: EPIDEMIC

Mad World: SANCTUARY

Mad World: DESPERATION

ROMANOV

The Paladin Princess series:

#1: The Pirates of Moonlit Bay

#2: The Pirate Queen

#3: The Lost Treasure

#4: The Pirate Prince (September 2019)

#5: The Death of the Queen (Fall 2020)

#6: The Fountain of Youth (Fall 2020)

#7: Magellan's Tears (Fall 2020)

The Lost Treasure

The Paladin Princess Series Book 3

Samaire Wynne

Black Raven Books

This is a work of fiction. All of the geography, characters, organizations, and events portrayed in this novel are either products of the author's imagination or are used fictitiously.

Black Raven Books

ISBN-13: 9781948594141

First Edition: August 2019

10 9 8 7 6 5 4 3 2 1

Dedicated to the people who recognize the magic that surrounds us.

The Lost Treasure

Chapter One
Blood in the Water

"CHARLOTTE!" My head whipped around at the frantic cry. I looked up, and Tam was calling from the crow's nest, his arm pointing like an arrow down off the starboard bow.

I raced over and leaned across the railing. Then I saw it.

The sea was red: red with blood.

We were in about three or four fathoms of water, off the coast of western Alkebulan, just returning from our journey to the northlands to visit Swerighe and allow Caroline to retrieve her daughter Greta, and then to the east to drop off Jim, Tupu and her baby boy.

Tupu had been eager to see her family after giving birth, and Jim had insisted on accompanying them, having grown quite attached to Tupu in the last year.

According to custom, the baby's naming ceremony had to occur on the third full moon, and in her village with the whole family in attendance, so the babe still didn't have a name when we got there. Tupu wasn't revealing anything; it was bad luck she said.

I wasn't sure what had happened, and he wasn't offering any explanations, but a week after we left them there near Tupu's village on the outskirts of Tambibo, Jim had returned alone. Alone and tight lipped.

I'd asked him if Tupu and the baby were all right, and all he would do was nod.

When I asked him if he was all right, all he would do is shrug.

The entire journey east and then north had taken months, during which we'd all explored the different way of being bored on a pirate ship. At least we'd been able to release the baby kraken we'd been hosting in the large washtub. Kym had been delighted with her new pet, but after he got so big he kept flopping over the sides of the tub, even Kym had to admit it was cruel to keep the baby sea monster in such confined quarters.

We'd parted with the little thing, if you could call a growing baby kraken the size of a small cow "little," and had placed him in the far northern waters of the Mare Internum. He'd swum away quickly, seemingly eager to explore his new surroundings, and Kym had shed a few happy tears while waving goodbye. She hadn't spotted Caroline's eyeroll behind her, thank goodness.

Then we'd sailed north, to Swerighe.

Caroline had agonized over whether to stay behind in our homeland, and we'd stayed there a week, as I visited with my parents and Caroline weighed what she wanted to do. In the end, she had come back on board, bringing seven-year-old Greta with her. I had been relieved and overjoyed.

I'd held it together until I was alone in my captain's cabin, where I'd burst into tears of relief and happiness that they'd decided to stay with the ship. Mother and Father had been understanding, and relieved to see I was fine. They said they knew I would be okay the hour they heard I'd been kidnapped: They'd actually felt bad for the Alkebulan pirates, they told me, laughing. They knew how determined and resourceful I could be.

Yeah, right, Mom. Okay. I remember rolling my eyes internally while smiling at them.

Oh, brother. The things people tell themselves to avoid guilt. I shook my head, remembering. Scarcely a year had passed, but I was a different person now than I'd been then: more resilient, less naïve and a whole lot tougher.

Now, I stood here, leaning over the railing and staring at the dark stain of blood welling up from the body floating in the water, the land in the distance. It was still dark, but there was no mistaking the sight.

The body was dark, with long, black hair undulating in the water, fanning out from the head, which was face down. The arms were submerged, but we could see the tail, at least twice the length of the body, greenish-black in color, the scales still winking with the iridescent rainbow hue distinctive to the sirens that dwelt in the Mare Internum. This particular specimen was about ten feet long: clearly an adult, and clearly dead. The blood fanning out from her circled her body at a distance of at least eight feet all around, making for a macabre undulating circle of death.

"Fish her out, mates," Tam called out from the rigging six feet away, then dropped down to the deck and approached me.

"This is the third one in as many days," I said, turning to him. "What do you think's causing this?"

"Same thing as the other ones, I'd guess." He leaned over for another look at the body. "Belly ripped open by predators shortly after her death from poisoning." His voice was grim, as grim as I'd ever heard him. And we'd buried his brother last month.

"Drop anchor here," I directed. "We've got to stick around for a bit while Khepri investigates." I gestured to another sailor to fetch the healer from below.

Everyone jumped to obey me, and I smiled at how fast they responded.

The siren was being hoisted up out of the water, and swung, dripping, as the lift-arm rigging brought her in, over the deck.

"Easy there, now," Tam cautioned the sailors. "Don't damage the body. We've got to keep it intact so we can examine it." He turned to me. "This is starting to really rattle the crew," he said quietly, out the corner of his mouth, for my ears only. "I hope Khepri can find a new clue from this one. I don't appreciate whatever is doing this to sirens in my waters, it's predatory and giving me the creeps."

The crane was lowered and released, and the siren dropped heavily to the deck inside the net we'd used to fish her out of the sea.

He spat a wad of chewing tobacco over the railing and into the water. "Not that I have any love for these creatures, but what happens when it runs out of sirens to kill? What's next? The mermaids?"

"If it is some 'thing' that is doing this, I don't think they'd stand a chance with the mermaids," I mumbled. "They'd slice it to bits before it got the chance to do them any harm." I remembered the sharp spears the mermaids hunted with, and the sharp spines running along their tail fins, something we hadn't noticed right away.

"And how is a siren any less deadly than a mermaid, I ask you? Wicked sharp teeth and claws that can skin a fish in seconds," Tam nudged the toe of his boot against the siren's arm. Her fingers were pushed against the deck and fanned out, each ending in a razor-sharp claw.

I looked closer.

The claws on her fingertips were about three inches long, and the ends wicked sharp.

"They can normally retract the things, but here it's clear she was fighting or clawing something to the very end," Tam said.

Khepri rushed up then. She tightened the belt on her cloak against the chill morning air and bent to examine the corpse.

I looked closer. A chill ran through my body as I looked at the gaping wound in her belly, her internal organs splayed out grotesquely on the deck. Remnants of flesh were embedded in her claws, strands of stringy tissue trailing from her fingers, pale remnants of the battle she had fought and lost.

The gashes on her torso bore the same distinctive tissue.

Could she have ripped open her own belly?

Khepri was wrapping up the body and directing the sailors to bring it to the makeshift exam table she'd rigged up belowdecks. Khepri followed as they carried the dead siren away.

I turned back to our discussion.

"The part I don't understand is the poison. How would you easily poison three sirens in an inland sea?" I said.

Tam didn't hesitate. "Poison the water."

"But there are ten thousand animals in this sea – at least – and none of them have been affected."

"That we know of."

"Maybe the sirens are especially susceptible to this particular toxin."

"I don't know, but I think we'll head for the islands, and ask the mermaids. I wonder if they even know what's been happening."

"They may not. The first two bodies were found in the eastern reaches of the sea, near Tambibo."

"I actually thought it was some contagion originating near Moonlit Bay."

"Well, we're nowhere near there now, so I think we need to look elsewhere for answers."

"I'll be very interested to know if Khepri finds any new information," he looked toward the door they'd disappeared through.

"Let's give her time to examine the corpse. This one looked a lot fresher than the others. I think we caught it within an hour of her death."

"Clearly."

I inhaled deeply, breathing in the salty sea air.

Tam remained beside me.

I closed my eyes for a minute, holding on to the ship railing, my mind receding from the week's troubled findings of corpses floating in waters. I felt myself relaxing, the stress melting out of me.

I envisioned tall trees swaying in the breeze and fields of flowers splashing bright colors on hillsides. I had enjoyed our stop back home more than I'd let on. The land of my birth was green and beautiful, and I had missed its fair lands. I took another deep breath, letting it out slowly.

"Charlotte." Tam's quiet voice brought me back to the present.

I kept my eyes shut, murmuring, "What?"

"Would you like some hot tea?"

I opened my eyes. Tam was facing away from me, looking out to sea.

Had I heard wrong?

"What did you say?"

He turned back to me, smiling. "I said, 'would you look at that sea?' It's weirdly glassy this morning."

Huh?

He peered closer at me. "You feeling all right, Captain?"

"Yes, yes, I'm fine." I looked out onto the water. The sun had risen high enough that the sea could be viewed in the bright sunlight.

He was right. The water looked funny.

"Why is it so calm and glassy? It almost looks thick, almost viscous, like oil." I shaded the side of my face, where the sun was shining bright, and scanned the seas. It was odd. One or two pockets of calm water were normal at sea, but I was looking out on a heavy, unmoving flat expanse so alien to these parts that it was jarring.

"I came out so fast I didn't bring my brass sight," I said.

"I'll get it," Tam turned and disappeared into the cabins.

He was back in a minute and handed the old brass tube to me. I opened it and surveyed the open water.

Strange.

"Charlotte." Kym walked up to me. "Good morning." She looked down on the deck, still bloody and strewn with the scraps of guts that had fallen from the wound on the dead siren. "Ugh, gross."

A sailor came up with a mop just then, set a bucket of water down and began to scrub the deck clean.

We walked away a half dozen feet.

Kym turned to me. "Another siren?"

I nodded.

A worried look settled on her young face.

Just then, Greta ran up, a riot of soft light-brown curls bouncing on her head, and I glanced at her. She looked very much like Caroline, except she had a dreamy faraway look in her eyes most of the time. She spent much of her time on deck daydreaming. Her mother was convinced she would become an artist, or a poet.

"Hello everyone," said Greta. "Fine morning, don't you think?"

Kym gestured over at the blood on the deck the sailor was scrubbing. Greta gasped and turned white.

"Another siren death," Kym whispered in her ear.

Greta's eyes gazed, mesmerized, at the red liquid swirling in the soapy water as the sailor worked.

I raised my eyebrows, glancing at Kym, who met my look with one of her own. Christianne joined our group and quickly took things in. I dipped my head in the direction of the door to belowdecks, nodding at Greta. Christianne smiled grimly.

"Come on, Greta, let's go get some breakfast." She gently guided the younger girl away.

I took a deep breath.

"Charlotte!" Khepri was walking quickly toward us. I turned to her, hoping she had some news. "That body, it's like the others but it's the freshest we've found. I need a sample of the seawater from this location."

I gestured to one of the sailors, who lowered a bucket to collect the sample.

"I'll have some results for you soon, Charlotte," Khepri said.

"I'll help you," said Kym.

"I wonder if the siren clawed out her own belly; it looked like it, from what I could see," I said.

"I don't think you're wrong, actually," Khepri nodded. "What I want to find out is the nature of the poison: Is it in the water, or was it something they ate? This specimen will help me learn more than the others, since it's so fresh."

Kym walked up, the bucket of seawater in her hands, and they both made their way back belowdecks.

"Shall we pull anchor, Cap'n?" a sailor asked.

"No, let's just hold tight here for a few hours. She may need more information on the area." I turned to go back to my cabin.

As I entered, I could see subtle movement on the floor. A rock, about seven inches in diameter, was moving slowly and burrowing its way under a blanket.

"Chowder, are you stuck?" I leaned down and picked up the rock demon and sat down on the edge of the bunk, idly petting its rocky top. We'd found the little creature inside the volcano on the second island we'd visited last fall. It had quickly bonded to us, and I'd grown quite fond of it. *I couldn't very well leave it behind, could I?*

We'd brought a number of creatures away from those islands after our visit, and Chowder was the last one left. It hadn't needed much care, and seemed to be happiest, so, unlike the Kraken baby, and the centaur boy who'd come along for a short jaunt, we'd kept Chowder on board.

Chowder was purring.

"What do you think is killing the sirens?" I asked the drowsy creature.

I got no response.

"If the water has poison in it, where do you think it came from? And how can we remove it?"

The purring got slower, then stopped.

"I guess naps are more important to you," I chuckled, then carefully lowered the rock demon onto the blanket nest, and covered it with a flap of the soft material.

I decided to go visit Khepri; I didn't want to wait on her report. *Curiosity is a virtue, right?*

I closed the door quietly behind me, and walked down the short corridor and down the steps to the hold.

I found Khepri and Kym with gauze masks and seaweed gloves, examining the corpse closely.

"Found anything?" I asked.

"Mmmmm," Khepri murmured.

"Charlotte," whispered Kym. "Look at this." She motioned to a waxed wooden tray with a specimen lying in it. I peered inside. A small organ lay there.

I looked closer.

"Is it supposed to be that color?" I sniffed and smelled an ammonia odor. I straightened up and looked at Khepri. She was bent over the midsection of the body.

She lifted out a second organ, and Kym brought the tray over. Khepri plopped it beside the first organ and straightened.

I waited. I'd learned long ago not to rush the healer.

"Well, that's her liver and her heart." She gestured at the first organ. "This liver smells of ammonia and looks light grey because it has stopped functioning entirely and ... " she reached forward with her knife and slit the organ open, "... see here," she gestured at a dark line, "... and here, these are blood vessels that constricted completely in the body's desperate attempt to protect the organ from further poisoning. Unfortunately, the lack of blood served to kill the organ completely, which is why it's grey, and death followed very quickly." She straightened and arched her back.

"The smell you detect is the poison itself. I wasn't sure with the others, but this corpse was so fresh I have no doubt. The poison reacted with the body's chemistry, and the body's defenses, in a desperate attempt to reject it, produced the ammonia smell." She nodded to Kym, who produced a small glass vial of oily yellow liquid. "The poison was in the water. It entered the body through the gills."

She lifted the side of the body, exposing the siren's gills. They looked shriveled and blackened, and dripped with the yellow residue.

"See, the gills not only act to remove oxygen from the water so the siren can breathe, they also serve as the body's first filter against any foreign contagion." Khepri gestured at my chest. "Like our own lungs." She looked back down at the corpse. "The poison quickly killed the siren, in particular, because sirens have a particularly sensitive liver. They must live in clean water or they quickly die out."

She raised her eyes to meet mine. "Should the oceans ever become badly polluted, these sirens will be the first to go extinct."

I frowned.

"So, the yellow poison was in the water?" I asked.

"Yes. It's in the water. Where, I am not sure. I didn't detect much of anything in the water sample I drew near Moonlit Bay, but the one from this morning showed traces of it." She led the way to another table. Glass bottles were held over flames, and the contents of vials bubbled vigorously. Khepri pointed to a sheet of papyrus.

"See this?"

I looked closer at the paper.

A wet stain darkened the bottom, and had slowly leached up the paper. The dark splotch showed a subtle rainbow hue as it went up.

"Look here at this," Khepri pointed at a spot maybe a hand's length up the thick parchment. I could see slight shininess.

"It looks oily, and yellow, a little."

"Smell it," she said.

I took a whiff. The same ammonia scent reached my nostrils.

"This is the seawater creeping up the papyrus?" I asked.

Khepri nodded.

Without a word I turned and hurried out.

Chapter Two

Poisoned Waters

"Tam, Jim, gather some sailors. We've got to do a dive." I gestured over at the anchor. "Hold that steady, men."

"What's up, Cap'n?" Tam asked.

"We're in about three and a half fathoms of water. I need to investigate what's down there." I walked to the railing, gripped the wood and leaned over.

The water was usually crystal clear, but seemed a bit cloudy today.

Jim walked up to us. "Charlotte, do you want me to dive and search? I heard about the siren."

"Yes, if you could. We're looking for anything out of the ordinary, really. Anything out of place," I said.

"Gotcha, boss. I'll just ..." Jim did a kind of wriggle-shudder and transformed into his true form, the magnificent Djinn.

He went from a smidgen over six feet tall, with dark tan skin and mildly well-muscled, to nearly ten feet tall, very muscled, and with green-blue-purple hued skin. It was hard to describe. But the effect was powerful.

I smiled.

He'd conjured up a swimming outfit that was inspired. What looked like dark blue iridescent mermaid scales covered him from knee to ribs, and flexed with him as he moved to the railing.

I walked closer to him and whispered, "Are you ever going to tell me what happened with you and Tupu?"

The Djinn turned and gave me the most inscrutable look I've ever seen, and, without a word, launched himself over the side and plunged head-first into the water.

We all leaned out and watched him swim down to the bottom. Normally we would have been able to track his every move in the ordinarily crystal-clear waters of the Mare Internum, but today, as he got lower and lower, his outline became fuzzier, until he was just a dark splotch moving along the lighter sandy bottom.

"That is weird," murmured Tam beside me.

"I am really worried about this. It's getting worse," I whispered.

The Djinn's movements carried him farther from the ship. After an hour, I retreated to the galley in search of sustenance, returning shortly afterward with some jerky. I munched on it and looked out at the sunny skies and low swells of water.

The sea was still glassy and still, the slight rippling of the water its only movement.

As we watched and waited for the Djinn's return, Chowder rolled up to me and nudged my boot. I looked down. The rock demon had its mouth open. A small pink tongue lolled out the side.

"Hungry, too?" I asked, smiling.

Caroline walked up and smiled. "I've got some sand over in a tray," she said, bending down and picking Chowder up. The rock demon shivered in delighted anticipation. Caroline smiled at me, "I'll just take him to his food."

I watched them as they walked, thinking on my little pet. Nobody had ever encountered a rock demon before, and there were no texts mentioning any such creature in either Alkebulan or Swerighe, Khepri had assured me.

The centaurs had thought him a remnant from the volcano's magical portals, but Kym'd had the most tantalizing suggestion: that Chowder had come through one of the portals in the mountain that led to the alien planet we'd visited.

We hadn't seen any rock demons while we were there, but Earth wasn't the only place connected to that world: Races from other planets had visited there, as well. Kym surmised he'd come from one of them, and had either been left behind, or been the last survivor. Wherever he'd come from, he had found the perfect hiding place in the rocky cavern beneath the volcano where we'd found him.

That planet we'd visited had not been exactly friendly to us. Between the ravenous hedge maze and the other poisonous plants, and the transplanted life forms that had retreated underground and had been desperate enough to rationalize cannibalism, we'd been happy to eventually leave that world and return home.

My thoughts drifted to the magic tome we'd won and returned with. *The Book of Mysteries.* I'd kept it under lock and key, safely in the hold, and Khepri had started to decipher it. The first thing she had to do was decipher what language it was written in. We'd consulted with scholars when we visited Swerighe, and their insights had helped us progress far more quickly.

And Khepri's knowledge had progressed as well. Strangely. Wonderfully. It was almost as if the book was teaching her, whenever she spent time with it.

And it glowed.

The Book of Mysteries was priceless, and we guarded it, and we kept it a secret, which was important.

Not even the sailors on our ship knew it was there.

You can keep something safe if no one knows it exists.

I walked over to the bow and peered over the edge. The Djinn was no longer in sight. *Hmmm.*

Khepri suddenly popped open the door and ran up. "Charlotte? CHARLOTTE!"

"What's up?"

"Has anyone gone in the water? Just now?"

"Yeah, Jim went down to search for anything odd, he's in Djinn form."

"Get him back. GET HIM BACK! NOW!"

My heart started to race.

I saw Tam halfway up to the crow's nest.

"TAM!" I called. "Can you see him?"

He hurried the rest of the way up and started scanning the seas.

I swung around on Khepri. "What did you find?"

Her face had blanched white.

"The poison is caustic. It'll burn his skin. The siren's skin was peeled away. I didn't realize it until Kym pointed it out." She paused to breathe.

"What?" I said.

"I was examining the corpse, and Kym was helping me." I nodded and she continued. "The skin is all burnt off. Kym pointed it out: You can see the remnants of the outer skin in between the toes. The ocean water is full of this stuff over here. I'm hoping sirens are more delicate and easily hurt than Djinns ... but ... he could be in real danger."

I thought for a minute.

"What about the mantas?"

"Oh. OH! I forgot about them. We need to check on them right away. They have thick skins, but they could be in real danger." Khepri looked sick to her stomach.

19

I raced to the railing, looking down into the water.

"Check the mantas!" I called out.

Khepri stepped beside me.

"Is there anything we can do to go in the water to check on them?" I asked.

"I could whip up a salve, but. ..." She hesitated.

"Do it."

Khepri turned and rushed back belowdecks.

"Hey!"

I turned around.

The Djinn had reappeared. His head popped out of the water, and he called out again.

"Hey, I found something," the green-purple figure lifted his hand out of the water.

"I'll get it," said a sailor, extending a net.

"Need a bucket," called the Djinn.

"Oh." The sailor withdrew the net. Someone threw a bucket out into the water, a rope attached to it.

The Djinn plopped something into the bucket, and it was hauled up.

"Hey," I called. "How are you doing?"

"I'm okay, I guess," he answered. "It stings a bit, but I'll live."

"Can you check on the mantas?"

He gave me a thumbs up and dove down again.

I followed the dark figure through the strangely murky water as he swam out to the giant manta rays that were tethered to the front of the ship. They hung in the water mid-depth, idle.

I waited.

And waited.

I saw the dark figure moving to each of the large creatures, five in all. Their wingspan was close to fifty feet, and we tried to baby them when we could, feeding them fresh fish and checking them periodically to be sure they were healthy and uninjured.

It had been less than a week since we had examined them.

I straightened from the position I'd slowly slipped into: curled over the railing and half hanging out over the water. He was coming up.

The Djinn surfaced and slowly rose into the air, reaching me in a few seconds.

"We need to talk in private," he said quietly, looking at me unblinkingly.

I nodded and turned, leading the way to my cabin.

"The manta rays will be okay, but they have burns on them," Jim transformed into his human form to better fit in my cabin, and sat perched on the cushion bench under the porthole.

"Do they need a rest?" I asked.

"They need to get out of these waters immediately, is what they need. I suggest hastening to the islands for the mermaid's pearls."

The last time we'd visited the mermaid's lagoon, on the coast of the southern island in the Mare Internum, they had given us some pearls as a gift. I'd thought at the time they were just pretty trinkets, but they were a medicine.

Khepri had crushed the pearls, with instructions from the mermaids, after we'd returned from the quest for *The Book of Mysteries*, and the resulting powder, when mixed with the gel found only in their lagoon, had provided a rapid cure for all skin ailments.

It had cured a bad burn in less than an hour.

But not just any pearl would do: the oysters the mermaids had harvested the pearls from were found only in the grotto adjoining their lagoon. And the gel was gathered off the froth from the magic sea cucumber species, so far found only in their lagoon. We'd been on the lookout. Nowhere else.

"We'll head there immediately." I rose and opened the door, motioning for the sailor who always stood guard in that hallway to fetch Tam, the unofficial helmsman of our ship, *Pride of the Sea*.

Tam was there in a minute.

"Make rapid course for the islands." I glanced back at Jim. "They can fly?" He nodded.

"All speed," I instructed Tam. He nodded and left to make preparations and ensure my orders were carried out.

"Tell me exactly," I closed the door and sat back down, "what were the issues you found with the manta rays?"

"They had visible burns on their gills, on the edges and reaching maybe a meter in. The gills suck in seawater at a rapid pace, the poison in the water would have a much more acute affect in these areas. I also saw mild burns on the rest of their bodies. But I think the main system affected is their gills. So far."

I nodded.

"We don't know if the poison could reach their other organs. The siren's liver, for example, which no doubt was working double time to cleanse their bodies of the toxin."

I sat back.

Jim lifted the bucket he'd brought in, and showed me what was within.

"Coins?" I asked, peering in. I was astounded.

We'd found buried and spilled treasure both on shore and in the coves we'd passed. None of it had been leaching poison. I lowered my head and sniffed delicately. Rearing back, I wrinkled my nose. "Ugh."

"Yeah. Ugh is right," Jim agreed. "Look what picking it up did to my hands."

He lowered the bucket to the floor and turned his palms up.

His skin was red, and angry raised ridges blazed a deeper red.

"And they looked worse when I was in my djinn form." He looked at his hands, fingering the burns delicately. "Transforming seemed to have healed them some."

I offered him a jar from my table. "Khepri's special salve, for your hands."

He took the jar and dug out a glob of the stuff. "Thanks," he said, rubbing the balm on the burns liberally. "It feels better already."

"It's not as powerful as the mermaid's unguent, but it'll help until we can get there. In fact, I should stock some onboard."

"Mmmm," Jim murmured, and I could see the redness fading a bit.

"Do you have burns anywhere else?" I asked.

"No, the water itself burned my skin when I was down there, like a bad sunburn, but transforming healed it." He smiled.

"Good. Now, the question in my mind is: How did these coins get here, and Why are they poisoning the water?"

24

Chapter Three
Mermaid Answers
and
Island Legends

"Land ahoy!" the sailor called out from the crow's nest.

I had just finished speaking with Tam on the status of the mantas, and the sun was still new in the sky. Khepri and Christianne had tested the ocean spray hitting the side of the ship, and had found it to be contaminated. And the water's toxicity was growing higher as we sailed west.

This was not good.

Within a half hour, we were docked inside the southern island's atoll and were rowing to shore. Mermaids and centaurs waved at us cheerily, the former from their lagoon on the northern edge, the latter from the beach. I was glad to hop into the shallow water and splash ashore.

"Iilcendorr, my friend," I embraced the black centaur, and got a hearty pat on the back from him as he laughed in delight.

"What brings you to our shores? Is anything amiss?" He must have caught the serious look on my face.

"Yes, and we need to talk. Can we convene a gathering?" I looked around the island shore. "You've made enormous progress, I see."

"Yes, we're extremely busy, even now. The crops planted this spring are growing well, the native trees are yielding fruit, and our friendship with the mermaids has grown." Iilcendorr glanced over toward the lagoon, then back to me. "Of course, we ruffled a few feathers initially, but soon smoothed them out. We'd neglected to run some of our plans by the mermaids, but we do now, and don't make a move on building or planting unless we have their approval." He smiled heartily.

I knew how important diplomacy was, and I was glad to hear they had ironed things out with the fierce mermaid tribe. We did not need those two groups at odds with one another.

"Charlotte, we're going to go visit the mermaids," Kym said beside me. Christianne smiled eagerly and took Greta's hand, leading the way.

"Okay, I'll be along shortly."

Later that morning, I sat in a circle with the troupe, the centaurs, and the mermaids. The lagoon's waters lapped gently at the shore, creating a calming rhythm in the background.

Earlier, we'd shown the bodies of the dead sirens to both groups, and Khepri had filled them in about her theory.

The mermaids had taken possession of the siren bodies, with the intention, they said, of affording their close cousins a proper ocean burial. I felt for them, their eyes downcast as they departed with the lifeless bodies. My mind was on the bigger picture, though, and what the poison in the ocean waters meant for the rest of the creatures in that ecosystem. There were literally millions of lives at stake.

"We need to get to the bottom of where this poison is originating, and try to remove the source," I said firmly.

"We can supply the tincture you need, of course, Princess," said one of the mermaids who had learned our language, "and we are extremely worried about the poison. We found the bodies of several sirens close to the island, ourselves, last week, and again two days ago. And the angelfish have been affected, too." She held up a banana leaf with a large, very dead, fish laid out upon it. The fish, naturally striped in silver and black, was deeply tinged with red, a sign of internal bleeding.

Khepri rose to examine the body more closely. She conferred in a whisper with the mermaid, then gently took the banana leaf from her and moved off to the side to examine it more closely.

"These coins were fished out by the djinn; we think they are part of what is poisoning the water." Caroline passed around the bucket with the gold Jim had collected. The centaurs and mermaids examined the contents carefully.

"These coins," said Iilcendorr, carefully sniffing the bucket's contents, "they are made of a very pure gold, and they have been imbued with a serious poison, very likely during smelting." He passed the bucket to the centaur next to him, and it slowly made its way around the circle of people. "I cannot ascertain if this was done maliciously." He looked at me. "Or if they used the poison in smelting but had no idea it would be toxic."

The mermaids all peered into the bucket, and recoiled when they smelled the odor. They whispered among themselves, then glanced back at the bucket of coins. Then the first mermaid came forward.

"We do not know of these coins or the poison; we had thought the sirens had been attacked by some predator, Princess, although what could defeat and slay a siren in this manner, I do not know. Perhaps only a kraken might best a siren."

"I doubt these coins are from the kraken, though."

"No, we do not think so. But ..." She glanced at the other mermaids, then turned back to me. "We have legends of gold that is fabled to be poison to the touch. ... We thought it was just the rantings of an elder, but ..."

I leaned forward. "You have an elder who knows of this gold?"

"Well, sort of. He is a treasured elder who is blind, but has an incredible history. He speaks of a legend his grandmother told him. The story has since been lost to the ages ... he is the only one who remembers that story ..."

"Can we speak to him?" I held my breath, hopeful.

"I will ask," she said.

"What may we gift him to please him?" Caroline asked.

"He requires nothing, I believe. He takes his joy from his great-grandchildren."

"How old are his great-grandchildren?" I asked.

"Very young."

We reconvened later that afternoon, when the sun was beginning to dip below the horizon. I had brought rum to share with everyone, and a tulip encased in molten glass, from Swerighe.

"Look, Charlotte, look!" Kym was breathless.

"Don't point, it's rude."

"I know, I mean, I'm sorry. Oh, you!"

"Don't shove, it's rude."

"He's so old, I can't believe it."

"How long do mermaids live, Mama?"

"Oh, many hundreds of years, Greta."

"Actually," rumbled Jim quietly, "I think it's several thousand years, at the very least."

"Wow."

"I think he's probably ten thousand years old."

"Stop staring."

"Well at least she stopped pointing."

"At least."

Greta began to giggle and couldn't stop. Then Kym got the giggles, and Christianne looked crossly at them both.

"Shhh, stop it. They'll hear."

"I ... can't ... ha ha ha!"

Caroline held Greta's hand and drew her tightly to herself. "Greta, shush!" she whispered.

"I'm trying, Mama."

"Oh my god," Akim said, just running to catch up to us. "That's one elderly merman!"

Kym laughed even louder.

"Shhhh!"

Oh, my god.

"Everyone?" I turned toward my group and put on my most serious face. "This elder has news on what is killing the sirens and poisoning the ocean. We've all seen the evidence of what this danger can do. We all know what it WILL do if left unchecked." I stared at them silently for a moment. "I suggest we have a little decorum. Yes, he's old. That means he's tough and to be reckoned with. It means he has lived through some incredible things, and has a lot of wisdom to impart. Have a little respect." I turned back to walk again.

"Sorry, Charlotte."

"Sorry."

"I'm sorry, Princess Charlotte."

Sigh

We walked on.

The centaurs had lit torches along the beach in the twilight. Behind the island's mountains the sun was ablaze, and the entire sky was a riot of colors. Orange mixed with red and yellow, before melting into blues, which were slowly becoming darker and transforming into purples. The stars were beginning to appear, promising to speckle the night sky in a vivid show of lights.

Akim raced ahead with Kym, Greta and Christianne, while Caroline, Khepri, Jim, Tam, and I walked on more slowly. I watched the youngsters run ahead with exuberance, and fleetingly missed the excitement of youth. Then Tam lightly bumped against me as he stepped through the sand.

"Sorry, Princess."

I smiled.

Tam had caught my eye in the last month. Caroline told me he'd been taking on extra duties just to put himself near me, but I didn't believe her, until I caught Khepri smiling and ducking her head.

"Is he really?" I had smiled.

Caroline's eyebrows had threatened to disappear up into her hair. "He is, indeed."

I paid more attention for a few weeks and, darned if she wasn't right. He WAS trying to spend more time near me.

Tam stumbled in the sand, catching himself before he fell.

"You okay?" I asked.

"Perfectly okay, never better." Tam said.

We walked on.

The gathering was enormous. Word must have spread about the emergency, because I saw centaurs there I had never before seen – dozens more. And while we normally didn't see more than eight to twelve mermaids together, there were several dozen here, and more idling in the lagoon waters farther out.

I saw the old merman Kym had first spotted. He was surrounded by several mermaids, his granddaughters, I would guess, and half a dozen merchildren frolicked at his feet. He had a broad smile on his face and held an infant merchild in his arms, and he was whispering to the baby and wiggling his fingers at her to make her smile.

Several mermen were in attendance, and I found myself staring. We'd been led to believe that the males of the species were heavily protected, with numerous mermaid guards following them everywhere. The mermaids had told us that the birth of a male was an uncommon occurrence, and was highly celebrated when it happened. The ratio of females to males in the mermaid kingdom was 20:1 and so these creatures were rare and important. And now I could see why.

The mermaids' skin was differing shades of green, with blue and pearly white mixing in here and there. They were very beautiful. But the mermen looked otherworldly: They were pearly gold, their eyes an unearthly green with gold rims, and their tails sported such brilliant gold scales they shone with an inner light. I could see why the mermaids would treasure and guard them, not only were they rare, but they were gloriously beautiful. I would hide them, too; the sheikhs would kill to obtain such a treasure.

We all settled down to a feast, and it was only after satisfying our hunger, and presenting the elder merman with the bottle of rum we had brought, that everyone settled down to hear what the senior stateman had to say.

A large fire had been built on the beach, and a ring of rocks brought in to act as seats for us humans. The ring spanned halfway on sand, and halfway in the foot-deep water of the mermaid lagoon. The centaurs stood on the sand, creating half of the ring around the bonfire, which was nearly at the water's edge. A mermaid swam up to us all, as we sat on rocks in the shallow lagoon.

"Our elder believes the poisoned coins you discovered in the ocean are part of a legend, and he will now tell you the entire tale. You should know, he rarely speaks more than a few words to us, but he felt this was so important that he wished to address you in person." She bowed and withdrew to sit near the old merman.

It was clear the mermaids had told the elder everything we had discussed with them. There was intelligence in his face, and worry, too. His voice was gravelly and deep, and we sat, listening closely, to every word he spoke.

"My grandmother ... was a thousand years old ... when she told me and my sisters this tale, ... and she was deadly serious in the telling. ... It was more ... a warning ... than a story. And I am now going ... to tell it ... to you." He paused.

"This story ... has never been shared ... outside our tribe ... But I sense dangerous things ... are happening ... and now ... it must be told."

He closed his eyes and took a deep breath, and began to speak.

"There is a ... faraway land," he began. "A land full of ... steep, steep mountains ... and ... deadly dangerous creatures." He paused and bent down to kiss the merbaby's forehead, then handed her to her mother next to him.

Then he continued speaking, his voice crackling with age against the backdrop of our reverent silence.

"The dense forest ... growing around ... the tallest mountain ... is said to be home to a multitude ... of dangerous beasts, ... each more terrifying ... than the last."

He took a drink of nectar from the flower his granddaughter offered him. "Thank you, love."

Then he turned back to us and resumed his tale.

"These beasts ... hunger for the flesh ... of travelers ... who enter that forest. The top of the mountain ... is said to be ... fifteen thousand feet high, ... and the path to its peak ... is blocked ... by huge glaciers ... of ice and snow, ... and a river of fire."

He paused.

We held our breath. We needed to hear more.

He began speaking again.

"At the top of the mountain ... is a sanctuary ... watched over by a forgotten ... order of mystics ... skilled in the art of battle ... and devastation." He took a deep breath. "It is fabled that ... in the rear of the sanctuary ... is a passage ... that leads inside the mountain ... and deep into the heart of the Earth. At the end of the passageway ... are catacombs ...

guarded by a beast ... so dreadful ... that it is said minds will go mad ... at the sight of it."

The elder paused.

The fire crackled, startling us, but we did not take our eyes off his wrinkled, wizened old face.

"The door ... to the catacombs ... can only be accessed ... by defeating the beast. Inside the catacombs, ... concealed by a hideous shroud ... and an ancient poison, ... lies the lost treasure ... of El Dorado. ... It is ... El Tesoro De Oro. ...The golden treasure. ... It is fabled ... to be imbued ... with a poison ... that kills ... whatever ... or whomever ... touches it."

The elderly merman fell silent, gasping.

His daughters held him close, rubbing his back and whispering love to him.

Chapter Four

Heading to the New Continent Iq Ameq'el

Wind blasted my face as *Pride of the Sea* plowed swiftly through the waters, thanks to the mantas pulling the ship along. As I sat in the crow's nest with Kym, my eyes sought out the setting sun ahead of us. We had been making great time in our drive to get to the source of the poisoned coins, the continent of Iq Ameq'el. It was west of Alkebulan and southwest of Swerighe, and only one person on board had ever seen it. It was fabled to be wild, utterly wild, and awash with all manner of ferocious beasts and exotic sights.

The old sailor Jack, who had been on board the ship over the course of four owners and three name changes, regaled us in the evenings of his memories of Iq Ameq'el, holding us spellbound.

"T'last time I was thar, I was nobbut a lad, 'bout twenty summers old." He chewed on a blackroot twig and shifted it from one side of his cheek to the other. "T'ship been dock'd offshore 'n' t'Cap'n had us land a skiff on t'far shore. Twelve of us'd land'd on t'beach, but only ten got back off. T'snakes unner t'sand had got t'two men, I swear. T'was sunset an' we'd been land'd only an hour, and t'men were off explorin' t'jungle. Me 'n' three others stay'd wit' t'boat t'guard't. We heard t'men scream. They come runnin' fast'r than anything I ev'r seen. Mos'ly dark by then. T'was a huge ripplin' in t'sand come af'er them men. Runnin' like t'devil'r after t'em. Most made it bac' aboard t'skiff. T'last two were half in, I had t'hold of one of 'em. Dreaded worm pull'd t'man right out'a my hands. T'screams ... t'blood ... Sand was soak'd red. We high tail'd it out o' thar so qui'k I lost m'fav'rite hat." He took off his hat and wiped his eyes with a filthy handkerchief, unable to continue.

Tam patted the man on the back, murmuring to him.

I blinked, looking out to nowhere, lost in thought.

Two days after leaving the southern island, about the point where the Mare Nostrum had given way to the Okeanos Aithiopos, we came across a ghost ship. Listing in the headwaters of the Aethiopian Sea, the ship had been smaller than *Pride of the Sea*, and in very poor shape.

We boarded the vessel, which crumbled under our boots in some places, and discovered no one alive on board. We found three sailors' corpses, deep below in the hold, huddled together at a table, several empty bottles of rum strewn about.

The captain's log was nearby, and the last entry read as follows.

"We have had nothing but bad luck and death since leaving the nightmare land. Half the crew's dead, and all we have to show for it is a bag of gold we took from the monster's room. The men are convinced the gold is cursed; I think it's the ship itself. Since we dropped anchor at that forsaken beach, nothing has been right. We've made good speed these summer months, but it's all for naught. We've been throwing coins overboard as we sail, hoping to appease whatever gods have brought this jinx down upon our ship. A handful here, a handful there, and we had clear sailing until we sighted the far coast of home.

Then the men started dropping dead. Their hands turned black at first, then the black traveled inside, until they were screaming in agony and clawing at their midsections. It was a horror, and only at the end did I figure out it was the coins themselves, not the ship, that had been cursed. I regret ever sailing west. My love to wife and child. I fear I shall never see them again ..."

The diary was held in the clutched hand of a corpse so thoroughly rotted it had turned white in the salt air. The other hand clutched a sack, mostly empty. I extended my scimitar and poked it, and was rewarded with a faint clinking. I poked it harder, and the sack, rotten with age, parted, dropping a dozen gold coins on the floor at the corpse's feet. They shone as brightly as the coins we'd found.

We fled the old ship then, not touching anything. Tam reckoned it had been adrift for years, the gold slowly leaching out its poison into the water.

After that, I locked away the coins we'd found. I didn't want the same thing to happen to our own ship.

"What are you planning, Charlotte?" Christianne asked one night as we gathered in my cabin for conversation. "You aren't trying to retrieve the cursed treasure, are you?"

"I want to find the gold and perhaps discover a way to eliminate the poison from the ocean."

"But we have no idea which path that old ship took, or where the sailors tossed the coins," Khepri said.

"I know, but I want to get to the bottom of this. I have to. What if the poisoning grows worse and the seas are washed of all fish? What if the source of the gold also contains the cure for the poison?"

Caroline, sitting in a corner, did not say a word, but had a deeply troubled look on her face.

"We will be careful, I promise."

By the time we'd been at sea for six weeks, we'd found a dozen more siren corpses floating in the water in a nearly direct line from the Mare Internum to Iq Ameq'el. In a grisly efficiency, we'd used the bloated, decaying corpses as navigation aids, as the mermaids had told us the continent of Iq Ameq'el was huge and we'd needed to pinpoint where the poisoned coins had originated.

We'd found several maps near the old sea captain's corpse, but I was unwilling to bring anything from that cursed ship on board *Pride of the Sea*. It might have been superstition, it might have been real scientific caution. Either way, I needed all the luck we could get for this voyage.

The call from the deck below brought me back to the present.

"Aye, Tam, there's another one!" One of the sailors stationed on the starboard bow was leaning out over the ship railing and pointing.

Several sailors ran over carrying hooked poles to fish the thing out of the water.

I brought the brass sight up and extended it, pointing it down at the water.

There. A dark figure floating face down, hair extended for several feet in all directions.

Huh. That was weird.

Wait. No, that wasn't hair. Well, part of it was hair and part of it was entrails, floating out in a fanned pattern, from the midsection of the corpse.

We'd formed a plan to deal with events such as these. Tam lowered a skiff into the water and jumped in along with several others. Khepri ran up and joined them, her medical bag flapping against her leg.

They used a canvas tarp and pulled the body from the ocean, laying it out in the large landing boat's bottom. Khepri performed her examination right there, taking samples, examining organs, using tools so she wouldn't have to touch the body herself.

Contamination was a real threat when dealing with this poison. We'd taken steps to avoid going into the water at all, if possible. The corpses were doubly dangerous, having been infiltrated with the stuff enough so that it had killed them.

I'd never seen so many dead sirens in my life.

I'd never seen so many sirens in my life, period.

They were elusive creatures at best, staying hidden even while luring young sailors to their watery deaths.

I focused again as movement caught my eye. Khepri was waving at the sailors to toss the corpse back overboard. She's tied a red cloth to its neck, marking it as having been examined and discarded, should the currents bring it back within our range.

That was fast.

It had taken her just under ten minutes to complete her inspection: She was getting faster and more efficient.

The streamlined process wasn't a luxury. Less than ten days into our voyage, we had accumulated no fewer than a dozen fresh siren corpses down in the hold, each dutifully examined by the good healer, and each placed in a sealed hold designed for the preservation of game. Lined with salt and wax, this large locked oak hold had filled up so rapidly we had no place to store any more corpses. Besides, the smell was getting to everyone. Siren corpses rotted quickly in the heat of summer. Khepri and her unofficial assistant, Christianne had taken great care not to let the contaminated matter get tracked into the rest of the ship, and the hold they were stored in was sealed with wax and salt. Still, because the top was unlocked and opened for every fresh find we fished out of the ocean, there was no stopping the stench. It drifted until it encompassed every square foot of *Pride of the Sea*, until it permeated everywhere, even the kitchens, overwhelming the aroma of the food being cooked there. The stink of death was everywhere. It got into the cloth of the sails. It got into our clothes. It was in our hair, for goodness sakes.

It was disgusting.

So, we'd decided not to keep the corpses on board, after all. Following a quick examination, samples taken and placed in stopped vials. Then off the corpses went back into the sea. Khepri's examinations often entailed puncturing the bloated corpses and releasing the gasses that had blown them up and set them afloat on the surface. Without those gases, they sank to the depths of a proverbial watery grave.

I assuaged my guilt at leaving the poisoned things in the water by resolving that I would do everything in my power to find the source of the poisoned coins and the cure to the poison itself.

"Charlotte!"

I glanced down at Tam, who was waving up at me. I swung over the basket's top edge and shimmied down the rope ladder to the deck below.

"Hi there, Princess." Tam grinned easily at me, shading his eyes.

"Oh, is the sun behind me?" I moved to the side so he could see me more easily. "What's up, Tam?"

"Khepri says this one is different."

Oh, dear.

I followed him down to the hold where Khepri was just washing up after her examination.

Christianne was there, fixing a vial of liquid in a metal bracket and turning a flame below it on low. She glanced at me and smiled. The fifteen-year-old was getting to be quite the scientist. With Khepri's help, she'd make a wonderful healer someday soon.

"Charlotte," Khepri turned to me, drying her hands thoroughly on a cloth. "I know we're going as fast as we can, but there's a new urgency."

"What's up?" I asked.

"Well. ..." She glanced at the notebooks she had been making notes in, fingers twitching to write down the notes on today's find. She looked back up at me. "It was nothing new regarding the poison. It was a bit more concentrated than average, but nothing we haven't seen before. But in this case, the siren had not ripped open her midsection during her death throes. Instead, the torso had been ripped open by a shark, I believe. The bite radius matches a mid-sized shark, maybe seven or eight feet long."

My eyebrows rose.

"It looks like just one bite. The shark probably wriggled until the organ fell out. It likely got a taste of the poison that killed the siren, and left the rest of the corpse alone. But it did get that one bite in." She looked at me pointedly.

"So, the poison is starting to move across the food chain. The poison will spread more readily now, and will reach that much further. We must hurry if we are to nip this in the bud."

I swallowed with worry.

"All the marine life in the ocean will be endangered if this poison continues to spread."

Christianne spoke then. "Not just the ocean. Food from the sea accounts for the bulk of the world's food supply. If the sea birds eat toxic fish, they could carry the poison hundreds of miles inland and infect predators far from the seashore."

Khepri nodded. "We could see widespread infection and starvation if this gets out of hand. And it's threatening to."

I shuddered involuntarily.

Caroline poked her head through the doorway just then. "Meal time, Miss. Come and get it!"

After the conversation we'd just had, my stomach roiled at the thought of food. A moment later, though, it rumbled in hunger. I hadn't eaten today, and it was past noon.

Sigh.

"I will do my best to stop this, Khepri." I nodded at the healer and thanked Christianne for her help before departing.

Returning to my quarters, my thoughts turned to the giant manta rays that pulled the ship. *Pride of the Sea* was vitally important to the troupe, and to me. If the five giant mantas, with their fifteen-meter wingspans, did not have food, they wouldn't be able to pull the ship. The winds had never been enough to pull the large ship where it needed to go. If not for the mantas, this seven-week-long journey to the faraway continent of Iq Ameq'el would take five times as long, and that would be with luck on our side.

The mantas not only got the lion's share of their meals from the black skipjacks and bluefin we caught each day and fed to them, they also screened thousands of gallons of seawater through their gills, filtering our plankton and small sea creatures, to augment their rich fish diet.

They would probably be affected sooner than any of us, sooner than the fishing industries on the coasts, sooner than the inland grizzlies in Swerighe that caught ocean-going salmon that migrated up the rivers to inland spawning grounds, sooner than most animals affected by this danger.

I was moody and lost in thought as I speared pieces of fish steaks off my plate that Caroline had prepared, and nibbled them halfheartedly.

"You'll need a full stomach to be able to fight this problem, Miss." She ate on the other side of the room, opposite me. Greta sat next to her, eating daintily from her own plate of fish steaks.

I smiled at her. "You have always been able to read my mind, Carrie."

"It's a requirement of the job, Miss."

Chapter Five
Land Ho!

"Khepri."

The healer looked up from the massive book she was studying. "Do you think you'll be done deciphering that tome soon?" I was very curious. We'd traveled to the ends of the stars to retrieve the thing, and the scholars back in Swerighe had badly wanted to get their hands on it. We'd kept it on board, and Khepri was slowly but surely deciphering it, page by page.

"It's not that it's in a foreign language," she'd told me the day she started, "it's that the material provided needs to be interpreted correctly, or it won't make sense." She leaned over the page and pointed. "For instance, see here? This one took me a week to decipher. It reads, 'plyck the wyry dark green seagrass foynd yn the shallows yn the farthest land during the fyll moon, so they are at theyr most powerfyl, then stew at low fyre yn a pot made of dark faerye-hated ferrym untyl they are boyled down to a gel. Collect thys gel and bottle yt yn a clear glass contayner, and expose to the new moon yn wynter for seven snowy days strayght yntyl yt tyrneth whyte. Only then will yt serve as the perfect healyng yngyent for the lyng rash found when the coygh wyll not qyyt."

I blinked. *Wow.*

"I'm sorry I disturbed you. Carry on. I know you're working hard."

Khepri laughed. "It's just ... it's an adventure. It'll take me years to completely decipher the whole book, but I am working at a steady pace, and I am confident I will finish." She bent down and continued examining the book, pencil and paper in hand, jotting down notes every few minutes.

I sipped my stew, and spooned a chuck of potato into my mouth. It was delicious, a thick broth with vegetables and fish together with herbs.

"Caroline, this is really good!"

"Thank you, Miss. I've been perfecting the recipe."

There was a knock at the door, and Jim poked his head in, looking around.

"Come! Join us! Have a bowl of Carrie's good fish stew!" I beckoned the djinn into the room.

Caroline handed him a steaming bowl, and he settled into a chair.

He inhaled deeply. "Mmmm! Smells wonderful!"

I had been waiting for an opportune moment to question the quiet man, and this seemed just the time.

I waited ten minutes, through idle chatter among friends, until he'd had a chance to eat half of his stew. I put my finished bowl aside, and brought my knees up in my chair, wrapping a blanket around them for comfort.

"So, Jim," I said quietly.

He looked up, chewing.

"You never told us why Tupu didn't come back with you. Is the baby all right?" I asked.

Khepri and Caroline stopped what they were doing and looked up, listening.

Jim shifted in his chair.

"Last I saw, the baby was very well. He has Tupu's eyes."

"Ohhh!" I smiled. Tupu had violet eyes with the most luxurious color.

Jim fell silent.

I waited.

And waited.

Finally, he took a deep breath and said, in a voice that was almost a whisper, "Tupu and I had a fight."

My eye watched him, I tried not to blink. Jim was not to be hurried. I didn't want to pelt him with questions and have him shut down. So I waited.

He remained quiet.

Caroline put her hand on his shoulder and squeezed gently. "Jim, relationships can be very hard. Especially if they are unequal." She took a deep breath, then continued. "My own husband and I argued a lot, after Greta was born. He was very unhappy that I was splitting my attention between him and my newborn. He resented her, and told me so. He grew sullen and began drinking more, making things much harder on us all. Then he was killed suddenly, in a farming accident. It was a very hard time. But listen: I've been through hard relationship times. I think many of us have. We can try to understand what you're going through." She sat back.

Jim stared at her, lost in thought, for a long time. Then tears welled up in his eyes, and he spoke again. "I just miss her so much. I'm not even sure what the argument was about."

He put his head down, then looked up a minute later. "Wait. I remember. She accused me of coddling her, of being too protective of her." He sighed sadly.

I nodded in understanding.

"Jim, Tupu is a fierce warrior. Her expecting and bearing a child doesn't change that one bit. It's a part of her soul. She's a very intense person." I paused, looking at Jim.

"To be honest, you were a bit overprotective when we went for *The Book of Mysteries*," Khepri gave him a sheepish look.

Caroline just raised her eyebrows and pressed her lips together.

"Oh, God, I knew it," Jim sobbed. He shuddered and seem to catch himself.

I handed him a handkerchief and he blew his nose.

He looked up at us, "What can I do to fix this?"

"Jim, I don't think it's something for you to fix. Tupu is intelligent and knows you were just worrying over her because you were developing feelings for her. Hopefully she'll come around." I looked around at the room at large.

Caroline and Khepri looked embarrassed.

Jim finally spoke, "we exchanged angry words. I said things I now regret. Then when it was time for us to return here, I asked her if she was ready, and she just said she was going to stay with her village for a while."

"Oh."

"Her family was not supportive of us being together, if I'm honest." Jim said.

I frowned.

"Her mother did not like me. When she heard us arguing, she stood in the doorway looking judgmental: Her arms were crossed in front of her like this," he raised his arms and folded them across his chest.

"Hmmm."

"Oh, dear."

"Jim," said Khepri, "Mothers can be a real pain in a relationship. And it can be hard for a daughter to go against her mother's wishes." Khepri looked thoughtful.

"Although," said Caroline, "Tupu is very headstrong. If she was being pressured by her mother, your argument may have forced her to side against you, even though deep down she might have not wanted the result that came about."

"I waited an extra day, hoping she'd change her mind," Jim said miserably. "In the end, she just stood there, her mother beside her holding the baby, and Tupu had her arms crossed in front like that, and refused to say a word. She didn't even say goodbye." Jim's eyes had a sad, faraway look in them.

I felt horrible. "You never know, she may wish she had come with you, she may miss you, right this very minute. You never know." I patted his hand.

We continued eating in silence.

Minutes passed.

Then – "Do you think she might have had a change of heart? Do you think I should return and ask?" Jim sounded so hopeful.

"No, sweetheart. Just wait for her move, the ball is in her court," Khepri said.

Caroline nodded in agreement.

Jim and I strolled on deck an hour later, both of us needing fresh air and wanting to check on the progress of the horizon, and we were present when the sailor on watch in the crow's nest called out.

"LAND HO!"

With an ear-to-ear grin, I looked up and saw the sailor's arm and hand outstretched and pointing, unwavering, off the port bow.

"WHOOP!" Jim let out, and instantly transformed into his djinn form, rising up in the air to get a better look at the new land.

Kym ran up, Greta in tow.

"It is Iq Ameq'el? Have we arrived?" Kym jumped up and down, her braids lifting and falling with her. Greta looked at me, wide-eyed.

"Well, I sure hope so, but we've got to confirm." I pointed in the air at the rising djinn. The purple and greenish-blue figure was growing smaller and smaller, until he was hundreds of feet above the ship.

It was a tense moment, everyone on board wanted the voyage to be over. We'd been sailing for nearly eight weeks. The mantas had made the voyage far quicker than it would have been without them, but still, everyone was just slightly on edge. Miles and miles of ocean water, every single day, will do that. We needed a change of pace. We needed something new to do. We needed land.

I shaded my eyes and peered up again at the djinn. He was very high, and seemed to be hovering there. Then he dropped back down to the deck, and approached him.

"Well?"

"I believe we've arrived at Iq Ameq'el, Charlotte. It's a huge expanse of land. Covered with jungle and mountains, but the beach ahead looks very rocky. Recommend we sail south along the coast and look for a better place to drop anchor."

I nodded, this seemed smart. But we had to get closer to the land first. I stepped up to the fo'c'sle and held the railing as I leaned out. Tam was beside me a minute later.

"Turn south to search for a good spot when we get closer, Tam."

"Aye, aye Cap'n" He stood there for a minute longer, both of us watching the land get closer. Trees taller than I'd ever seen grew dense along the coast, right up to the water's edge, with large boulders peppering the shallow waters near the beach.

"Looks like an untouched land," Tam murmured.

"Nearly, I think," I said, spotting a dark figure in the water. I turned and cried out to the helmsman.

The sailor in the crow's nest was calling out as well.

I turned to Tam, "Do you think we should bother?"

"Might be different; might have new information. You never know," he replied.

We slowed the ship and spent an hour examining the siren corpses floating just offshore. While we were fishing the first one out of the water, a second surfaced. Then a third.

I grimaced. Things were coming to a head. We needed to get to the bottom of this.

Two hours later, we'd examined all three siren corpses, taken samples, and had made progress sailing south along the coast of this new land.

Ten miles later, we'd found a cove with a sandy beach.

Jim strode up to us, a new bucket of coins in hand. "These were collected near the bodies we found an hour ago, Charlotte. They're different."

I looked in the bucket he held out with interest.

"WHOA!" I reared my head back in surprise.

"Yeah," Jim said.

Inside the bucket were twenty or thirty more gold coins. But they were different.

"Fresher, I think," said Jim.

The new coins had the same caustic smell as the others we'd collected. But these coins smelled far stronger. And that wasn't the worst thing.

"EWWW," Kym exclaimed. She'd ran up and looked curiously in the bucket Jim held out. His shadow had been falling across the mouth of the bucket, and so the coins inside were temporarily in shadows. So, naturally, Kym had leaned her head farther, almost inside the bucket.

"Is that blood?" she asked.

The coins Jim had collected that day were bleeding.

I shook my head, meeting his eyes.

He understood. As he turned to go down belowdecks, he said over his shoulder, "I'll just take these to Khepri."

Kym looked at me, her nose wrinkling. "Those were gross."

Blood had speckled the coins, and clumps of seaweed. But the blood that had come from the coins themselves had looked ...

"Cursed," whispered Kym in my ear.

"Shhh!" I put my finger to my mouth, swinging my eyes toward the sailors, then back to Kym. I gave her a knowing look.

"I know, I know," she whispered.

"Know what?" asked Greta, walking by.

"Nothing," I said. "Absolutely nothing."

"Nothing at all," nodded Kym, smiling at the child.

I turned to my other side, calling to the helmsman.

"Approach to five fathoms and drop anchor," I ordered. "Prepare the landing party."

Tam got to work.

Christianne walked up, her scimitar sheathed and strapped to her side. "Charlotte, will we be just the six of us? Or will we bring a seventh, since Tupu is absent."

I thought for a moment. Seven had worked really well for us on the quest for *The Book of Mysteries*. Seven was our lucky number, and I didn't want to change now. I shivered momentarily.

"Superstitions getting to you?" Christianne looked at the sailors working to drop anchor. "Yeah, I get you. They've gotten to me, too."

The sailors aboard *Pride of the Sea* were a superstitious lot, and since we'd been finding all the siren corpses, they'd become positively eerie. Several of them had brought cats aboard, declaring them good luck, and able to ward off evil spirits and jinxes.

Not one to invite an unwanted enchantment, I tended to side with them in their beliefs, when it suited me, that is.

I turned to Christianne. "Invite Tam to come along." I glanced over at the handsome sailor, then back to Christianne. In a low voice, I said, "Make sure his scimitar is sharp and in order." I winked at her.

She laughed and went to go talk to our first mate.

I guessed he'd come, and I wasn't wrong.

He left several able sailors in charge.

Caroline left Greta in charge of things, or so she told her.

"My darling, we need someone to guard the lockbox with *The Book of Mysteries* inside. You're the only one I trust to do this," Caroline told the seven-year-old. I'd locked the book in my cabin safe, attached to the wall itself. The key was on a cord around my neck. The spare on a cord around Khepri's neck.

"But Mama, who might come to steal it?"

"You never know, my darling. It could be anyone. Why, just last week Jim had been telling us of djinns who do evil things."

Greta's eyebrows rose.

"You must protect the book."

Chapter Six

The New Land Greets Us

We rowed our small landing craft to the shore, hopped out, and began dragging it up onto the beach. There was seven of us, Tam joining us, a look of relish on his face when he found out.

"Remember what Jack told us," I'd cautioned on the way over.

Sure enough, there was a rumbling in the distance.

I put my hand on the hilt of my scimitar, scanning the beach.

"There!" Tam pointed.

"Ohh, man."

"Back up!"

"Nope, look behind us."

"Oh, hell."

"Grab my hand."

"Lemme at 'em!"

I watched as something under the sand rushed toward us, something big. Then I saw three others, and a fifth behind us, all zeroing in on our location.

"They're coming fast, be ready."

3 ... 2 ... 1 ...

A large snake head reared up out of the sand five feet in front of me.

It must have been about two feet in diameter, and its mouth was open wide, teeth extended, hoping to secure its prey. Me.

I stepped to the side and swung my sword to the side, bringing it down expertly behind the head. Or where I thought the head would be.

"They've got two heads!" Caroline cried.

"Three! This one has three!"

Luckily, the giant sand snakes did not maneuver too quickly. I sideswiped another head, bringing my sword down and cleaving a foot-deep cut in the thing. The head went limp.

Two heads down. One more to go.

The sand snake I'd engaged brought its third head up and snapped at me, moving faster than the other two had.

Surprised, I stumbled backward, nearly losing my footing.

It came forward, hissing.

I caught myself just in time and thrust my scimitar up from the ground, spearing its head. My sword stuck in the creature, and it went limp.

"Lord ..." I mumbled, putting my boot on the thing and yanking my weapon out.

I swung around.

The troupe had dispatched more of the beasts, but Kym was still ...

What is she doing?

Kym was atop the last head of a four-headed giant sand snake, and she was riding the thing as it swung back and forth, trying to toss her off its back. She whooped in delight as the head whipped back and forth.

"Kym! KYM!!" I ran toward the thing.

Kym looked toward me, a wide grin on her face, delighted. "It's like the old days on Lissy!"

"Kym, that is NOT Lissy! That thing is NOT your friend!" cried Khepri.

"KYM GET DOWN OFF THAT THING RIGHT NOW!" I screamed.

She slid off the sand snake in shock, swinging her scimitar into its neck almost as an afterthought, staring at me all the while. "You don't have to scream, Charlotte."

Breathe.

"Okay, yes, I know, and I'm sorry for screaming, but you have to be a little more cautious, Kym." I walked toward her, grouchy.

Kym walked forward, silent and sullen.

I took her hand and sat in the sand. "Listen, we've had this talk before. You've got to take things more seriously, okay? You may be fierce, but we've never seen anything like these snakes before, and we don't know what they're capable of. It could hurt you. Are you listening?"

Kym was not listening.

I fell silent and looked around, checking to make sure everyone was okay.

I'm acting like a mother hen, for God's sake.

"Come on, Kym, let's explore!" I jumped up, laughing. "Everyone snap out of it. I'm weirded out, too."

I cleaned off my scimitar in the sand, and walked over to the edge of the jungle.

Caroline and the others joined me.

The trees were a lighter green that we were used to, and they grew taller, much taller. Palm fronds reached hundreds of feet into the sky, a cloudless azure blue.

"It looks like there's no trail, not even an animal trail," said Tam. "Where do you want to start?"

I took a deep breath.

There had been five of the giant sand snakes, with two to four heads each. The sand was littered with their bodies, and red blood splattered across the beach.

I closed my eyes and listened.

"Do you hear that?" I asked the group at large.

Everyone paused to listen.

"I don't hear anything, Charlotte," Christianne whispered after a moment.

"Exactly," I whispered back.

I took a step into the thick foliage.

Another snake exploded out of the greenery at me, and I fell backward in the sand.

The thing ran over me, scraping me from my boots to my head.

"ARRGGGHHHH!"

"Get it! GET IT!"

"Watch out!

"HOW MANY ARE THERE?"

"GET IT!"

"I got it."

This last was Tam's voice, I could tell. Deeper. A rich, deep voice.

I scrambled to my feet. I'd lost my sword.

Turning around, I search for it in the sand.

"CHARLOTTE!" Christianne screamed.

I whipped around.

Two new sand snakes were attacking her at the same time. There were a total of ... lots ... of heads involved.

"WHERE'S MY SWORD?" I cried out to no one in particular.

Jim reached down at my feet.

"Move, you're standing on it."

Oh.

I stepped to the side, glancing up at the same time.

Khepri, Kym and Caroline were dispatching the two monsters advancing on Christianne.

Jim handed me my scimitar. "Here you go, Charlotte."

I glanced at him. I saw he had an amused look on his face, before he ducked down and ran off to join the fight.

I brushed myself off and jumped after him.

"RAWR!" I cried, swinging my sword down on the nearest sand snake. I swung with such force it nearly took the head clean off. It certainly killed it.

I swung around. Were there any more?

Jim was dispatching one himself, he'd transformed into the large blue-green-purple djinn and was cleaving heads right and left.

Tam and Khepri worked to kill another, two of its heads were limp and dead, and two remained, rearing and hissing at them.

Kym and Christianne had just stabbed another, and were circling it as it floundered in the sand.

"Miss?" Caroline was beside me. "Everything okay?"

I nodded, grinning.

Another giant snake had appeared, and we jumped after it together. This one had the most heads yet: Five of the waving, toothy monster heads lunged at us. We quickly moved to the side, and the snake slowly tracked us, unable to keep up.

I chopped with my scimitar, on one side head; while Caroline took care of the other side.

Five heads were quickly pared down to three.

Then one.

Then it was dead, bloody in the sand.

I panted, my hands on my knees.

"What a workout, huh?" I looked over at Caroline.

She smiled and shook her head. "Those were easy, Miss. The only hard part was that there were so many of them."

"Luckily there's many of us, too."

I stuck my sword in the sand, reaching down to wipe sand across the bloody blade.

"We haven't even gotten a hundred feet in from the water, and this land is already trying to kill us," Tam said, walking up.

"No kidding," Christianne said, joining us along with Kym and Khepri.

"This is actually pretty normal," said Kym, laughing.

I rolled my eyes and grinned.

Tam looked mildly alarmed.

"She's kidding," said Khepri.

"Am not."

"Are too!"

"Not!"

"Kym, you know you're kidding. Giving the new guy a hard time just for fun!" Christianne laughed.

"No, I'm not. Well, yes, I actually am." She skipped away as Tam lunged for her, laughing.

"Okay, people. Let's gather round." I called to everyone. "Listen, this is obviously a bit more hostile than we expected. We're going to need to be on our toes at all times. Eyes peeled. Ready for anything. Got it? There's no telling what else is out there."

Caroline and Khepri were panting.

So was I.

"Let's find a place to make camp," I said.

We hiked into the jungle, thankfully encountering no more giant sand snakes. We walked single file, winding our way through the trees as we went. The ferns and low plants that grew in abundance turned out to be pretty flimsy, and we were able to just stomp them down. I led the way, clearing a path for the others, and after about an hour, I was exhausted.

"Here, let me do it," Tam said quietly, behind me.

Grateful, I fell back and let him break the trail.

It was hard going.

I walked behind him, watching him stomp through the enormous ferns, raising one knee high and then the other to navigate the dense undergrowth.

Caroline walked behind me, then Christianne and Kym, then Khepri, with Jim bringing up the rear.

We hiked several more hours in, Jim taking a turn in front, then the others. Christianne and Kym tried, but they weren't big enough to make much headway alone, so they stomped in front, side-by-side. It actually worked better than one person blazing a trail.

After hiking inland about ten miles, we came to a meadow.

"Thank goodness." Kym dropped to the ground, sweating.

I scanned the tall grass, looking for any threat.

A massive bird squawked noisily overhead, and we watched as it drifted west, its wingspan huge, on toward a massive mountain.

At least I think it's a bird. I had seen no feathers on its leathery wings, and although its long head resembled a bird's beak, its body looked more like a huge version of the small water dragons we'd seen diving for the fish parts dropped in our wake from cooking.

It let out another loud squawk and disappeared into the mountain forest.

"Is that our destination?" I asked.

The mermaids had told us, roughly, where their legends said the poisoned treasure was.

"Since no one seems to have been here, I think either the other crew came to the mountain from a different path, or, it was so long ago that the plants have had a chance to grow back over their path," Khepri said.

"Not that they likely made much of a path," said Caroline.

"Nope," I agreed.

"How do we even know we landed in the right place?" Christianne asked. "Or that this is the mountain we're looking for?"

"We don't," Tam answered.

That was hardly reassuring. Still, the mountain did look immense and seemed to fit the description of the one we were looking for.

I looked around. The edge of the meadow seemed as good a place as any to make camp. Shading my eyes and looking forward, I could see we still had to cross a meadow, which looked like it was several miles across, then get through the dense forest at the foot of the mountain.

Tam looked up at the peak. "It's a steep slope. I hope there's a path."

"You and me both," I replied.

We prepared for night, bedding down and building a fire. Hiking through the virgin jungle had exhausted us all; and we ate a light meal and settled in as soon as night fell.

We could hear various animals screeching and chittering; I thought I could identify some from their calls, but I had no clue what others were. One in particular was especially troubling.

"Miss," Caroline whispered, "do you hear that moaning?"

"Mhmm, I hear it." I shifted in my bedroll as I whispered. "Do you know what it is, Carrie?"

"No, Miss. It sounds like a ghoul."

Oh, god ...

Whatever it was let out another cry, it was a low-pitched shriek, like the grunt of a koala, but louder and more drawn out. It faded into a groaning sound. I shivered, feeling a cold iciness crawl down my back.

Another of the same creatures answered the first, and I closed my eyes and pulled the blanket over my head.

"That thing is freaking me out," a voice said in the darkness.

I whipped the blanket off my face.

Kym was sitting up in her blanket, staring out into the black jungle. The fire flickered, but was low enough that all I could see clearly were her eyes. They were wide and unblinking.

"Sweetheart," Caroline whispered, putting a hand out to touch Kym's arm. "We'll explore more tomorrow, we'll probably see what the animals are. But first you've got to rest and sleep."

Smart Caroline.

"She's right. We all need to get some rest," I whispered. "Feel secure: Jim has taken first watch. We are safe. Try to sleep, everyone." I turned over and shut my eyes, trying to be a good example.

We settled down again. All was quiet. I must have drifted off.

Until.

My mind awoke halfway to a stomping sound nearby.

Then a shriek, and that moaning again. Very nearby.

Then several shrieks.

My eyes opened, and I quickly pulled on my boots and jumped to my feet, grabbing my sword in the same motion.

Tam and Jim were already standing, and both had torches raised high.

Kym was suddenly huge: the chimera bounded to her feet and lowered her head and gave a massive RAWR.

There was a scrambling of hooves and a shriek of surprise, and then whatever had been sneaking up to the campsite was dashing away in panic.

A chimera roaring into your face will do that, to anyone, or anything.

It was going to be a long night.

Chapter Seven

That's a Neat Trick

We slept in the next morning, having lost so much sleep in the middle of the night. Examining the campsite in the light of day, we found footprints from some animal we couldn't identify.

"Looks like a large antelope of some kind."

"It's a cloven hoof?"

"Yes."

"But it's huge!"

"Could there be centaurs here?"

"I don't think so. It doesn't feel like ..."

"Thing came right up to us, sleeping here."

"It may have been after our food."

"Who knows?"

"By the way. Kym?" the little girl turned to me. "Thank you, thank you!" I hugged her. It was hard to express my happiness at having such a friend nearby. She was an incredible asset to our little troupe, and I hoped she never got bored and left. It would be devastating.

It was bad enough to have Tupu gone.

I let her go and smiled, wiping my eyes. "Happy tears!"

"Hey, anyone see my stocking?"

I laughed.

We finished preparing for the climb up the mountain. We had brought makeshift grappling hooks as well as ropes, which we normally packed. I had lost count of the times a rope had come in handy. Just ask a certain centaur youth who fell halfway down a dadgum waterfall.

"I think we will enter the forest there, just at the northern end." I pointed across the meadow. "What do you think, Jim?"

The djinn looked and nodded. "Seems like it's a bit less dense over there, so yeah."

"Miss? Here's the gel you asked for." Caroline handed me the ampule of aloe vera sap, which I tucked into a corner of my pack. It would come in handy for any bug bites I might get. The insects seemed to love me, although the feeling was definitely not mutual.

I scanned the jungle around us. It was already growing warm.

"Everyone ready?" I glanced about, and they all looked back expectedly. "Okay, let's head out."

We crossed the meadow with little trouble – other than a throng of strange, light-green caterpillars that seemed to be everywhere in the tall grass. By the time we'd made it to the other side, dozens of the creatures were stuck to our upper legs.

Khepri brought forth an empty ampule and caught a few inside. She stoppered the glass bottle and looked up at me. "You never know."

I smiled.

Khepri was always looking for new ways to create medicines and treatments for the various conditions that afflicted the crew. Especially since we acquired *The Book of Mysteries* and she'd begun to interpret it.

It was a long process, but I had really good feelings about it.

This morning, Jim led the way, I followed closely behind, then Kym, Christianne, Caroline, Khepri, and Tam at the end. The sailor had taken a protective role in the group, and I wasn't going to tell him otherwise. He'd find out fast enough that we were all fierce warriors, every last one of us.

We were at the tree line.

Jim and I stepped into the forest at the same time.

The forest was as spooky as anything I'd ever encountered. We entered the forest past the clearing, and the sun was bright in the sky, but as soon as we plunged into the thick trees, we encountered an unnatural darkness that could not be explained by the forest cover alone.

A cry pierced the air through the trees *AIIIIGGHHHHRRREEEE!!!*

"What the heck was that?" Christianne whispered, ducking as if something had flown overhead.

"Was that a bird?"

"I don't think so."

Something massive moved through the trees off to our right.

"WHAT WAS THAT?"

"Okay, everyone calm down," I said. "Let's be ready with our swords."

There was a sound of metal against leather. I pulled my scimitar from its scabbard and twirled it in the air.

We walked several paces more through the dark forest.

"Are we sure this is the only way to that durn mountain?"

"This is so spooky."

I heard Kym giggle.

"Kym, are you afraid of anything?"

"No."

More giggling.

Then ...

AIIGHEREHAHAHAHAHAHA!

The troupe were all on my left side and behind me. We kept walking ...

Something grabbed my arm on my right side.

I jumped a foot into the air.

Pain shot through my arm as something sank its teeth into my flesh.

"RUN!"

"AHHH!"

"UGGGHHH."

"AGGHHHHH!"

"Jim? JIM!"

I ran, clutching my arm, trying not to lose the grip on my sword. "TAM?" I called out.

Something heavy fell against me.

"I GOT IT!"

I pushed at the weight that was falling against me and froze.

It felt like a warm bear. Only not a bear.

"What is that? HELLO?"

"Charlotte, come here?"

"I'm trying to. Where are you?"

I looked wildly around for the others. I thought I spotted Caroline and Khepri, far off to my left.

"CHARLOTTE!" Tam appeared at my side. He glanced beyond me, and his eyes went wide. "LOOK OUT!"

I ducked, and Tam brought his sword down on something.

An inhuman cry pierced the silence, louder than any person could have made.

I stood up again and turned, my scimitar ready.

Tam was struggling with some huge hairy beast, their arms locked as they wrestled and tumbled down and to the side.

"Tam, I can't get my sword to it! I might hit you!" I cried out.

"JUST ..." he tumbled again, and the thing growled ominously.

"It's like some kind of maricoxi or something," Jim called out.

I swung around, and saw Jim fighting another hairy beast.

A mari-what?! These things looked like a cross between a man and a bear. Or a gorilla.

I grabbed Tam's leg as he flipped past and pulled. He slid out from under the thing, and I brought my scimitar up and lunged at the thing before it could get to its feet.

I was rewarded with a cry, but then the beast went nuts, thrashing about and grabbing at my legs. I backpedaled furiously, trying to get out of its way, and at the same time trying to land another blow.

Tam ran around it and came at it from the other side, and lunged at it, striking gold.

The thing wailed and thrashed even harder.

I stabbed at it and withdrew my sword, then stabbed again.

The thing finally stopped moving.

I lifted my sword and saw the blade was covered in black blood.

What the heck...?

There was a howl not far off, and a growl, and two more of the beasts came lurching toward us, running half on their knuckles and half on their feet.

They were far larger than gorillas, and I got a decent look at the closest one before I brought my sword up.

The hairy face was grimacing at me as it brought it huge arms up to strike. Long, sharp talons extended several inches and looked razor sharp in the dim light.

"Watch out!" Tam brought his sword up beside me, and I saw that a third was coming from the other direction.

"There's too many, let's regroup!" I called out, and grabbed his sleeve and ran back toward where I had seen Jim.

We ducked in and out of the trees, winding our way to the others where we could mount a proper attack. Or defense, depending on the situation.

"Miss! MISS!" I swerved toward the sound of Caroline's voice and found her and Khepri high in a tree, with six or seven of the beasts climbing up after them.

Jim ran up, panting. He nodded at me and Tam and we all attacked the beasts with a ferocity borne of desperation.

One of the things had gotten close to Caroline and she brought her sword up and plunged it into the thing's neck. It screamed in pain and fell back out of the tree, but Caroline's sword stuck in it, and she was nearly pulled out of the tree along with it. She wrenched her arm sideways, and the sword came free of the beast, and it tumbled the rest of the way down, hitting branches as it came.

I looked up at her, and she saluted me, letting me know she was all right.

I jumped to the other side of the tree to help Jim. He had gotten the attention of two of the beasts, and they were advancing on him from two different directions.

I brought my sword up to strike at the nearest one. I never got the chance.

"CHARLOTTE WATCH OUT!" I heard Tam scream right before one of the beasts that had climbed halfway up the tree after my friends decided to drop on top of me in an ambush.

It roared as it came, and I looked up as the thing fell onto me heavily.

"ARGHHHH!" I cried out, as the thing forced me onto the forest floor, my right arm crumpled beneath me. The wound I'd sustained earlier had been all but forgotten, until now.

Tam ran up and grabbed at the thing, but it turned and slashed at the sailor and shredded his shirt sleeve, and blood blossomed down the length of it.

"DARN IT!" Tam cried out, half in pain, half in anger. He grimaced and yelled out," DUCK!"

I dropped my head, and Tam brought his sword down on the thing's arm, burying it deep in bone and muscle.

It cried out in pain and tumbled off me, and I was able to get to my feet. Tam had worked his sword free of the beast and was slashing down again, his face furious in the heat of battle.

I brought my own scimitar down on the thing, slashing a deep wound in its belly, and it finally lay still.

"OVER HERE!" I heard Jim call out from a dozen feet away.

He was grappling with three more, they had tried again to get up the tree to reach Caroline and Khepri. One was halfway up the lower branch, and Khepri had stuck her sword into its eye. Blood ran down its front, and it moaned, but then began climbing again.

I heard a familiar roar behind me and turned to see the chimera jumping toward us. She stopped and batted her massive lion's paw at an approaching beast, and the thing went down without a fight.

So good to have a friend like the chimera.

Christianne was running toward us through the trees. "Charlotte! I killed two on my own!"

"Great, kid," I called back. "Don't get cocky!" I brought my scimitar in a great arc and slashed at the legs of the climbing beast.

Tam was fighting one he'd been able to pull out of the tree, and Christianne joined him, both of them slashing with their swords until black blood flew through the air.

I wanted to laugh in glee.

This was too easy.

Then I heard Caroline scream and saw her fall out of the tree.

One of the beasts had come from the next tree over, and had launched itself at her. They fell together, the hairy thing had its claws buried deep into Caroline's sides.

"CARRIE!" I jumped forward.

Jim got to her first. He brought his sword down on the creature's neck, and the blade sunk in and stuck, but did not slow the monster down at all.

Caroline screamed again.

"AAHHHHHH!"

I grabbed at her, trying to pull her away from the creature. It was stuck fast to her, its long, razor-sharp claws had somehow burrowed deep into her sides.

Her outfit, like all of ours, was a kind of leather armor that protected us from severe blows and lashes, and teeth.

And claws, I hoped.

I frantically tried to pry the darn thing off my friend, but it had hooked in. I could tell from her face that the claws had pierced through the leather and she was feeling the points in her flesh.

"AHHHH!"

"Stupid thing." I got to my feet, took aim at the head of the thing that was chewing on my poor Carrie, and glanced at her one last time.

"Okay?"

She nodded.

"Duck," I said quietly, and brought my sword down hard, with both hands gripping the pommel. The blade landed at an angle, slicing into the head of the creature.

The top of its head came clean off, and blood poured out. It slumped and fell to the side.

"Ughhh, oh, gross ..." Caroline said, pushing it off of her.

The creature had little in the way of brains that I could see. It was mostly blood and red gore pouring out onto the forest floor.

I put my hand out and helped Caroline to her feet.

"You okay?" I asked.

She grinned at me, wiping a piece of monster head gore off her cheek, and said, "Never better!"

I laughed and we both turned to assess the situation.

Tam had taken two beasts down and was fighting a third. Jim was running his left as Christianne called out.

"Come on!" I said, and Caroline and I both raced to help Christianne.

She and Khepri were back to back, and five more of the beasts were circling them.

"God, where are they coming from?" I wondered out loud.

I slashed downward at the monster nearest me, a huge beast that must have been at least eight feet high and half that wide. It growled as my blade sunk into its back an inch, then shrugged its shoulder and turned. I brought my scimitar down again, and the thing grabbed it with its huge paw, much to my chagrin. I backed up, pulled at my sword, trying to grab it back from the beast.

It growled at me and reached forward with its long foreleg, claws extended and whistling through the air.

I ducked and let go of the blade.

Oh, no.

"It's got my sword!" I cried out, as I reached into my boot for my long dagger.

The monster advanced on me, and growled again, tossing my scimitar to the side like it was a stick.

I slashed with my dagger at its belly, trying to land a blow, but its forelegs were too long.

Suddenly, it jumped forward and slashed with both front paws.

I reared back, and the sharp talons just missed my face. They came so close I felt the wind whistle as they went by.

I stumbled backward and fell to the ground. I quickly shoved the dagger back into my boot holster and scrambled backward.

"Hey, Charlotte, need some help?" Tam called out from nearby.

"Nah." I scrambled back on my hands and knees as the beast growled, dropped to all fours and advanced on me. "I'm fine. I can handle this no problem!"

I backed up again and noted two trees growing closer together that I had just scrambled past, and I rolled sharply to the side, as the beast reached for me. It hit the trees, its claws embedded in the bark.

I jumped over it and ran back, dipping down and scooping up my scimitar.

I jumped back to the beast, which had just gotten its claws free of the trees, and brought my sword down hard on it, chopping deeply. It went down.

"See? I'm doing fine!" I grinned.

Tam threw his head back and laughed.

A hairy arm reach over and grabbed Tam's head and dragged him backward and up into the tree where the owner of the arm had been hiding.

OH NO!

I jumped forward, quickly transferring my sword to my left hand and wiping my right palm on a passing tree. It was slick with blood and getting slipperier as the minutes passed. As I approached the tree Tam and the beast were in, I transferred the scimitar back to my right hand, and grabbed my long dagger out of my boot again, in my left.

Looking up, I could barely see the beast and Tam.

It must be climbing up to the top.

"Tam!" I called out.

Nothing.

"TAM!"

Suddenly, a hairy body fell out of the tree, bounced once, and came to rest against the trunk.

"Watch out below!" Tam called.

"Ha ha! Very funny." I grinned.

I looked around.

Jim had subdued his opponent, and was also looking around at the scene.

Caroline and Christianne waved from the next tree over.

Khepri walked out of the bushes, cleaning her sword.

I couldn't see the chimera.

"Where's Kym?" I asked.

I think she went off over there," Khepri gestured to our right. "I saw her running after three of the things.

"I'm going to find her. Who's with me?" I said.

I hadn't taken three steps when I heard the chimera roar.

"She sounds irritated," Tam said.

A crashing sound through the trees made my eyes widen. "That sounds like ..."

I ran forward.

The others followed me.

We zigzagged through the trees and came to the chimera. She had knocked down a few trees and had two beasts cornered against a rock face.

They snarled at her as she batted at them with her massive lion paws.

I looked closer and saw a dark den in the rock face next to them.

Suddenly, they both launched themselves at the chimera at the same time.

She batted one down with her paw, smashing it to the ground with a snarl.

The other made it to her back and was grabbing at her tail.

Oh, this is not good.

The chimera was very sensitive about her snake tail. It was actually the head and body of a snake, like a huge cobra, with dark stripes running along its length.

The tail hissed at the hairy beast as it swatted at the thing with its sharp claws. The snake's hood was spread out, and its tongue flicked in and out of its mouth as it swayed and wavered in the air.

The beast made a grab at it, and missed.

The snake darted forward and sank its long fangs into the monster's arm. It screamed.

It was mostly hairy, but the fur was sparse, and you could see the dirty mottled brown skin of its arm through the hair.

This skin was now growing green and swelling to twice its size.

The beast screamed again.

The snake released its grip and reared back, hissing.

I thought I saw venom dripping from its fangs, a thick, fluorescent green liquid that beaded at the tips, then dropped.

The beast screamed again, gripping its arm, and fell to the ground.

The chimera leaped to the side and batted at the thing with its paws, but it was still.

The venom had got it.

"That's a neat trick," Tam winked at the chimera.

Chapter Eight

The Moaning Cry

We rested an hour, patching up cuts and bruises, then prepared to hike through the forest again. We hadn't taken a dozen steps before we noticed something odd.

The trees were very tall, and very full of branches and leaves. It was hard to see past them, since not much sunlight seemed to penetrated the rooftop foliage.

I suddenly heard a screeching cry that morphed into a long, low moan, then trailed off into silence. It sent a prickling feeling down my spine, and I shivered.

I peered ahead.

The leaves looked almost black.

Now why would that be?

From the meadow that morning, the forest trees had looked a normal medium green color. Now, deep inside the forest, the lack of sunlight and the apparently dense, deep green leaves combined to make it dark in these woods.

Very dark.

"I'm lighting my torch," Jim said.

"Good idea."

"Me, too."

"Yep."

"Can I light mine from yours? Thanks!"

"Got mine right here."

"Oh hey: much better."

I smiled.

My friends often got chatty when they were spooked. It helped us to deal with places that creeped us out.

Me, too.

I lifted my lit torch high. We all carried lit torches now, and the effect was to banish at least some of the darkness.

"Better," I said, smiling.

In the flickering light, we moved with more confidence, but the going was still slow. The forest trees grew thickly, and the darkness seemed to swallow up the light from our torches. It barely illuminated our troupe as we hiked; a few feet beyond was the darkness.

And that darkness seemed to be growing.

"Shouldn't the sunlight make the forest grow lighter?" Christianne wondered. "It's not even the noon hour, and it seems to be getter *darker*."

I nodded grimly.

We hiked onward.

Suddenly, another screeching scream sounded, much, much closer. It trailed off into the same long, low moan as before, then silence. I put my hand up and we stopped.

What WAS that?

I felt I should know the sound, something tickled in the back of my memory, but I could not put my finger on it.

I shrugged, and we continued hiking. Jim moved to my side, with Kym not far beyond.

It was quiet in the forest now. Too quiet. I couldn't hear the nature sounds I'd heard out in the meadow. It put me on edge. I was almost expecting something ...

Complete and total darkness flooded the area. Our torches seemed to provide no more light than the flame of a single candle.

I paused again.

Then...

"AHHHHH!"

"OH GOD!"

"Miss! MISS!"

"Jim, transform. NOW." I crouched next to a tree. I could not see what was happening.

"Charlotte?" This was Kym.

"Here." I reached out, fumbling. The darkness was now so thick I could not see the end of my arm.

Lord almighty.

"Okay. OKAY. ... WATCH OUT!"

"EVERYONE GET DOWN. COME TOGETHER."

"Where are you?"

"Kym?" My hand brushed against someone. "Is that you"? I grabbed at a pant leg.

"Yeah, it's me," Kym said.

"Transform, please. Right now." This was an emergency. I needed my people at their most ferocious.

I heard a faint pop.

Huh.

I'd never realized her transformation made a sound.

"AIEEEEE!"

That was Tam. *Oh, god. The new guy.*

"TAM?" I called out.

I heard a faint groan and a whisper.

I'd had enough.

"DJINN, CHIMERA, COME TO ME." I stood up, raising my torch high into the air.

Something kicked it out of my hand.

That's it. I'm angry now.

The djinn was there, wrapping his arms around me. The chimera was there as well.

"Up. Just like we practiced." I commanded.

I was lifted high onto the chimera's back. My torch was placed in my hand.

"Can you two see through this?" I hoped against hope they could. Being magical beings, the djinn and chimera were often affected differently by magic, and often not affected at all.

"I can see just fine," the djinn's low voice sounded grim.

"Me, too," came the growling voice of the chimera I was riding.

"What is out there? What's the danger?"

I raised my torch high again, gripping it tightly, in case the thing that had knocked it out of my hands should try that stunt again.

"It's ...," the chimera's voice pronounced a word I couldn't understand.

"What?" I asked.

"Monoceroses," said the chimera, more clearly.

"A what?"

"Charlotte," the djinn said in a low voice, "it's unicorns."

Oh, no.

I scrambled to remember my History of Magical Creatures class. It had been more than seven years.

"I'll take out the leader, if I can," the djinn sounded grim.

"Yes, do that," I ordered. Then, "Kym?"

The chimera shifted underneath me, and made a sound like, "hmm?"

"Let's help him." I was angry.

The chimera plunged into the thicket, avoiding trees like it was second nature. I held my torch high, but it did little good. The darkness was almost a physical thing. And it had a source.

I heard the djinn plowing ahead, knock trees aside, and then ...

A scream. Almost a squeal.

A wet, tearing sound.

Then ...

Sunlight flooded the forest, sweet blessed sunlight. I actually blinked from the brightness.

"THERE!"

"GET THEM!"

"Oh my God! KHEPRI!"

"IT'S BEHIND YOU!!"

"WATCH OUT!"

"I GOT IT!"

I slid off the chimera and ran forward into the fray. There were a dozen unicorns. I could see them clearly now, the sunlight glittered through the trees and illuminated an almost surreal blur of horns, hooves and fur. They were white, but a few of their horns were splashed with blood. It was on their hooves and teeth as well.

The animals screamed and rushed at members of the troupe.

I swung my scimitar at the nearest one, burying the weapon deep in its neck. It dropped like a stone. I jumped to the next unicorn.

"Watch out!" someone called out. I turned and saw a unicorn charging me, a murderous look in its eyes.

I ran to the side. It followed me. It could maneuver well in its forest home.

The thing's eyes glowed red and silver.

The horns struck out at us, slicing arms, knocking us down, trying to skewer us.

I hopped around the trunk of a tree and swung my sword around the other side, catching the thing at the back. My sword stuck in its spine as it went down, and I had to step my boot against it and pull hard while wiggling the blade back and forth. It finally released.

I whipped around to find another trotting nearby, gathering up a head of steam as it prepared to gore the chimera from the side. I leaped forward and lunged with my scimitar, and at the same time the chimera swung around and roared, swiping at the unicorn with her paw.

She caught it on the side of the head, and its jaw came half off. It hung there, bloody, swinging in the air to and fro, and the unicorn fell to its knees, my sword stuck a foot into its ribcage. It screamed a dying cry that ended in the moan we'd been hearing.

That's really creepy.

I withdrew my sword and stuck it in again where I thought its heart was. Blood spurted out of the wound I'd made and covered my hand and arm.

Oh, yuck.

"Kym, step on it for me?" I asked.

The chimera turned and place a paw on the body of the expiring unicorn. Its breath was raggedy and slowing. I pulled out my sword and tried to wipe my hand off so I could use it without it slipping.

Turning to survey the fight, I saw Tam and Jim each fighting a beast, and Kym jump on a third. Tam's torso looked bloody, I wondered how badly injured he was.

Then I saw Caroline.

She was bent over someone; the thick ferns obscured my line of vision, so I couldn't tell who. But I could see she was frantic.

I jump over to her.

It was Khepri.

She was laid out on the ground, a massive gash on her leg.

"Khepri!" I knelt down at her head.

Caroline was tying off a tourniquet on her upper leg, biting the cloth to pull against it to tighten it. I surveyed the damage.

The gash was maybe six inches long, but it was deep.

"Oh, that's not so bad, Khepri." I gulped down fear.

Khepri was drifting in and out of consciousness, groaning.

"She took a horn bash to the side of her head," Caroline said.

I looked around, still kneeling. "Christianne? CHRISTIANNE?!" The girl came running.

Christianne was basically a healer in training, under the tutelage of the woman now laid out on the ground.

"Oh, no." Christianne knelt at Khepri's side and took over her care; Caroline remained to aid her.

I stood up, a sad look on my face. Blood was splashed everywhere. Across my clothes, on my boots, up my hands and arms, against my face, in my hair ... It was everywhere. I looked around and saw my friends looking much the same.

"Here, Charlotte, take this," Tam handed me a wet cloth. He gestured behind him. "There's a stream just over there. We were actually quite close to it when they attacked."

I looked at him. I finally found my voice. "But, *why* did they attack?"

I looked out over the forest floor. I was mesmerized for a minute; the unicorns' horns were an ivory white, blood pooling on their crevices. Crimson red human blood and, in a few cases, the brighter red of Kym's blood, and the darker red of Jim's blood. Sprays of blood crusted on the beast's snouts, and their teeth were tinted red with it. I remembered the moaning cries of the unicorns, the grunts, the low tones of their calls. And now silence and a blood-soaked forest.

It looked like a war zone.

We made camp on the far side of the stream, several miles down from the battlefield. Tam pointed out that the dead unicorns would likely draw scavengers. I'd had enough of fighting things with teeth for the day.

We used the stream to wash ourselves and our clothes and belongings.

Unicorns fight savagely, and the queen has the power of Instant Darkness, which they use to blanket an area they are preparing to attack in. The unicorns themselves can see just fine through the blackness, just as other magical creatures can. Humans and other nonmagical animals, however... are usually doomed.

Thank god for Jim.

"Jim, thank you for bringing down the queen," I said. "We wouldn't have had a chance if that blanket of darkness had stayed up."

"You're welcome, Charlotte." He stared into the fire moodily. "But I should have sensed the unicorns long before they were a threat. I know the groaning cry they make, I just hadn't heard it in hundreds of years, so I didn't immediately place it."

"I understand," I said. "Don't feel bad: We were triumphant in the end."

Jim glanced over at Khepri, who'd been injured the worst, then back at the fire.

I stood and walked to his side, sitting again. "Khepri will be okay. She's a tough woman. And Christianne has things well in hand." I looked over at Khepri and Christianne. "Don't you?"

"Yes," Christianne smiled. "She's going to be okay."

Khepri gave a weak smile and a thumbs up sign.

The gash in her leg had been sanitized, stitched up, and bandaged, and a neat beige wrap was all that showed.

Tam had been gored by a unicorn horn – thankfully just on his side – and tossed into the air at one point. He had a few of Christianne's stiches, and a cloth wrap was tied around his side. He was sore, but would be all right.

Christianne had proven well up to the job of healer, not only in sanitizing and stitching wounds, but in the liberal application of Khepri's magic salve, which vastly accelerated the healing process. Left untended, the gash on Khepri's leg would have taken weeks to heal, had it not become infected. With Christianne's ministrations, it would be healed in a matter of days.

All of us had scrapes and bruises from the fight.

My own face had a massive scrape across the cheek that had been doctored with the salve and was starting to heal. It smarted a bit, but after seeing Khepri's leg wound, I felt fortunate.

We would all take a few days to heal, but we'd be okay.

Chapter Nine
The Mountain

The next few days found us resting and recuperating. Christianne was taking care of Khepri, Jim was hunting for food, Kym and Caroline took care of the mundane cooking tasks.

And I found myself keeping Tam company quite a lot.

"Seriously, you cannot still be hungry." I gathered the wood sticks we'd been using to roast wild rabbit, and tossed them into the fire. It crackled and sparks shot up into the air. The rabbits of this land were fatter than we'd had before, and they were a lighter color. But they tasted just as good, we'd found out.

Tam burped gently. "I'm full."

"That's what you said an hour ago," I said, laughing.

"No, really. I think this time I've had enough." He looked up at me. "Here, come sit with me and tell me about your homeland."

I could not resist.

"What do you want to know?" I sat opposite him, and pulled a blanket over my shoulders.

It was late afternoon on our fifth day camping in this spot. I was starting to get antsy. This might provide a little diversion.

"Well, did you have any pets growing up?" Tam asked.

"I had a small Gotland pony. She had a blonde mane and tail that I would braid."

Tam smiled. "Okay, how 'bout any indoor pets?"

I thought back. "Mother and father had hounds, but I didn't have any personal pets that came inside." I thought for a minute. "What about you, Tam?"

He smiled. "I grew up with a pet hawk. It was one of my uncle's hawks, he had a collection of hunting hawks, which a lot of people did in Alkebulan." He thought for a moment. "Still do, in fact."

"And what did you do with your hawk?"

"Hunting, mostly."

It went like that for the rest of the afternoon.

A few nights later, we were gathered around the fire eating our evening meal when Khepri cleared her throat.

"I think I'll be okay to continue tomorrow," she said, smiling.

My eyes grew wide.

Kym let out a "WHOOP!" and jumped up, giving Khepri a hug.

"Are you sure?" Caroline asked.

"Well, according to my doctor." She grinned at Christianne. "I've been getting stronger every day. Christianne has been wonderful. She's been very careful and taken very good care of me."

Tam spoke up then. "I'm good to go as well." He grinned.

"Well then, is everyone in agreement? Shall we start up the mountain in the morning?" I asked, looking around.

"YES!"

"Yes, definitely."

"Yes, I can't wait!"

"Let's go tonight!"

I laughed. "Kym, I promise we'll set out at daybreak." I winked at the eager six-year-old girl.

And we did.

The next morning, I was up before dawn I was so excited. Well, that, plus Kym bounced me awake.

"Charlotte!" she said in a whisper.

My eyes popped open. I had been in a light sleep for at least a half hour, waiting to get up, but not wanting to be the first one up. That was usually Kym. Nearly every morning, in fact.

I smiled, jumping up. "Finally!" I whispered back.

Khepri, Caroline, and Christianne were still asleep.

Tam was poking the fire. He'd had second watch, so he'd been up for hours.

I rubbed my eyes.

"Tam, how'd it go last night?" I grabbed the bowl of stew he handed me.

"Quiet and still and nothing amiss, Charlotte. In fact, the forest animals made a bit of noise, but it was all normal."

"I heard an owl, I think," Kym said.

I pulled on my boots, grabbed my scimitar, and walked down to the creek to wash up, and Kym followed me. We took care of our toilet, and then I crouched to wash my face in the cold water.

"Brrr!" Kym exclaimed, splashing around.

"The water is snowmelt from the mountain, most likely." I stretched and swung my arms about to limber up.

"Charlotte, what do you think we'll see today?"

"Not sure. But that reminds me, I should check my sword when it's light."

Kym squinted at the treetops and wrinkled her nose.

I squinted at the sky as we walked back to camp. The stars winked at me. The pale light of a beautiful crescent moon shone down on us.

Back at camp, Kym began to wake everyone while I picked my bowl back up and began to eat.

Tam brought his bowl over and sat next to me, and then Jim and Caroline joined us. We all ate in companionable silence for a few minutes until my stomach decided to comment on the stew and growled noisily, followed almost immediately by a loud burp coming out of my mouth.

Everyone burst out laughing, and our day began.

We began our hike by heading directly toward the mountain, which loomed larger and larger in our field of vision. It grew so large in the sky that it seemed we were right on top of it, but the hiking continued and the mountain just kept getting bigger.

Several hours passed.

Khepri seemed fine, and I was amazed at how well her leg was doing.

"You don't even have a limp," I said, walking up alongside her. "Does it hurt at all?"

She patted the leg and I was wondering if she'd wince, but, "No, it feels as good as ever!" She smiled at me, and I smiled back, delighted.

I hurried back to the front. Tam was there, hiking alongside Jim.

I fell into step alongside them. "I don't know why I always want to be out front." I said.

Tam smiled.

"Probably because you want to know what's there," Jim said.

I nodded. "I can't wait to see what's up ahead, every time we go hiking." I swung my arms and jumped into the air a few times as I walked.

After a while, our hike brought us to a rock face.

I looked up. This was the mountain; I was sure of it. It was so steep and sharp, and it rose higher than any peak I'd ever seen.

We stopped for a ten-minute rest, drank from our waterskins, chewed on dried rabbit meat and berries. Caroline had brought baked bread that was crusty and tough on the outside, but soft on the inside. She handed a small loaf to each of us, and I bit into the savory bread with relish. It was delicious.

I turned to the troupe. "Okay," I said. "This is it." I glanced back up to the mountain. "Let's try to find a way up."

"Pick a direction," said Tam.

I turned to the left, which was roughly southwest, and started hiking alongside the rock face. The others followed.

We quickly realized the rocky terrain was tricky.

"Hold my hand," I told Khepri. We took turns bracing ourselves and letting the others climb.

The going was rough but we made steady progress.

Until ...

"What's that?" Caroline pointed.

I followed her finger to a dark recess in the side of the mountain base, about fifty yards away.

I blinked.

"Uhhh, not sure."

I squinted in the bright sunlight.

"It looks like a cave," said Christianne. "Do you think it's empty?"

"I don't know. Let's hike!" said Kym.

"Okay, okay. I was just wondering." grumbled Christianne.

We continued on.

I wondered about that cave.

"Jim, maybe you should scout on ahead?" I said. The general rule of thumb we had was for Jim and Kym to try not to transform on land. At sea, when we were alone, with no other ships nearby, it was fine. The entire crew knew about the two magical creatures, and had seen them transform many times. And I trusted my crew. We all did. You had to, when you were at sea, because anything could happen. You had to be able to count on everyone aboard. I trusted the crew with my life. I wouldn't be able to sleep soundly otherwise.

Here on land, we'd had to break that rule so they could transform for the battle with those murderous unicorns. We wouldn't have had a chance otherwise. When Jim took the lead unicorn out, that had cleared the Instant Darkness spell it had laid on the forest. But unless it was that kind of emergency, we tried to be careful: You never knew who was around.

Speaking of which ... I glanced around, listening and looking up the mountain, to both sides, then back the way we had come. No one. We'd not seen another sentient soul since we'd landed on the shore of this faraway land.

But you never knew.

I eyed the dark recess in the rock wall. It sure looked like a cave.

And anything could be inside.

"Jim," I said quietly. He came to my side. "Scout ahead. Look in that cave. Check everything."

He nodded and was gone.

I watched as he rose into the air, now in his djinn form. He leveled off at about twenty feet, and sped ahead.

We continued hiking as the djinn scouted ahead. I had to look at my feet so I didn't fall on my face; when I tried to look up and follow the djinn's progress, I immediately stumbled.

Tam had caught my arm before I fell.

"Thanks." I smiled, although I felt shaken up.

"No problem," Tam answered. His voice sounded funny. I looked up at him, and he was grinning at me. It was quite the devilish grin, too.

I need to watch out for this one, or he'll steal my heart.

I stumbled again, even though I'd been looking straight at the rocks and going slower.

Now where the heck had that thought come from??

I shook my head as I hiked.

I have absolutely no time for anything with any guy. None. Zilch. I do not need this right now.

I stumbled again.

"Princess, do you need to grip my hand as we go?" Tam's voice broke into my thoughts, and I glanced up at him.

I spoke without thinking.

Why, oh why did I speak without thinking?

"Just stop flashing those dimples so I can concentrate, will ya?"

Tam threw back his head and laughed. He stopped, his hands on his hips, one booted foot on a higher rock that the other, and had a good belly laugh.

I scowled and hurried on ahead.

Where was Jim?

I drew up alongside Caroline. "Do you see him, Carrie?"

"No, Miss, but I think he ducked into that cave, probably to check it out.

A minute passed. Then another.

Then, *did I just hear a cry of surprise?*

"What was that?" I said to no one in particular.

"What?"

"I heard it, too."

"Wait. Look."

"Oh, no."

By this time, we had gotten close to the cave. We were about twenty yards from the mouth when the djinn flew out, floating about five or seven feet off the ground. He was going FAST.

And a second later we could see why: right on his heels, leaping out the cave with a roar, came a ... a ... what the heck was that thing?

"Oh, no. It's a mountain ogre," said Tam behind me.

My heart leapt into my throat.

The djinn seemed to glance our way, then turn south toward the horizon.

He's trying to lead the ogre away from us.

But at what cost? The djinn was fast, but so was the ogre.

The monster was about fifteen feet tall, and thick. He looked humanoid in that he had a head, two arms, and two legs. But that's where the similarity ended.

Its body was very thick and muscular, and heavy. Legs like tree trunks. Arms that looked extra long, and murderous. Its face was lumpy. There was no other way to describe it. Large, angry looking eyes, a large bulbous nose, and a wide mouth. The mouth was continuously open, and we could see blunt, broken teeth inside.

It was naked as a jaybird.

It jumped from rock to rock as it pursued the djinn, and its butt wobbled every time it landed.

I looked closer.

What was that?

"Ewww, it has poop on its buttocks," cried Kym, holding her nose.

Oh my God.

"Kym," I said in a whisper. "Shhhh!"

But it was too late.

I suppose every creature has its strong points, and this one's was apparently a keen sense of hearing.

Just as I shushed Kym, the ogre came to an abrupt stop and turned, blinking its eyes stupidly.

Oh, no.

Oh, yes.

The ogre had spotted us.

Chapter Ten

An Unfortunate Occurrence

The thing stopped and looked at us. I think it was surprised we were behind it. I glanced around it and saw the djinn had stopped too.

Everyone was stopped, at a standstill, just looking at each other. We stared at the ogre and took him in.

It was more than fifteen feet tall. Its teeth were too big for its mouth, and stuck out from its lower jaw, the side canine points reaching almost to its nose.

The thing's skin was a kind of pearly-grey. It reminded me of something.

What was it?

I had it: It looked like the underbelly of a fish that had been dead two hours. Before it started to stink, and when it was still shiny.

The ogre had rough bristly hair sprouting from just about every bit of it. The bristles coming out of its ears were thicker.

His. It was definitely a male.

I stared at it as it stared at us.

"Shouldn't we run, Charlotte?" whispered Kym, finally being quiet.

"I ..."

"Come on, Charlotte," Tam grabbed my arm and led me back down the rocks.

We ran back toward the edge of the forest, and just as we stepped off the rocks at the base of the mountain and hit the flat earthen floor, the ogre roared.

It can only be called a roar.

The massive creature raised its face to the sun and let out this horrendous roar that sounded a lot like Kym's chimera roar, only much, much louder.

I saw the trees tremble from the sound wave.

Ohhhhh ...

Then the thing jumped.

It landed on the forest edge, grabbing at the trees to steady itself, making the ground quake like a temblor no more than twenty feet from us.

The shock of the tremor nearly threw us off our feet, and we stumbled before regaining our balance and racing for the trees.

I hoped we could lose ourselves in the thick forest; that the giant ogre would have a hard time getting through the dense growth. I was wrong.

It plowed through the trees and brush like they were nothing. Like a normal person might run through a field of wheat.

"Charlotte, this way!" Caroline called, turning north again. I glanced back briefly. The djinn was there, at the head of the ogre. Actually, *on* the head of the ogre.

The djinn had ahold of the ogre's ears; he'd grabbed both large ears and was pulling the monster backward. It worked: It came to a standstill and then it, I mean he, tumbled backward. The ground shook as the massive thing landed.

"We're going to have to kill it!"

"I think you're right."

"It'll just follow us and try to kill *us*."

"Okay then."

"Come on!"

"Let's do this."

The ogre was floundering on his back, like an upended turtle. We had a chance to get the upper hand.

The djinn was hovering above the ogre, gesturing to us to finish him off. He looked comical. I would have laughed if I weren't faced with the task ahead of me.

"I can't," I said.

"What?! Charlotte, come on, it's on its back, we have an opening ..."

"Yeah, come on!"

"I can't either," Caroline said.

Tam looked at us, his hands on his hips, and exasperated look on his face.

"It's just that, I have never attacked anything that's not attacking me," I explained.

"He was *chasing* you! Isn't that close enough?"

"KILL IT!" called the djinn.

The ogre was trying to get up.

"Oh, gods ..." I raced forward, drawing my scimitar. The others ran after me.

Leaping up, I drove my sword deep into his huge belly. Kym and Christianne speared him as well. Caroline drove her weapon into the ogre's throat. Khepri stabbed at his side, Tam alongside her, stabbing too.

Well, this is easy. I feel guilty.

The ogre groaned, then roared again.

I thought for sure that ...

He flipped over and got to his knees, roaring again.

"Oh, come on!" Tam yelled, as the ogre got to his feet.

"This might take a while," I said, running up to the monster again.

We sliced at his huge legs, unable to get to the thing's torso.

The ogre grabbed a nearby tree, uprooted it, and began swinging it like a club.

"Oh, that's it. THAT IS IT!" I heard Kym say.

I turned and saw her transform.

She was the massive chimera, her size now a match for the ogre's.

They came together is a roar of sharp talons, sharp teeth, muscled arms and that tree it swung like a club.

The two huge creatures circled slowly, sizing each other up and looking for an opening.

The chimera screamed and leaped forward, swatting at the ogre with a powerful paw, claws extended.

The ogre reared back, the chimera's claws only grazing the flesh, although they left deep scratches along the ogre's leg.

The chimera leaped again and again, both front legs thrashing back and forth, trying to catch the ogre as it backpedaled. The chimera's snout wrinkled in fierce anger, her mouth open in a lion's scream, her fangs bright in the dappled sunlight coming down through the trees.

At last, weary of the chase, the chimera crouched and sprang at the ogre, flying a dozen feet through the air and landing full-force on the creature, her fangs coming up to the ogre's neck and biting down.

The chimera brought her hind legs, huge goat hooves, sharp as a blade, up to scrabble against the ogre's large rotund belly.

Blood flew from the wound, and the ogre screamed and grabbed at the chimera, wrenching her off and throwing her to the ground. Then, quicker than I thought the thing could move, it brought the giant tree-club up and ...

The chimera shrieked as the ogre brought the giant club down on her back.

"KYM!" I screamed in horror.

The chimera rolled out from under the giant club with a roar, bringing her huge foreleg up and swinging a massive paw, claws spread wide, against the thing's belly.

The chimera's talons were at least eight inches long, thick and strong and wickedly sharp at the points. And each front paw had five of the things.

The chimera's muscled foreleg bulged with strength as the blow hit.

The ogre's belly, with several gaping wounds from the sharp goat hooves, and multiple stab wounds in it already from our scimitars, split open like a ripe melon.

Its weakest point.

The amount of gore that fell from that ogre was astounding. It showered down on us, coating everything.

Great. More laundry.

The ogre lay there, groaning in its death throes. It pawed at its own organs as they spilled forth from the massive disemboweling wound.

I'd seen the chimera use that same move to take the head off Malik the rapist without a thought. Clean off.

It was a terrible blow.

The ogre was dying. Bleeding to death. Thick blood, which was red with black flecks, poured from multiple wounds onto the forest floor.

The monster floundered, its arms reaching out to weakly grasp whatever it could. Fistfuls of flotsam from the forest floor, branches from trees, even its makeshift giant tree-club.

Its movements got weaker and weaker as it bled out.

Its eyes searched around for any compassionate face, its groans grew weaker, and I felt terrible.

I saw Tam jump up then and stab at the ogre's neck with his scimitar, trying to hasten the death.

The ogre's eyes grew wider with fear.

Tears sprang to my eyes.

With a final groan, the ogre's eyes closed and it seemed to lose consciousness.

We kept watching it. The blood poured out slower and slower, until the thing's heart stopped.

It was sad.

We took an hour to wash off the gore in the stream which, as it turned out, ran along the side of the mountain after it left the forest about a hundred feet south from where we'd battled the ogre.

"Man," Jim said, scrubbing at his pants. "This whole adventure has been mostly doing laundry so far."

"Ha ha! Yeah, it has," I laughed.

It was a chore. But we did it. As it turned out, ogre guts stink to high heaven.

Kym was washing her clothes out a second time.

"I swear, Charlotte, I can still smell the ogre poo."

I was amazed the blow to her back while in chimera form hadn't broken any bones. The chimera had limped away a few steps, her back not broken, but severely bruised. She'd transformed and had felt much better. It turned out it's very hard to hurt a magical creature, which is why it had been so hard to defeat the ogre.

"You're amazing, Kym," Christianne said, scrubbing her own clothes. "The way you fought that ogre, I will never forget it. It was epic."

Kym, grinned, very pleased with herself.

An hour later we were hiking again along the side of the mountain, our damp clothes drying quickly in the warm sun.

"Hey, let's explore the ogre's cave? We might find something useful in there," Tam said.

"An enterprising young man, wouldn't you say?" Caroline whispered to me, smiling.

I raised my eyebrows and grinned. "No way to tell, actually. I need to gather more information."

"Oh, brother," Caroline laughed.

Kym skipped up then and raced ahead, Christianne following her.

Those two are a pair.

We climbed up to the ridge where the dark cave was, and peered in.

"Careful," Khepri said, pushing her toe against some flotsam just inside the entrance. "You never know what could be inside."

"Hmmm. What would I have inside my cave if I were an ogre?" said Jim.

"Well, you might have ... um ... I don't actually know," I laughed as I looked into the cave.

My laughed echoed in the dark depths. I shrugged and pulled out my torch and lit it with my flint and steel.

The others did the same, and we were soon ready for exploration.

"Spooky, Christianne said, her voice sounding small in the huge, dark depths.

The cave was large inside.

As it would have to be to comfortably fit the ogre.

I lifted my torch high and saw the ceiling far above.

Caroline picked up a fist-sized rock and flung it overhead, disturbing some bats. They squeaked and flew out the cave entrance in a cloud of wings.

One flew low and lit on a stalagmite that rose from the cave floor. There were many such rock formations along the sides of the cave, I noticed.

"Cute little thing," I said, studying the small creature.

It stared back at me, its eyes beady in the torch flame light.

Khepri and Jim walked farther in.

Chapter Eleven
Trodden Feet

"There's animal bones in here," Khepri called, her feet making a crunching sound.

I walked over to her and looked.

"Huh. Mostly rabbit and fox, but I see a few unicorn bones, I think." I pushed the toe of my boot against the white stack. "Ugh."

"What's over in the corner?" Kym asked, lifting her torch. "OH!"

"What is it?" called Tam.

"Just, more gross stuff," Kym said. "I think this is where it slept or something."

I walked toward Kym.

Tam was ahead of me. "Be careful. The cave floor is unsteady," Tam called over his shoulder.

I heard a large tumble and then the lighter, almost tinkling sound of sticks falling.

Sticks ... or bones?

I turned back to the others closer to the cave entrance. "Hey, Caroline, you there?"

"I'm here, Miss."

"Is Jim there?"

"I'm here, Charlotte."

"I'm going to the back of the cave. Kym is already there. If ... ha ha ... if you don't hear from me in five minutes, send out a search party ... ha ha ha!" I chuckled.

I heard Caroline and Jim laughing.

Okay, Charlotte. Let's see what's back here.

"Kym?" I called out, picking my way through the pile of bones. There was no easy way to get through the cave.

Not that I expected the ogre to have a raised walkway through its home, but it would have been nice ...

I held my torch out and concentrated on placing my feet in a firm, steady spot, before shifting my weight.

But the best-laid plans ... go awry ... I guess ...

I slipped.

"OOF."

I landed on my side, bones flying away from me as my boot slid sideways.

"Oh, gross," I mumbled.

I quickly got to my feet, and brushed my hands off, then reached for where my torch had fallen on the ground.

Raising it again, I looked around.

I'd come so far into the cave that it looked dark. I looked again. I could see a faint torchlight far ahead of me.

That must be Kym.

I scanned the area around me. As my eyes searched, I noticed a faint light coming from the cave walls.

Bioluminescence.

It gave a faint glow to the surrounds near the walls, and its illumination extends perhaps a few dozen feet out from the walls. This left most of the cave in darkness.

I guess the huge grotto was at least fifty yards across and four or five times as deep.

Or more.

I heard a faint *"halloo!"* call, and wondered if came from Caroline or Christianne near the cave entrance. As I picked my way through the bones again, I called out, "Hey, Kym, wait up."

My torchlight flickered on the walls as I made my way to the far wall. It helped if I stayed close to the sides: The white bones were shallower there, and walking was easier.

"Here, Charlotte," Kym called from up ahead. I looked and saw her waving her torch. I waved back and picked up my pace.

"Miss?" Caroline called from behind me. I turned and looked.

She was moving to join me, but it looked as if she was hopping through the bones.

"Carrie, go slower. You might ..."

I saw her fall.

"OOF!" came her cry.

Her torch fell as well.

I started to walk back to help her, but she waved her hand. "I'm okay, I'm okay."

I stopped and watched her pick herself up and make her way to me.

"Hey!" I grabbed her hand and pulled her the last few feet. "You okay? I fell, too."

"I'm okay. Just maybe a bruise. The pile of bones actually cushioned my fall." She looked up, brushing her hands off on her legs.

"Where's Kym?" she asked.

"Over there," I gestured over my shoulder. "She's way ahead of us. I think she may have gotten to the back of the cave." I turned and looked. Kym's torchlight was bobbing up and down as she moved along what looked like the back wall of the cave.

"So, Khepri's staying near the mouth of the cave. She says it's time for lunch, and I helped her build a small fire. She's making soup." Caroline laughed.

I smiled. "She's always cooking something, huh?"

"She or me, ha ha. Christianne went back out to shoot at a rabbit she saw. So, it's probably going to be rabbit stew, or maybe carrot stew, with rabbit kabobs. Or something."

Caroline shifted her pack on her back, and moved her torch from one hand to the other. "So, she said. "Where's Jim?"

I gestured over to the other side of the vast grotto. Jim was examining something on the ground he had found. He was about a hundred feet away.

"Okay," said Caroline. "Hmmm," she said, looking around. "So, where's Tam?"

"Oh, um," I looked around. "Hmmm. He was just here." I turned all the way around, slowly, looking in the distance for Tam. "I just saw him, about five or ten minutes ago, about halfway to Kym. But I was back there." I gestured. "This right before I fell, I think."

"That's weird," Caroline said.

"Tam!" I called.

"Tam!" called out Caroline.

A faint *"halloo"* sounded again.

"What was that?" Caroline said, turning.

"TAM!" I called again.

"TAA-AMMM!" Caroline called out.

We fell silent, listening.

Nothing.

Then ... *"Halloo?"*

"Where is that coming from?" asked Caroline, searching the darkness.

I turned to the rear of the cave. "KYM?"

"YEAH?" came Kym's voice calling back.

"COME OVER HERE," I called back.

"*Hallooo!*" came the call again.

"I think it's coming from over there," Caroline pointed across the expanse.

"Really? I could've sworn it was coming more from that direction," I pointed off to the side.

"The sound is echoing off the walls. It's impossible to tell where it's coming from," Caroline said.

"Nothing is impossible."

"You know what I mean."

"Well, yeah."

"Okay."

"I think that's Tam, by the way."

"Well, of course it's Tam."

"Do you think he fell somewhere?"

"Hey, hi," Kym scrambled up to us on the side we were standing on. The bones rose to a gently slope there. "What's up?"

"Tam is missing," I said.

"Uh-oh." Kym looked around. "This place is so huge."

"Charlotte!" Jim called out, halfway to us.

"Here, Jim!" I waved.

"I think he can see you."

"Ha ha. I know."

Jim waded up to us. He had sunk deeper into the pile of bones.

"I think this cave has been an ogre den for far longer than the ogre we slew has lived in it," Jim said. "I found some artifacts that look very old." He pointed back to the opposite wall.

"Tam's missing," Caroline said.

"Oh?"

"We called out, and we thought we heard his voice, but we can't be sure," I said.

Caroline turned and cupped the side of her mouth and called out, "TAM!"

We listened. Sure enough ...

"Hallooo!"

Kym jerked her head to the side. "I thought. ..." She took a deep breath. "TAM?!"

"Hallooo!"

"He's down this way," Kym turned and began wading through the bones, back toward the rear of the cave.

We followed her.

She turned to veer off to the right, toward a spot she had not walked across as she'd returned to us.

We stopped and called out again. "TAM!"

"Here!"

"This way." Jim pointed, veering more to the right.

We hurried through the bones, holding our torches high.

"I don't see him at all," Caroline said.

"I think he must be in a recess or a dip or something," said Kym.

"But why can't he just stand up or wave or something? I think he might have fallen down somewhere ...," I said.

"He might be injured," said Jim.

We hurried on.

We reached the side of the cave and still hadn't found him.

"TAM?" I called out.

"Here!"

"This is insane, his voice is coming from the path we just crossed," Caroline said.

"Hmmm," I said, wading back into the bones in the middle. "Fan out. He may have gotten stuck in some low point, under the bones."

"Under the bones?!" Kym said.

"You never know." I stepped carefully through the bones, holding my torch out to see if it would reach through the white pile, but the torchlight just bounced off the bones, partially blinding me.

"TAM?"

"Here!"

I walked forward. *Had Tam's voice been closer?* I continued to call out.

"Tam?? TAM!?"

"Here!"

That had definitely been closer.

I looked up and saw I was about thirty feet from Caroline, who was nearest. Jim and Kym had fanned out and were searching farther.

I kicked at the bones, and they made a tinkling sound.

I walked forward a few more feet.

"Tam?" I called out.

"Here!"

"Keep calling out, Tam. I'm getting closer to you!" I called out.

"Okay!"

I walked forward, changing direction as he called out, and slowly made my way closer to where I thought he was.

As I walked, I grabbed a nearby branch of wood that had been discarded. It was about four feet long. I used this to sweep through the bones as I waded through them, searching.

"I think I'm close, Tam!"

"Be careful!"

His voice sounded far off, yet close.

"Where are you?"

"Down here! I fell through. ..."

I walked forward another few feet.

Fell through? What does he mean?

I walked forward, waving the branch ahead of me.

Five more feet forward ...

Another three steps forward ...

"Here!"

It sounded like I was almost on top of him.

"Tam?" I called out, taking two more steps forward.

"*Here ...*"

I took a step, then another, then a third ...

Suddenly, the ground was not there.

"OOF! OOOOF!" I fell straight down, plunging through the tinkling white bones, and finally fell heavily to the ground, my feet hitting first, and collapsing beneath me.

I fell to my side.

I grabbed my ankle as pain shot through it.

White bones fell around me.

These bones were long leg and rib bones, with an occasional skull bone tossed in.

"Charlotte?"

Suddenly Tam was there. He grabbed my arm tightly, and held on.

I screamed in surprise. "AHH!"

"It's me. It's me!" The rest of the sailor appeared, out of the bones.

I blinked, trying to get the bone dust out of my eyes.

Coughing, I said, "Tam?"

"Yes, it's me." He sat down beside me.

"What is this place?" I looked around. long bones fell around us.

Tam held his arm up to block some of them, and they made a small space where we could see each other.

Despite being next to each other, a few smaller bones fell between us. Tam put up his other arm to block the bones better.

"I fell down here a while ago. I've been calling and trying to climb out ever since." He looked around us. "But I think we're down pretty far."

"Why don't the bones over us crush us?" I asked the question I had first wondered.

"I think these bones are from large birds." He indicated a long bone in front of us. "They're hollow. See?" He pushed against a bone with his boot, and it snapped easily.

I looked around.

"It's like being at the bottom of a large pit, and having straw thrown on top of you," he said.

I coughed again.

He looked at me. "Lift your shirt over your mouth if that gets to be a problem. I had to do that at first." He looked around again. "But then the dust settled, and it got easier to breathe.

I shifted my legs around, and more bones dropped, making a tinkling sound.

"How are we going to get out of there?" I said.

"I have been wondering that same thing for the last half hour," he grinned.

"Oh, right." I smiled. "Sorry. I was supposed to be the rescue committee, I guess."

"I WAS hoping to be rescued, I won't lie, ha ha!" he laughed.

We have to get out of here.

"Okay, tell me what you've tried so far," I said.

"Well," he gestured with his hand. "I've tried climbing out. The bones just break after a while. Or they shift, and I fall back down."

"Is there a side to this pit?" I asked.

"Yes, It's not a large area, maybe a dozen feet or so in diameter. I tried making my way to the side and climbing up that way, but the walls actually get smaller as you go up." He looked up through the bones. "I think the opening is actually quite small. I scraped against it when I fell. It's probably just a few feet wide," Tam said.

"That's probably why we could hear you," I murmured, looking around.

"Okay," I said, "I'm going to try standing up. Help me? I think I hurt my ankle."

"Oh! May I look at it?" he asked.

"Okay. It's covered in my boot, but ..." I said.

"I won't remove the boot," he said. "Which one?"

"My left."

He moved to my front, blocking the bones from falling on me.

Well, mostly.

One bone fell on my head, making a hollow sound, and I chuckled.

"This could be a comedy, if it we weren't stuck in here."
I smiled.

He grinned and bent over my left boot.

"I'm just going to. ..." He reached out and grasped my ankle in his hands, and tried to flex it back and forth.

I winced as the pain hit me.

He squeezed the boot without turning the ankle, and looked at me.

I breathed, my senses down by my foot, then looked up at his face.

"I don't think it's broken, thank goodness," he said.

"Nah, it's just a turned ankle. I'll be fine."

I tried to get to my feet.

"Here." He rose and extended his hand.

I grabbed it, and he pulled me up.

Bones fell around us, and I began coughing again.

Tam pulled his shirt up and over his mouth.

I put my arm over my face as everything settled around us.

This was ridiculous.

"Wait. I just remembered," I said between coughing. I reached back and fumbled in my pocket. "Aha! I knew I had it here," I said, pulling out a large handkerchief.

I promptly dropped it.

Tam chuckled.

"Here, allow me, Princess." He bent down and pulled the handkerchief out of the bones.

I closed my eyes as a particularly vicious bout of coughing overcame me.

I bent over, trying to catch my breath, and felt his arm around me, supporting me.

"Here," his gentle voice was close to my face.

Ohhhh, what is happening?

I slowly straightened, and his arm stayed around me as I did.

"Here, Princess," Tam said softly, stretching my handkerchief against my face. "We don't want it too tight."

His eyes locked with mine, and we paused there, staring.

My heartbeat quickened.

He has gold flecks in his brown eyes, something I had never noticed before.

"Thank you," I said slowly, staring back into his eyes, unable to look away.

He reached around and tied the cloth together, then used his fingers to adjust the cloth on my cheeks.

"How's that?" he whispered.

My heartbeat was so loud in my ears I thought for sure he could hear it.

I nodded, unable to speak.

We fell silent as we stared into the other's eyes, unblinking.

A new cascade of bones threatened to tumble down on us, and a shower of dust fell on my head.

I blinked in reaction, and the spell was broken.

"Hey, you guys okay?" It was the djinn, upside down, poking his head into our little bubble in the world.

Tam glanced away, his arms held up to keep the bird bones from falling on me. "Yeah." He cleared his throat. "Uh, yes. Thank you, um ..."

I stared at Tam as he fumbled for words, my smile obscured by the handkerchief tied around my face.

"You two lovebirds want more time alone, or can I help you out of this bone pit?" the djinn asked.

I ducked my face down, laughing.

Tam had a foolish grin on his face.

"Please help the princess out of this bone pit, djinn. She's been coughing. I think the dust has gotten into her lungs," Tam said.

"Right-o!" the djinn held his arm out, and I took it, and he grabbed me firmly around the waist and lifted.

Tam and I were both out of the pit and settled in front of Khepri's fire, our faces and hair washed. The camp Khepri had made was just outside the cave, I realized, on the dirt and rock ground.

An extra blanket was wrapped around my shoulders against the evening chill.

I glanced back into the cave as evening fell, my mind lost in thought.

"Here, Charlotte." Khepri handed me a medicinal tea, and I cupped the hot mug in both hands and brought it to my face, inhaling deeply.

Steam rose from the liquid and slowly drifted across my face.

I wiggled my ankle.

Khepri had taped it well, after apply her magic salve, and it already felt better.

Tam sat nearby, he had refused any examination, insisting he felt fine.

I glanced at him across the fire and saw he was deep in conversation with Kym, while holding one of the bones in his hands.

I stared into the fire, hypnotized by the flames.

A few minutes later, I looked away, sighing, and caught Jim's eye.

He smiled and nodded, glancing from me to Tam.

I blushed and ducked my head.

What was happening?

We continued hiking around the base of the mountain.

"You know, all I saw was animal bones."

"Yeah, me too."

"I don't think ogres are known for hoarding anything interesting. Are they?"

"No, I don't think so."

"You're free to go back and check, ha ha!"

"Come on. Let's just find a path up the mountain."

We hiked on. And on. It was a few more hours before the rocks gave way to more dirt and trees, growing right up the side of the steep slope.

"The sun will be setting in a few hours," Christianne said, wiping sweat off her brow.

"Let's just push on a bit farther," I said. "You never know what will be around the next corner."

We hiked on.

The stream was nearby, and flowers grew by its bank. Butterflies, a brilliant dark blue, fluttered near the water.

"Hey, look!" I turned to the voice. Khepri was pointing at the mountain.

What's she found?

"Oh cool!" said Kym.

"YESSS!"

"Finally."

I hurried over. The forest grew up the side of the mountain. There was a spot, Khepri was still pointing to it, that looked like an old path, a path trodden feet had created, either animal or magical creature, it didn't really matter.

It was a path up the mountain.

Eager, we starting up, and did not stop to make camp until twilight had fallen and it was hard to see the path before us. We camped next to an old stone shrine, it rose high into the air and provided shelter from the elements when we set up camp on its lee side. There was a recess near the top where a large puddle of oil resided, a lamp. We lit it and it provided a welcomed brightness in the night.

Chapter Twelve

Be Careful Where You Rest

The next morning, we had camp packed and boots on and were ready to start hiking up the mountain before the sun had even risen.

"Ah, the warm glow of barely-night! How I love it!" Tam laughed.

"I can see my breath," said Christianne.

"So can I," said Khepri.

"Tam, have you filled your waterskin?" I asked.

"Right here, m'lady. Ready and packed," Tam lifted his bag and wiggled his eyebrows.

"You're in a good mood." I smiled at him.

"It's a good day to be alive. After fending off a murderous unicorn attack and an ogre that would've gleefully eaten us alive down to our bones, I am happy to be alive!" He thumped his chest and laughed.

I checked everyone's pack, took one more stroll around our camp, and then spoke.

"Okay, I think we'll continue on this path, but let's stick to the edges, in case we come upon any other unfriendly life forms," I said.

"Sounds good, Charlotte," said Kym.

"Ready when you are, Miss." Caroline said.

"Let's walk."

We hiked until midmorning before stopping for a rest. Sweat poured down my temples, and the sides of my hair clung damply to my skin.

It had been six hours.

"Let's stop for a break here, guys." I dropped my pack off my shoulder and sat on a large rock sticking out of the side of the mountain.

"Whew." Caroline sipped from her waterskin, then splashed some onto her hot face.

"It promises to be a scorcher today," Tam said.

"Maybe it will cool off higher up the mountain," I said.

Jim turned his head back and looked up, shading his eyes. "I don't think it'll get cold until we're up another three thousand feet."

"How far do you think we've climbed today?" Christianne asked.

"Maybe five or six hundred feet," Khepri said.

"Ugh."

I munched on dried rabbit and blackroot and sat observing my troupe.

Kym played on a rock farther up the trail. She climbed to the top, which was nearly ten feet high, then jumped off, giggling, into a large pile of dried grasses. Then climbed up to repeat the whole thing. Over and over.

I heard the rumbled of thunder in the distance.

"Huh. Wonder if we'll have rain," Khepri said, looking up.

I glanced above us and saw a few white fluffy clouds scattered in the deep blue of the sky. The sun blazed hot down on us.

Weird.

"Must be off by the coast," Khepri said.

The rumble of thunder sounded again.

"Wow, that sounds like it's nearly overhead, but I don't see any rain clouds, do you?" I asked Tam, sitting nearby.

He got up and walked out to the edge of the trail and looked up, shading his eyes.

"Jim, do you see any rain clouds?" Tam asked.

"I do not." Jim glanced into the sky and over to the mountain that loomed above me. Then he dropped his eyes to the mountain behind me and froze.

A rumble of thunder sounded still louder.

Jim's gaze slipped to the left, up the hill, to where Kym was climbing back up the large rock to jump again.

Jim swiftly ran to Kym, catching her as she jumped, then ran.

"Charlotte, everyone: run!" He called over his shoulder.

I jumped up, staring at Jim, then glanced at Caroline, shrugged, and ran after him.

I had learned long ago to trust my troupe.

Jim ran, Kym slung over his shoulder like a sack. He ran over the edge of the trail, and down the slope of the mountain.

Thunder rumbled again, but this time, much closer.

Dirt and rock rained down on me as I grabbed Caroline's hand. We ran after Jim, not glancing back. Christianne and Khepri ran alongside us, holding hands to stay stable.

"Hey!" Tam called. He ran next to us. "What's going on?"

"Don't know. Jim saw something." Caroline said, puffing as she ran.

It was a good thing we held hands, because running down a rugged slope was more jumping and falling than running.

Tam cried out, "Oh no!"

I think he looked.

We ran halfway back down from the elevation we'd reached, before crouching behind some bushes alongside Jim.

"Okay." I breathed hard. "What ...what did you see?"

Jim just pointed.

I looked up to where we'd been resting and saw the rocks moving. Dirt was pouring off the boulders as the ogre who'd been asleep across the trail moved to sit up.

Oh, my God.

I saw the large rock Kym had been jumping off move and scrape to the side. It was not a large rock, it was the ogre's knee.

The ogre's knee.

I blinked.

The rock I'd been resting on had moved as well, and it also was no rock. It was the ogre's chest.

The thing was sitting upright. It looked as if the ogre had been asleep across the trail, and had tucked his face into the side of the mountain.

That sound like thunder must have been its snores.

The ogre stood and stretched and yawned, then looked sharply down the slope of the mountain at us.

With a roar, he crouched, then jumped off the side of the mountain, straight at us.

The thing was moving so fast the wind whistled as it passed, and when it landed, the ground shook.

BOOM! THUD!

It landed with one foot forward, the second foot behind it, and slid.

Rocks and dirt flew past as it skated down the mountain a few dozen yards, until it came to a stop barely ten feet from me.

I held my breath.

Did it see us?

With a growl of rage, the ogre swept its arm along the dirt like a scythe, scraping the ground and catching us up in the sweep.

"Ahh!" I screamed along with the others as we were hurriedly shoved, dirt and bushes and rock and all, off to the side of the slope, and into the canyon next to us.

We dropped about twenty feet onto a huge mound of dried grasses and bushes, and I silently said a thank-you to fate, because without these dried brambles, we would surely have been injured.

As it was, my legs were scraped up pretty bad, and several long tears appeared on my pants.

Great.

We tumbled down and watched as the ogre flopped on its belly and reached over the side of the canyon edge and grabbed a handful of brush, about thirty feet downhill from us.

It brought the vegetation up to its nose and sniffed, then stuffed it into its mouth and chewed with relish.

"Come on!" I scrambled down the dried grasses and my boots hit the ground running. I grabbed Caroline and Tam, and raced after Jim, who was high-tailing it up the canyon, away from the ogre.

Glancing back, I saw the ogre take another handful of brush and shove it hungrily into his mouth.

This is so weird.

We scrambled out the dirt bank of the canyon at its highest point, and clambered up a short slope to the path again, curving around so the ogre wouldn't see us.

"That was a close one," breathed Khepri. She patted Jim on the shoulder as he walked past. "Good one, Jim."

"Yes, Jim, well spotted. Thank you," I breathed hard, trying to catch my breath.

"I can't," she puffed loudly, "believe that," puff puff "I was jumping," gasp of air, "on a giant ogre's knee," Kym flopped to the ground, gasping.

"I can't believe we got away without it wanting to fight us," Caroline said.

"I think it did see us," Jim said.

"It definitely saw us," Tam said.

"It was distracted by the dried brush in the canyon," I said. "Not sure why."

"Wild animals eat plants when they have an upset stomach," said Khepri. "Maybe it had a bellyache?"

"Where's Christianne?" I said, looking around.

"What?"

"CHRISTIANNE!" I called.

"Charlotte, she's here," Kym pointed.

Christianne was lying down on the other side of Kym, her hands on her middle, breathing hard.

"So ... sorry, I'm ... just out ...of breath." She gulped in large breaths of air.

"Okay, let's rest and drink some water. That was just ...crazy." I shook my head.

This adventure is utterly nuts.

Ten minutes passed.

"Is it gone yet?" I peeked over the edge of the cliff beside the path.

I could see the ogre farther down; it had made a place for itself in the canyon, and was munching on the dried vegetation. It groaned and turned on its side, and I felt a twinge of pity for it.

Khepri crawled up next to me.

"I wonder what it ate that gave it indigestion?" I said.

"I hope it wasn't related to the coins," said Khepri. "We haven't seen much evidence of the poison in this land, except in the waters offshore, but that thing is huge, so it could travel to the shore in no time."

"Mmmm. It could have been the poison, then. It's affecting more and more creatures. We have to get to the bottom of this mystery," I said.

"Well, hopefully this ogre will eventually be all right. It's such a massive creature, it probably has a good chance of recuperating, from whatever ails it," Khepri murmured.

We watched as the huge beast groaned and grabbed another handful of dried brush, which it stuffed into its mouth.

"Charlotte?" Kym flopped down on my other side.

"Mmmm? What, sweetie?" I asked.

"Caroline and Jim think we should hike up to at least the next shrine before making camp. What do you think?" Kym asked.

I backed away from the ledge and jumped up.

"I think that's a great idea." I grabbed her hand and swung it back and forth. "Come on, kiddo, let's hike!"

Chapter Thirteen
Little Path of Horrors

"Let's go!" Kym was practically bouncing off the trees in her excitement the next morning.

"Okay, okay, Sweetie. Just let me get my boots on and wash my face." I felt groggy. "Ugh, I don't think I'm sleeping that well."

"Here," said Khepri, fishing around in her medical bag. "Let me brew you a tincture that will help that."

"Should I take it at night?" I asked.

"No, take it now. It's not a sleeping potion, it's an herbal remedy that will enhance your body's natural states. So, when you are awake and pumped, it quickens your reaction time and makes you hyper vigilant. And when you lose your eyes to sleep at night, it helps you to enter the deep sleep of midnight quicker than you normally would."

She lifted a packet of herbs from her stores and went to work heating water over the fire.

"Huh. But what if we're attacked at night? Won't I be groggy?" I asked.

"No, you will be awake and reactive to any emergency." She smiled at me. "Basically, this herb enhances whatever state you are in. And has no lasting effects."

"That actually sounds wonderful," Caroline said. "Maybe we should all be taking it."

"If you want some, just let me know," Khepri said.

The water was boiling and the tincture was ready in no time.

I cupped my hands around the steaming tea and took a sip. It was mild and delicious, and I drank it quickly, as Caroline did hers.

"I think we'll head out soon. How's everyone doing?" I said, feeling instantly better. I whispered in Khepri's ear, "I would like some of that herbal tincture morning and night from now on, Khepri." I patted her shoulder.

She beamed in happiness.

We set out a short while later.

As we hiked, Khepri kept an eye out and plucked medicinal plants frequently.

"I'll restock my herbal stores every chance I get," she said. "We've suffered a lot of injuries already on this trip, and there's no telling what lies ahead."

"Speaking of injuries, Khepri, how is your leg feeling?" Tam asked.

"Much better, thank you," Khepri did a couple of deep knee bends, flexing her legs to show she was back to normal.

"Hey, is this foxglove?" Christianne asked, crouching to examine a plant.

Khepri walked over to look, crouching alongside her.

"Yes, I do believe it is. Foxglove, also known as digitalis purpurea. An excellent herb for conditions ailing the heart." They harvested the leaves, which were carefully placed in the herb bag.

The path led us quickly up the mountain, and turned toward the far side. The way was earthen, and the larger rocks had been pulled to the sides, forming a clear if somewhat overgrown passage.

Birds sang along the path, squirrels scampered, wild rabbits and field hares ran up and down the mountain.

This mountain has more wildlife than the meadow below.

We found wild blueberries growing in abundance for a good mile, and filled our bellies and packs with the delicious fruit.

We hiked for several more hours with no issues. The rocky terrain on the footpath was mostly free of rubble, with steps every dozen feet or so, as the path curved around the mountain.

On either side were plants, mostly familiar, but with a few surprises. One of the biggest was that, the higher we got, the larger the plants we'd never seen became. Khepri had a theory about less gravity and humidity, but I wasn't convinced.

Jim thought the larger plants seemed more prehistoric and larger in nature.

We rounded a corner at midday and found a natural plateau where we decided to rest for a bit and have some lunch.

"Caroline, try some of these berries." I held out my hand. The new berry was a deep orange and quite large, and Khepri had declared it safe to eat. I'd eaten several handfuls already.

We were seated on a large flat rock, and our backs were turned to the inside curve of the mountain. Several new large plants grew there, and one in particular had caught Khepri's attention.

"This plant." She touched a large leaf that looked like a banana leaf only wider. "I wonder what the fruit to the tree is?"

"I've noticed not all of the new foliage has fruit on it. But it's summer," said Christianne. "It's strange."

"Mmm, yes. I agree, it's very strange. There should be some kind of fruit or flower on every plant during the summer," Khepri said.

"Well," Christianne turned to examine the large leafy plant. "This one has a massive stalk," she fingered the inch-thick stalk. "Hmmm," she stood to examine the plant more closely.

The trees at the edge of the mountain path reached far above our heads, maybe thirty feet tall or more. And the plants were very thick. It was impossible to see where one ended and another started. Or which fronds and leaves went to which stalk.

The trees hung over us as we ate our lunch, and shaded us so well we felt we were inside part of the jungle.

A spider dropped from the above plants on a silken thread and sat there, waving in the breeze a foot in front of our faces.

"This land is so wild and green," Caroline mused. "It's beautiful."

We finished eating and resting and prepared to begin our hike again.

I drank a last sip out of my waterskin and stowed it in my pack, which I slipped onto my back. Just as I turned around to check that nothing had been left on the flat rock, I noticed movement out of the corner of my eye.

"Oh! OHHHH!" Christianne cried out as a very large vine with a strange hinged end came forward, moving on its own and trying to touch her. She backed away slowly, and the vine followed her.

Suddenly, it reared back and lunged, quicker than the eye could follow, and caught Christianne up in its clutches. I saw the whole thing.

"OHHHHHH! AHHHHHHH!" she cried.

"AHH! WHAT THE HECK?" I yelled as I jump up, trying to reach her.

The massive stalk was maybe five or six inches in diameter, and the large hinged end grasping Christianne in its clutches was several feet long and wide.

Thin twigs grew out of the edges, and when it closed around her, these twigs looked very much like teeth.

Is this plant going to eat her? This is ridiculous!

As I tried to reach her, the stalk lifted her high into the air above our heads. I felt like we were back on that alien world we'd visited a year earlier, doing battle with the demonic hedge again. That plant had been deadly. I had no idea such flora existed on earth.

My God!

Christianne began to whimper.

"Hey! HEY! This thing's got some kind of sap or something, it's getting all over me. OUCH!" She let out a scream. "It's burning my skin! OUCH!"

Tam jumped up beside me and swung his sword, trying to cut the giant flytrap open.

I saw it was lifting Christianne just out of reach.

This cannot be.

It was almost as if the plant was intelligent.

I jumped down and rushed to the side of the path where the plant was growing from. Caroline followed me.

I heard a weird sound and glanced back to see Jim had taken his djinn form and was floating up to Christianne.

"Hold on, let me get hold of ..." he said.

Too late. I swung my scimitar against the stalk, and the whole thing shuddered.

It suddenly let Christianne go, and she dropped to the ground with a cry.

Khepri rushed forward.

"That was about ten feet, did the fall hurt your arms or legs?" I heard her say.

There was a whooshing sound, and I turned to look.

The giant stalk was waving back and forth: It seemed angry it had lost its meal.

Almost like an animal.

"Get out of the way!"

"Watch out!

"Here it comes again!"

Tam ran to Christianne and Khepri. "Any broken bones?" he asked hurriedly.

"No," Khepri said.

Tam grabbed Christianne's booted feet and backed up rapidly, covering maybe twenty feet in a few seconds, effectively pulling Christianne out of range of the wild, man-eating plant.

"Ha!"

"Whoa!"

"WHOA!"

"Heck with that."

The plant's thrashing stalk, the giant flytrap on the end of it flexing open and closed, whipped forward and grabbed ...

The djinn.

"NOT TODAY!" the djinn cried out, and suddenly, the plant was in pieces, the djinn ripping it apart from the inside the plant's jaws.

I don't think I'd ever seen my friend angry. He was such a calm and passive member of our troupe; you just never saw that side of him.

But we did now.

The djinn tore free of the giant flytrap, then whirled and descended on the thing, chopping at it with his bare hands. Grabbing the stalk and pulling, ripping, he turned the thing into a big pile of vegetarian mince.

He destroyed it right down to the nub coming out of the ground.

It took just a minute. He moved so fast he was a whirlwind of purple, green and blue.

He floated down to us, planting his feet on the ground, breathing fast.

He glanced at us as he transformed back into his human form, and looked sheepish.

"Sorry. Didn't mean to get so angry," Jim said.

We glanced behind him at the dozens of pieces of the plant that had, a minute before, been such a terrible threat, holding Christianne and leaking digestive sap on her.

I was speechless, my eyes wide and my jaw dropped open.

But Kym was not.

"That. Was. So. Awesome." She clapped her hands and laughed in delight.

Jim grinned and ducked his head, obviously embarrassed and happy at the same time.

Kym danced around the big man, clapping her hands, delighted with her friend's ferocity. "Now that's what I'm talking about!" Djinn in da house! HA HA HA!"

Khepri took samples of the plant, stoppering them tightly in several ampules, "Just in case the thing comes alive again."

I shook my head and smiled.

Khepri's scientific wonder had grown since the retrieval of *The Book of Mysteries*, and it was wonderful to watch.

I knelt by Christianne. "How're you doing, Sweetheart?" She was sitting in Jim's arms, looking weirded out.

"I'm okay, I guess. Plant just freaked me out a little, that's all."

"I'd be weirded out, too," said Khepri. "That plant was basically trying to digest you. It could have killed you if it had been able to keep you in its clutches long enough."

Christianne's eyes grew wide. "How long would it have taken?"

"Oh, maybe overnight."

Christianne relaxed.

"I wouldn't have let that happen to you." Jim patted her hand, and she turned and hugged the djinn.

"Okay, troupe, let's make sure we have everything, so we can get on our way again," I said.

Tam walked up the path a bit, scimitar in hand, remaining within our sight.

"Looking for more carnivorous plants, Tam?" I called.

"You bet I am," Tam called back over his shoulder and walked up a bit more.

He reappeared in a few minutes, his sword sheathed, looking relaxed.

"Everything looks okay," he said.

"Everything looked okay when we were eating lunch, before the thing attacked and grabbed Christianne," said Khepri. "We have to be on our toes, constantly. Anything could be a threat. Anything."

"Constant vigilance is the rule rather than the suggestion," Tam agreed. "We must be ready for anything."

I nodded.

"I will rephrase my 'everything looks okay' sentence." He cleared his throat. "I did not see any obvious signs of any more plants that looked like the one that grabbed Christianne." He smiled.

I laughed. "Good man."

Tam's eyebrows went up, and he turned his head to the side slightly, putting his hand to his chest in a *Who, me?* gesture, making me laugh some more.

We all stepped onto the path and began hiking again.

Tam took the lead, and I was able to watch him as he hiked up the mountain.

I think I watched him too much. Caroline moved to hike right beside me and caught my eye, a knowing smile on her face.

Kym skipped up the path, passing me, and Khepri came behind her, and I caught *her* eye. She gave me the same look Caroline had given me.

What the heck? I wasn't sure what they were on about. Tam was a sailor, and an extra sword on this adventure. That was all. *Wasn't it?*

I thought about it as I walked.

Chapter Fourteen
The Old Man

"Khepri, do you think there are other magical beings in this new land? I mean, other than the unicorns and the ogre and that crazy giant plant?" Kym asked.

"Actually, I think there's a good chance we'll see a lot more," the healer said. "After all, this land seems untouched by human hands, and so the magical creatures may have thrived, instead of becoming scarce because of human interference and being hunted, as they are in Alkebulan, child."

Kym seemed satisfied by Khepri's answer for a few minutes.

I held my breath, hoping the chimera child would reveal more of her thoughts. I wasn't disappointed.

"It's weird, but I feel at home here. Almost as if it were my oasis."

"Well, that makes sense, Kym. There *is* less danger here for a magical creature. Naturally. This land may seem dangerous to us, to humans, but to you it's comfortable."

I glanced over at Jim, walking nearby. He met my eye, and smiled and nodded.

My magical friends were comfortable, and that made me feel very happy.

The hike seemed easier.

A few hours later, we came around a bend in the uphill trek and saw ...

"Another cave." I said, stopping in my tracks.

"Do you think anything lives in it?"

"Another ogre, maybe?"

"Oh, lord, I hope not."

"It looks smaller than the ogre's cave down below, don't you think?"

"Yes, it does. Hmmm."

"Should we just hurry past it?"

"I want to have a look inside, don't you?"

"Aren't you curious?"

"Well, yes, but I just thought..."

"If there's an ogre inside, it'll come out as we pass, I'll bet."

"The only real access to this cave is the path we've just walked up, which seems a bit too small for an ogre to pass through," Jim pointed out. "At least without breaking a lot of the trees and bushes."

I looked around to make sure. "Trees and bushes look intact and undisturbed." I gave a thumbs-up sign.

"Let's go investigate!"

We hiked closer to the new cave.

Clouds slipped over the sun, casting a shadow over the landscape.

Uh oh.

Kym laughed. "You should see your faces! Ha ha ha! It's just a few clouds, not anything more! Ha ha!" She doubled over laughing, holding her middle.

I felt sheepish.

Chin up, arms out, I took the lead, hiking with purpose closer to the cave opening.

I hiked right up to the edge, and peered in.

Wait a minute. What was ...

"Come in, child."

He was wrapped in a tanned bear skin and deer leather, and had braided a lock of his hair on the side, with feathers woven through the braid. His skin was tanned and weathered, and his hands wore ornate silver rings on every finger. He tinkled with every step he took, bells hanging from his clothes jingling together and making a sound like a bubbling brook.

His wizened face looked amused at our presence.

The cave he lived in was dark at the front, but once we walked inside, maybe twenty paces in, the passage turned a corner and opened into a larger room that had been hollowed out of the mountain rock. This room was lit by firelight and candlelight. A small lantern hung on the far wall, as well.

Large cloths made of gauzy spiderweb silk were hung against the walls, their colors coming to life with the flickering firelight of the center ring.

Bearskin rugs were laid out around the fire, and the old man motioned for us to sit with him.

He waddled to the rear of the cave and fumbled with what appeared to be a clay oven. He moved a wooden peg and opened the oven door, then brought forth a delicious smelling cake.

At least that's what it looks like. It could be anything.

I looked around the cave. It seemed enchanted. Everywhere I looked I saw something new.

A cage hung from the far ceiling, and I walked closer, peering inside. At first it appeared empty, but on closer examination I could see a small creature curled up inside. It was hard to make out exactly what it was, but it looked like a tiny black cat with bat wings. My eyebrows rose in surprise.

Beside this cage was an old chair with a dark brown coat hanging from it. The coat seemed to be made of the same gauzy spider silk as the wall hangings, but much, much thicker. The odd thing about the coat was that it had more than two armholes. I blinked.

What manner of things are these?

I turned back to the old man, who had sliced the cake and was approaching, the slices spread out on a wooden platter.

"Sit, sit, let us warm ourselves and have a nice visit," he said.

He appeared utterly harmless, a unique character, and the only human we had encountered so far on this vast continent. We were eager to learn more from him, so we sat at his fire.

The cake was passed out, and I nibbled at the corner of my slice. It was delicious.

"Welcome. Welcome all. I have foreseen your arrival," the old man said.

We looked at each other, our eyebrows raised.

This was a surprise.

He nodded, as if we had expressed our astonishment out loud.

"Yes, indeed." He gestured at the crystal orb which sat on a black gauze-covered stand before him, a soft light emanating from it. "I saw it all in this ball."

Kym stood and came forward, peering into the large globe the old man had indicated.

"I don't see anything," Kym said.

The old man chuckled. "And you wouldn't, not unless you possessed the skill of second sight."

I could not look away.

"Sir please, how should we address you?" said Caroline.

"You may refer to me as 'the old man' – just call me 'old man.' It is how you think of me, so that will suffice."

He reached beside his chair and pulled forth a sack, withdrew a long black twig and placed it in his mouth, then passed the sack to us, gesturing to us that we should take one each.

He chewed thoughtfully on the twig.

We each took a twig from the sack, until it had made its way around the circle of us seated 'round the fire, and arrived back with the old man.

"What is this?" asked Christianne.

Khepri sniffed at it, then licked it. "It's blackroot, just a different variety. Tastes more potent. Be careful." She stuck the twig in the corner of her mouth.

The old man looked amused.

He then reached for another, smaller, sack beside him, and brought it forward.

He reached into it and lifted out a fistful of grey powder, and flung it into the fire.

It produced a loud FOOM! and a large cloud of gold smoke and sparkles rose from the fire and hovered near the ceiling.

I looked back at the old man and saw his eyes had shut, and that he was swaying gently to and fro. He lifted his arms into the air, and I saw each was adorned with metal bangles, which tinkled as he moved.

He whispered words that I heard but which fled my memory as soon as I tried to understand them.

He swayed and chanted his whispers for a few minutes as we chewed the long potent blackroot and watched him.

Finally, he stilled himself and opened his eyes, bending forward to place his fingertips onto the crystal ball before him.

I could see there was a cloudy swirling inside it, but could see little else from my angle with unstudied eyes.

"Mmmmm ... I see your futures ... mmmmm..."

He bent closer to the orb and looked pensive.

A few minutes passed, then he spoke.

"I see ... difficulties ahead ... I cannot ... reveal any more ... but ..."

He sat up and looked at us. "It is going to be bad."

What the heck?

"Can you tell us what you mean?" I asked, leaning forward.

"No, I'm afraid I cannot," the old man answered.

I sat back and stared at him. He stared back, a determined look on his face.

I tried again. "Look, telling us that 'it's going to be bad' but refusing to elaborate, well, well that's just ..." I found myself at a loss for words.

"It's mean," said Christianne.

Everyone began talking at once.

"But sir, what if we need to know?"

"You can't just ..."

"Listen, what do you mean by 'it is going to be bad'?"

"I am very curious myself, I admit."

"Please tell us!

"I cannot see why you wouldn't tell us," Tam said.

Caroline raised her hand. We all looked at her. She looked at Tam. "I can."

"What?"

"See why he wouldn't tell us."

"You *can*?"

"Caroline, you can't be serious!"

"Wait, wait, wait," I held up my hand. Everyone fell silent. "Let Carrie speak." I turned to face Caroline and nodded.

"Okay, what I mean is, ..." She turned to face the old man and carefully asked, "Why can't you tell us what you mean by 'it is going to be bad'?"

The old man smiled. "You are smart."

We waited.

He spoke again. "What I mean is that I saw several immediate futures. In the future I warn you with specifics, things turn out even worse."

What?

"You're kidding, right?"

"But if we know ..."

"If there's a danger we can avoid ..."

"Please tell us!"

The old man held up his hand. "My new friends, has it ever occurred to you that knowing a danger in advance does not necessarily make things better?"

We waited.

"Your instincts and skills protect you better than knowing of a danger ahead of time," he sat back.

Everyone started talking at once.

Oh, lordy ...

"Look." I held up my hand to silence the troupe. "We already know we're bound to run into difficulties. This is not news to us. Let's do what he suggests: Let's rely on our instincts and skills, and leave it at that."

"Are you out of your mind, Charlotte? I'll be a nervous wreck!" Khepri said.

"It is a bit nerve-wracking, I admit, but I don't see any other option," I said. "If he's telling the truth, it's best not to know. And if he's not, well, we can't just drag it out of him."

"I understand," Jim said. He looked around at us. "If we had known the unicorns were going to attack, or the ogre, those fights might have turned out differently."

"Exactly," I said.

"Well," grumbled Khepri, "I guess we have no choice." She scowled at the old man, who chuckled.

"This is not the first time I have upset someone, and I want you all to know it is not my intention to be, how did you put it?" he looked at Christianne expectantly.

Christianne look down. "Never mind."

We fell into a pensive silence.

A few minutes passed.

Then – "Sir, how long have you lived here, in this cave? In this land?" Caroline asked. I gave her a grateful look. Things had begun to get uncomfortable.

The old man seemed relieved as well.

"I have lived here in this cave for a very long time. When I was younger, my family came here from the northern mountains, which are a month's travel away. We settled here because the hunting was more plentiful."

"So, you and your family have always lived in this land?" Tam asked.

"Yes, we have. We always have, going back a thousand generations," he answered.

"We've come from across the sea. It took us many weeks to sail here on our ship," I said.

He nodded.

I wondered if he had seen our past as well as our future.

Khepri spoke up, her earlier grouchiness forgotten and replaced by curiosity. "We did not realize there were humans in the land. We'd seen no sign of any; plus, this place seems so wild, the magical creatures so plentiful."

"Oh, I am not a human," the old man said, smiling. "Although I can see how you might think as much."

Chapter Fifteen

Disgusting

By far, the most courageous member of our troupe was Kym. Although I might have picked a different adjective. Foolhardy. Or perhaps impetuous. Sometimes even reckless. But, as I thought about it, being that Kym could transform into a huge chimera in a flash, it was understandable. She had no fear.

And many times, it was a great time-saver. Really.

Like this afternoon.

"Sir." Kym stood and walked to the old man, right up to him, and scrutinized him thoroughly. Kym sat down in front of him, legs crossed, and her wide eyes examined the person before her, taking in every detail and nuance. Every scarf, bangle and charm, every smile, wink and laugh. From the purple feather in the old man's hair, to the slippers woven with golden thread at his feet.

We waited.

While Kym made her examination, the old man reached into the folds of the coat hanging nearby and withdrew an old wooden pipe. He proceeded to fill it with some herb from another pocket, then light it, then he sat back, puffing on the pipe, waiting, an amused look on his face. The light scent of eucalyptus filled the small room.

Finally, Kym spoke. "I cannot see what is nonhuman about you, but I will guess that whatever it is, you have covered it with a scarf."

The old man closed his eyes in amusement and chuckled. Then he stood, and threw off the bearskin he'd had wrapped around his shoulders.

Underneath, under a few colorful scarves, his garment looked like it was woven out of large leaves, and it lay on him very loosely, and seemed to flutter in a nonexistent breeze, as if the leaves were still alive.

A pair of delicate, latticework wings, very similar to dragonfly wings, unfurled from his back. They fluttered in the smoky air, and the old man smiled at us. A tail wiggled out from under his clothes and lay there, only its tip moving.

"I'm not a human," he repeated.

Christianne coughed.

With a wave of his hand, the old man cleared the smoke from the room, every bit. The scent lingered, and when he took another puff of his pipe, the smoke slipping from his lips vanished a few inches from his face.

"What are you, then?" Khepri whispered, mesmerized.

"I am one of the fae. We are known as weather faeries." He spread his arms in a gesture meant to encompass the entire cave – and outside as well. "We protect our forests, both the plants and the animals, from interlopers." He looked at us with glittering eyes.

I suddenly felt nervous. *Protect ... the animals ... from interlopers.*

Uh oh.

"Sir, we mean the land no harm ..." My voice tapered off, and I fell silent.

The old man held up a hand.

He sat back down, his wings folding behind him. We could see the edges fluttering a bit against the chair back.

"I know you've killed. I see everything." He paused, looking at us unsmilingly. "But you've acted in self-defense every time. You cannot be faulted for the lives you've taken as the creatures, in each case, attacked first."

I held my breath.

He continued.

"This is the only reason I have not acted."

Ohhh, man ...

I glanced at my friends. This old man, this weather faerie, was implying he had great power, and that he could use it at any time. We ... My heart raced. I had not realized the land was watched over by such a powerful being, who judged the actions of others.

Yet another uncomfortable silence had descended over the cave.

The fire crackled.

I felt sweat run down my back. My heart continued to race.

A log suddenly split and fell farther into the fire, releasing a small shower of sparks. This seemed to break the spell.

Jim rose and stood. "Well, we thank you for your hospitality. The cake was delicious, but I think we must be going now."

Khepri rose as well. "Thank you for the blackroot, it was certainly ... different ... from what we're used to, but Jim is quite correct, we really must be going."

As one, the rest of us rose and began to make our way toward the mouth of the cave.

The old man said nothing. He watched us leave, puffing his pipe, a thoughtful look on his face.

"Well, goodbye!"

"Thank you for your hospitality!"

"We'll just be going now."

"Have a nice day."

"Goodbye."

"Ta!

We hustled out of the cave, and by the time we emerged into the sunlight we were practically running.

I held my breath as I passed through the cave entrance, half expecting to be stopped by some force or magic.

We trotted out and back onto the trail leading up the side of the mountain, not speaking.

I glanced behind us as I ran, my pack bouncing on my back, my boots finding sure footing on the rocky trail. I did not see anything following us. After ten minutes I relaxed and slowed to a walk. We all were breathing hard as we continued hiking in silence.

Another few minutes passed.

Then, I caught movement out of the corner of my eye. Glancing up, I stopped in my tracks.

The old man was flying above us, and off in the direction of the coast. He was flying very swiftly, his wings beating furiously, and then he disappeared into the clouds to the east.

"Oh, wow." Caroline, her hands on her knees, was bent over and breathing hard form the mad dash up the trail.

"Wow, indeed," Khepri said, putting her hand on Caroline's back. "You okay?"

"Yes, I'm fine." Caroline glanced up and toward where the weather faerie had disappeared to. "That faerie, I am amazed we got out of there without mishap. I mean, everything I know about fae lead me to believe they are incredibly mercurial." She dropped her head, panting.

"Anything could've happened," I agreed, swallowing down worry.

"Well," Tam said heartily, "We got out of there and nothing bad happened, so ..."

Khepri glanced at him ruefully, "Nothing except the weather fae let us know he has been watching us."

Jim held up his hand. "So what?"

I stared at the djinn, waiting.

"So what if this faerie has been watching us? I have had a few dealings with the fae before and, though they are formidable, they are not all-powerful nor all-knowing." He flexed his arms. "We're a strong troupe. I don't think we should worry."

Kym laughed. "I agree."

I smiled.

We continued walking when the weather faerie did not make another appearance.

"Maybe he's gone to check out the ship."

"Maybe he's gone fishing."

"Maybe he's gone to visit the mermaids?"

"No, I don't think he'd venture that far from his cave."

"If he wanted to be helpful, he could go gather those poisoned coins up out of the water."

"I think he's only concerned with the weather and the forest around here."

"Well, the coins were dropped in the bay out there, so, you never know."

"Yeah. Well, we can hope he's helping."

"That blackroot was a little funny."

"I told you it was a potent strain."

"It made me lightheaded."

"And what was in the pipe?"

"Yeah, that smoke made me more lightheaded than the blackroot."

"Who knows ..."

Talking back and forth as we rounded a bend, we failed to notice what was up ahead.

A rumbling began, and the ground shook beneath our feet.

I dropped to the ground, and stayed there until the brief tremor subsided.

"Was that the mountain?" asked Christianne. "It felt like an earth rumble."

"Not sure."

The ground trembled again.

What was that?

The grass and trees on the side of the path began to shudder. Suddenly, the ground itself exploded upward, and a massive insect-like head rose up out of the ground in front of us.

"Oh, my gods!"

"Run!"

"Wait, WAIT!"

"What is that thing?"

"There's more than one, look!"

I unsheathed my scimitar and rose to a crouch. Tam and Caroline beside me did as well.

"Charlotte! There's one behind us, too!"

I whirled around. Two more had erupted out to the earth farther down the path.

"Are they trying to surround us?"

"Back up, BACK UP!"

I found myself with my back to the mountain as a total of four huge creatures, the size of large bears, crawled out of the ground and sat there, their antennae flittering about as if they were tasting the air.

A small wild rabbit shot down the path from above, frightened and panicked.

The largest of the giant creatures, which resembled long centipedes, lunged for the rabbit. A second after moving, a flame shot out of its back end, and a small explosion sounded, and the thing hurled forward a dozen feet, propelled by the blast.

The rabbit squealed as the thing caught it, its mandibles crunching the helpless creature with apparent relish. Behind it, I saw the grasses had been set aflame by the creature's flatulence.

A foul odor filled the air.

"Really?"

The other giant centipedes turned their antennaed heads toward us.

That was all the encouragement we needed.

We turned and ran up the mountain, skirting the nearest giant centipede while it munched on the unfortunate rabbit.

We kept our swords pointed in the general direction of the things as we scrambled up the slope, in some cases climbing behind a few trees, trying to get above them.

"WATCH OUT!"

I turned to see a new, massive bear-sized centipede directly in front of me. The rest were farther down, and this was the only one I could see in my path.

The thing reared up, its legs wiggling in front of it, its antennae moving fast.

Suddenly, flame shot out of its rear, propelling it forward rapidly, without warning. It was less than ten feet in front of me.

A rustling sound caught my attention, and as I watched the thing, I realized the sound was coming from its many legs as they rubbed together. The grasses behind it aflame, it reared up again and lunged for me.

"Charlotte!"

I stepped forward quickly as it came, meeting it in battle. My scimitar made a whistling sound as I made a wide, sweeping arc in the air about five feet high.

The giant centipede finally found its voice and screamed a shrill, high-pitched shriek as my sword found its flesh and buried itself deep in its side.

And stuck.

"Help!" I worked at wiggling my scimitar loose while Tam came forward to help.

The bear-sized arthropod was still struggling, and it was close, very close. My sword arm was vulnerable as I tried to pry my weapon it out of the creature. The thing's exoskeleton had a strong grip on my weapon, and I didn't want to let it go.

Tam leaped up and swung his sword and pierced the thing right behind where its head seemed to be.

It screamed again and reared back, taking me with it. I fell against the creature's body and found it was coated in a sticky liquid.

"Ohhh ... ughhhh." I shuddered involuntarily.

Christianne ran up and chopped at it near where my scimitar was buried, and completed the slice through the creature's body. It was now it two pieces, and both oozed an oily green blood that quickly coated everything.

"UGHH," Christianne said.

The giant centipede finally ceased its movements, but only after each of the two pieces flopped about for a few minutes.

I glanced behind us, down the trail, to see where the other massive creatures were.

Khepri and Caroline were battling one, and Jim in his djinn form had hold of another, squeezing it from behind its head, holding it up so it couldn't move. He straddled it almost like a horse, and the thing spit fire as I watched, driving it forward six feet and setting a tree ablaze. The djinn rode it and didn't fall off, and continued squeezing the thing until its movements slowed.

I saw, farther down the path, that Kym had also transformed and had a massive paw on the back of the last giant centipedes; she was pressing down, her paw almost buried in the things side. The chimera had reached down and grabbed the huge creature with her jaws, and her large teeth had pierced its flesh through the exoskeleton. Green ooze ran down the fur of the chimera, who was unwilling to release her attacker.

The giant centipede finally expired under the djinn's squeezing arms, and the one the chimera had in her teeth also succumbed at last. Caroline and Khepri's had sliced their foe in two, and it finally stopped movement as well.

I looked at the carnage on the trail up the mountain and felt the contents of my stomach roiling. It was the exoskeletons, I think, that grossed me out. And the green guts and blood. *Ughh.*

"This is just disgusting," Christianne murmured, trying and mostly failing to clean green ooze off her sword.

"Hey, let's go up farther," Tam said from his position in front. "I think I hear water,"

We hiked up about twenty feet and found a small spring gurgling out of the ground and running down the mountain in a stream.

"Let's clean up here, but then let's hike farther up and get away from those things," I suggested.

The stink of the flames lingered with us, wafting up the trail.

We busied ourselves cleaning our weapons of the green mucous.

Kym had transformed back into her human form.

"Ugh. I can still taste it." She spat to the side, then plunged her face in the spring water and kept spitting repeatedly.

"Those were ... pretty gross ... uh ..."

"Yeah."

"They certainly were."

Christianne just turned and vomited a bit into the grass.

"Did you see the way their farts ... uh ..."

"Soooo disgusting."

The djinn just plunged into the water downstream and then rose into the air a small distance away from us down the trail. Then he spun. He rotated so fast he was a blur. Moisture flung off of him far and wide.

I had to work to avoid vomiting as I cleaned my hands. It had gotten in my hair, as well, I discovered.

I had never been more grossed out than I was at that moment.

Chapter Sixteen

Up the Mountain

We had minor injuries from our battle with the giant centipedes. My arm had been caught by the legs of the creature I'd fought, each of which apparently ended in a barbed hook. We hiked a few hundred feet more on the curving path up the mountain, until we came to the edge of the dirt and rock path and found a series of carved stone steps.

Caroline and Tam also had wounds that needed stitching. Khepri and Christianne worked for over an hour patching us up, while Jim and Kym gathered firewood and made camp.

That night, we made a larger-than-normal fire, hoping to ward off any giant centipedes or bloodthirsty plants. At least we hadn't encountered any more unicorns.

Khepri found several new herbs along the trail, since we'd gotten to a higher altitude and new flora were growing abundantly everywhere.

"What do you think of those things?" Christianne asked no one in particular.

Several wild rabbits roasted on spits over the fire, the fat dripping into the flames and sizzling.

My stomach rumbled.

"I think this new land has many indigenous lifeforms that no one's, well, no *human*, has ever seen before," I said. "I will admit I would never have guessed 'giant centipedes,' but, I'm glad we could get the upper hand in the fight against them."

Christianne nodded.

Tam handed out bowls of vegetable stew he'd concocted. It wasn't half bad.

"I have never seen animals like those giant centipedes," said Khepri. "I wonder if we'll be encountering any other crazy-large insects?"

"Can you imagine?" I mused. "Giant wasps or hornets? Flying at you?" I shuddered.

"Oh, no, no, no. That would be really bad." Christianne said.

"Rabbits are done. Help yourself," Caroline said.

I reached forward and tore off a piece of the cooked roasted rabbit, and sat back down, taking a bite. It was delicious.

"Succulent," Kym murmured as she chewed.

"Delicious," said Jim.

"We should sleep soon. Something tells me today was only a taste of what this mountain has in store for us," I said.

"Indeed," said Khepri.

"I bet we'll see even worse dangers farther up," said Kym.

"We'll be ready for them," Jim yawned sleepily. "Of that I have no doubt."

I took first watch and sat staring into the fire as my troupe slept. I felt a foreboding. The weather faerie, who I had an easier time thinking of as 'the old man,' had warned us of the trials that lay ahead of us, telling us, *'It is going to be bad.'*

If the faerie had been watching us, and knew of our battles with the unicorns, the ogre, and the carnivorous plant, and had seen how fierce we were, something tells me he would not have mentioned that trials in our future were *'going to be bad'* unless they were going to be much, much worse than what we'd already been through. That kept me awake and alert on my watch. It was unsettling. Very unsettling. To think, something awaits us that worse than anything we've already met in this new land.

Jim relieved me at around one a.m. and I tried to fall asleep in my bedroll. I tried. I think I finally dropped off an hour later. But it was hard.

The morning came too early, and I yawned almost continuously as I washed my face and cleaned my teeth in preparation for heading out.

"It's a brand-new day, troupe, let's make the best of it," I said.

We'd camped next to the path, and on the lower end the trail was natural and smaller, but as I looked upward, there were wide stairs, carved out of the stone, curling to the right around the mountain.

If this mountain is fifteen thousand feet high, that's going to be a lot of stairs.

Caroline brought me a pack of food as I stood looking up the staircase that led up the mountain.

"You okay, Miss?"

I turned to look into her face, and saw she was concerned.

"Yeah, I'm just ..." I shook my head, trying to break out of the daze I felt in.

"Hey, everyone, listen up," Tam was calling out.

We turned to see what he was saying.

"Early this morning, right before dawn, I noticed a nest right over there." He pointed, then opened his other hand.

In it were six large blue eggs. "Who wants eggs this morning?" He smiled.

"Oh, Miss, you love eggs!" Caroline said.

I shook my head. "Let the others have them, Carrie. In fact, you go have some."

"Are you sure, Miss?"

"Very sure." I watched her go to the fire, where everyone was gathered, marveling at the blue eggs Tam had found.

I turned my head and looked up the stairs again, wondering where our path would take us. I knelt and touched the carved rock stairs. They were smooth. *This is very odd.* I wasn't sure what had me worried. Maybe it was nothing. Maybe it was the old man's prediction.

I looked back at my troupe; they were laughing and in good spirits, watching Tam cook the eggs. *My friends are so important to me. I don't want anything to happen to any of them.*

Now, Charlotte, you're on a dangerous adventure. Anything could happen.

I fingered the bandage around my stitched arm, my mind drifting.

"Charlotte?"

In a daze...

"Charlotte?"

I snapped back into the present and realized I'd been staring into Tam's face while my mind had wandered.

He had some egg in a bowl, and was offering some to me.

I shook my head, trying to clear the cobwebs, then looked down into the bowl. The bright cheerful yellow of scrambled eggs met my eyes. I looked back up at him and smiled. He smiled back, amused.

He extended a forkful of eggs toward me and, without thinking, I opened my mouth.

Tam gently placed the eggs past my lips, lifting the fork and withdrawing it as it spilled its contents into my mouth.

I chewed.

"Good?"

"Very good, thank you Tam." The explosion of flavor in my mouth finally woke me up the rest of the way, and my stomach grumbled loudly.

Tam laughed, and handed me the rest of the eggs. I took the bowl and the fork, and eagerly ate every bit while he watched me.

At one point, his broad cheerful smile shifted slightly, becoming subtler, more casual, and I realized he was staring at my mouth.

My eyes grew wide.

"Here you go, and thanks," I handed him the empty bowl and fork, and turned away.

I heard him say 'You're welcome' as I walked away.

You're being rude, Charlotte.

No sir, no I was not. I was being ...

What?

I could not answer myself.

The stone steps were about twenty feet wide here, and they curved gently up the mountain. We left the trees behind, for the most part. Small, scrubby looking windswept trees were the norm, now. Those and wild grasses, growing almost sideways.

There was a constant wind. It whistled through the rocks and made a low, haunting sound as we climbed higher.

Every now and again, we came upon a gold coin or two, dropped on the step seemingly haphazardly.

"It's almost as if they dropped them as they fled," Caroline mused.

I nodded. That's exactly what it looked like.

Every thousand steps or so, we came upon a large shrine to a deity we did not recognize, and a place to light an oil lamp. The lamps were rather big, and we lit them all as we passed them, to ward off the lonely moaning of the wind.

"Do you think these are large enough to be seen far away?" Tam asked.

"Oh, I'm sure they are," I said as I bent over to light the newest one. The bowl of oil was protected by a glass globe, with several small openings to extend a flame for lighting.

The bowls were more than a foot in diameter. Bright firelight burst into flame in front of us, and we prepared to keep climbing.

Then Kym said something I had been thinking but hadn't articulated.

"Who filled the oil in the bowls?"

Who indeed?

Khepri sounded cheerful. "Whoever did, I'm going to thank them if we finally meet them. These oil lamps are so cheerful against the stark, stark mountain."

"Me, too."

"They're warm, too."

"It's a lot of oil. Just makes me wonder."

Makes me wonder, too.

We encountered no other giant bear-sized centipedes and, stepping up the stone stairs, I was happier. *At least the massive monsters probably can't break through this rock.*

It was getting colder, the farther up we went. I bent my head upward, and I could see the higher reaches of the mountain, covered in snow. But I could also see a strange light emanating from one side of the mountain. *What could it be?*

About seven thousand feet up the stairs, we encountered a bear. A strangely large bear. It had come upon our campsite as we'd slept.

We'd been on our second day up the mountain stairs, Caroline had been on third watch, and had roused me about an hour before dawn.

"Miss, MISS!" she'd whispered urgently. "There is a new beast. It's coming down the stairs toward us and will reach us in a few minutes!"

That's all I needed to hear. I'd jumped up, grabbed my pack and had run after Christianne. We'd hidden high up on the inside curve of the stairs, behind the shrine. The oil lamp flickered, lighting up the area so we could see the giant bear plainly.

We were all huddled together, waiting.

The bear had lumbered into sight only a few minutes after we'd all gotten up behind the stone shrine. I looked down on it. It was currently nosing at the remnants of the cookfire. We'd left animal bones from our dinner lying next to the campfire.

"That's an Angustidens bear," Jim said with certainty. "I have encountered them before. We must take care."

The bear was huge: On all fours, it was at least six feet tall at the shoulder, and it looked to be all muscle.

"I'll bet that thing weighs thousands of pounds. It's huge," Kym whispered as we crouched together on the side of the staircase.

We all huddled there, watching it.

"It's almost like all the animals in this new land are bigger than normal. Bigger than our animals in Alkebulan," Christianne whispered on my other side.

I studied the beast. It sniffed the air, smelling our campsite.

"I wish I'd cleaned those up," whispered Khepri. "My bad."

We took turns preparing dinner, and last night had been Khepri's turn.

I made a noncommittal sound. "I guess from now on we should clean all that stuff up before we bed down for the night," I whispered. "The bear probably smelled it from pretty far away."

I watched the short-snouted animal sniffing the air again. I knew that wild animals had a keen sense of smell. *I should have known.*

The bear crunched every last bone left beside the fire, then sniffed and smelled every inch of the campsite, before ambling off down the stairs. By the time it was out of sight, the sun was coming up.

We prepared to continue our hike.

The troupe started up the stone stairs, but then I doubled back for my flint and steel pouch, which I'd left behind.

"I'll come with you, Princess," Tam said, a lazy grin on his face.

"Tam, stop calling me 'Princess' – really, now, I mean it," I said, trying not to grin as well.

The man had such an infectious smile that it was hard.

I was examining my pack and the campsite to make sure I hadn't left anything behind when ...

"CHARLOTTE! BEHIND YOU!" Caroline cried out from up above.

I swung around. The bear was back.

How did he sneak up on me?

I scrambled up the stairs, but the faster I ran, the faster the bear jumped after me.

Tam was ahead of me, reaching out to give me a hand.

"Come on, Princess," he grimaced. I looked down at the extended hand. It was rough and mildly calloused, very rugged looking. I looked back into Tam's face. Our eyes met.

Oh, lordy ...

I tripped.

Well, of course I tripped. The best time to trip was when a gigantic bear was after you, and I was not one to disappoint.

I heard Caroline scream.

Why does she have to do that?

I had my answer.

The bear was at my feet. It grabbed my booted leg in its mouth and began to pull.

This bear wants to eat me.

Of course, a dozen small rabbit bones were not enough to satisfy the bear, just to make it that much hungrier. *A nice Swerighe princess was what it really wanted to chomp.*

Lovely.

I don't know why, but I wasn't afraid.

Tam will help me.

And indeed, Tam was leaping over me, sword extended, to face the bear.

"AH-YEAHH!" he cried in a challenge.

"He's trying to lure the beast away from me.

The bear wasn't falling for it. It would not release its grip on me. I was being dragged, inch by inch, back down the stairs. *Probably wants to pull me to a nice, quiet spot where it can eat in peace.*

"YA! YA! YA!" Tam lunged at the thing, and I watched as his sword pierced the bear's snout.

That had to be on accident. No one's that accurate when fighting a moving giant bear on a stone mountain staircase. Are they?

I shook my head. The bear was screaming, and blood poured out of its snout. I kicked at it, hitting the bear's injured nose. It cried out in rage and pain. Then ...

It let me go.

I scrambled to my feet, ready to lend Tam a hand.

But Tam and the bear were both falling. As the bear tumbled down a dozen steps, however, Tam righted himself, ran after it and stabbed it again as it tried to clamber to its feet.

The bear roared.

Tam pierced the bear's thick hide again and again, in a pattern, almost in slow-motion.

He's trying to lure it over the edge.

And he was succeeding. The bear was paying no attention to its whereabouts. Tam had enraged it so much it was clear the bear wanted to tear Tam limb from limb. Tam advanced, over and over, then turned and scrambled across the stairs and down the other side.

The far, outside edge of the stairs was a steep drop, and the precipice had no mercy.

Tam kept advancing, piercing the bear, then backing up, until the huge beast was at the edge. The bear rose on its hind legs, and I gasped. The thing was three times the height of the sailor.

Tam showed no fear, and did not waver. He swiped at the bear with his sword, until the bear lunged in anger ... and they both went over the edge. My heart leapt into my throat.

I screamed. "TAM!"

I rushed to the edge and peered over. The bear was at the bottom of what had to be a two-hundred-foot drop, in a natural gorge, laid out, blood coming from its mouth. It moved then, shook its head, got to its feet and ambled off. It had had enough of us.

I looked around wildly. Tam was nowhere to be found.

"Princess."

I turned at the voice.

It was Tam, climbing up from the hidden shelf he'd dropped onto as the bear had followed him over the cliff.

Safe and sound.

His hand reached out, wanting a lift onto the upper ledge.

I stared at him for a few seconds, I could not believe he was okay.

I reached forward, grabbing his hand and pulling him up.

He climbed up next to me, standing and looked out over the edge.

"Guess he's had enough," Tam said.

"Guess so," I said, finding my voice.

Tam turned to look at me, and the rising sun was behind him, giving him almost a halo.

"Thanks," I said.

He grinned, cocky as ever.

Chapter Seventeen
Goodnight, Princess

The sky that evening was darkened by a flock of large crows, circling overhead.

Khepri nodded at them. "They bring omens of change." She glanced at me, smiling. "Of progress."

"What do you mean?" I asked.

"In the literature and legends of Alkebulan, a flock of crows overhead means that whatever is occurring will change, will progress. Something will happen," Khepri smiled mysteriously.

"Back in Swerighe, we have rooks. The seers say they signal bad weather." I laughed.

"All birds fly before bad weather. That is true everywhere." Khepri smiled.

Once night had fallen, I settled down to first watch. I looked over at my troupe, all fast asleep. The encounter with the weather faerie had been very odd, and had rattled me.

I scanned the skies for any sign of the tricky old man. I had always been careful of the life around me, and last year we had begun to not only keep our camp tidy, but to "leave no trace," as Kym had put it, after we'd left. We'd buried the remnants of our fire and our refuse, and even covered the area with underbrush, to help it return to its natural state.

But the weather faerie's warning had rattled me.

Were we being watched?

I looked around and up at the sky again.

I did not like being judged by faeries, mainly because I did not know the standards that were being used to measure me.

I shifted and reached for my waterskin, drinking deeply from it. I splashed a bit of wetness across my face. It was invigorating.

I stood and stretched, my arms extending sideways and upward.

It was quiet on the lower side of the huge mountain. A few crickets chirped, and a firefly lit for a moment, fluttering across my field of vision.

Some small animal skittered through a bush nearby, late getting into its burrow.

Probably a fox or a badger or something.

I decided to walk around the camp perimeter, and stepped away from the fire. My hand on the hilt of my scimitar, I walked slowly, glancing out at the wilderness, my eyes searching, my ears alert, but there was nothing odd out.

I wonder if that weather faerie is nearby.

He had disappeared over the side of the mountain, temporarily abandoning his cave home.

For dramatic affect.

Now, where had that thought come from?

The weather faerie might be a powerful being, there was no way to tell.

Powerful beings did not need to make a show for dramatic affect. Did they?

I shook my head and kept walking.

Passing near the upper end of the camp perimeter, I saw a few patches of leftover snow, and I kicked them. The white spray went far over the edge of the slope.

My ears picked up a noise back at camp, and I glanced over.

Tam was sitting up.

It was hours before his watch started; he didn't need to be awake.

Had he been roused by a nightmare?

I picked my way through the bushes and back to camp.

He met my eyes and nodded.

The rest of the troupe were still fast asleep.

Tam threw a branch onto the fire, poking it to make the logs flame up. Then he settled the metal pot atop the coals and sat back.

I approached and settled myself into the seat I had picked out from which to take first watch.

"Nightmares?" I whispered.

"No, not exactly. Just ... dreaming." He smiled at me.

I fell silent. The night was quiet, the sky was inky black, and the stars winked back at me as I gazed up into their depths.

Tam had his cup, and tossed in a few tea leaves.

"Want some?" he whispered.

"Sure. Thanks." I grabbed my own cup from beside my blanket and handed it to him.

"Beautiful night," he said, whispering. I looked up to the stars with him.

They were magnificent.

A streak of light made a swift arc across the sky, and I smiled.

Wish upon a star ...

A few minutes later, Tam handed me my cup back, and I brought the aromatic steam to my face.

He settled next to me, sitting back.

"Your watch doesn't begin for more than an hour, Tam," I whispered.

"I can't sleep," he replied.

He seemed very relaxed.

I sipped my tea. It was strong and delicious.

"So how do you like this adventure so far?" I had been curious as to how he felt, this being his first foray with the troupe. Although I missed Tupu greatly, I was enjoying Tam's company more than I was willing to admit.

Why was that?

I stared into the fire.

"I'm really enjoying it," Tam finally answered. "There's lot of action, which is very good. When you went to retrieve *The Book of Mysteries*, I'll admit I was a bit bored staying behind on the ship."

"But when the centaurs came through the underground tunnel, to colonize the southern island ..." I said.

"Oh, that was amazing. We were so excited to see them." Tam grinned, remembering.

"I'll bet the mermaids were surprised, huh?" I said.

Tam nodded. "They were very surprised. I think they must have had their own legends about what lived on the northern island, and the arrival of the centaurs confirmed some of those stories."

"I was a little worried the mermaids might not like the centaurs encroaching on their island, but it went smoothly, I guess," I said.

"I think the reason it went so smoothly is that the centaurs were cultivating the land, mostly. The mermaids' territory was the lagoon and the waters off the island. In fact, I remember someone said the mermaids' territory extended around the northern island as well. It's actually pretty extensive," he said.

"I'm quite fond of both people," I said.

"I think they're fond of you, too, Charlotte," he said.

I glanced at him. "How come you sometimes call me 'Princess', Tam?" I stared into the fire. "I used to think it was because you were teasing me, but lately I'm not so sure."

"I'm sorry I teased you," he said nearly inaudibly. "I didn't mean to."

I remained silent.

"Sometimes, when I'm feeling nervous about someone, I don't know how to act," he said finally.

"I know. I'm the same way. I usually just don't say anything. I get too shy," I said.

"You know, I would never have taken you for a shy lady." He grinned.

I chuckled. "I'm not usually shy at all, huh? I'll admit I have noticed myself getting more confident in the last year."

"Just in the last year ...?" he said.

"Well, yes. I sure didn't like what happened when I first got to Alkebulan. It took a while to ... What was that?" I rose up, my back straightening.

I'd heard a sound in the darkness.

A cracking sounded again.

I rose to my feet, and Tam rose beside me.

I glanced up and noticed the stars had disappeared.

What the ...?

I drew my scimitar and slowly walked toward where I thought the noise had come from. Tam followed.

I glanced back, met his eyes, and motioned for him to remain at camp. I hated leaving the encampment unguarded.

He nodded and remained where he was, while I crept forward.

Why am I sneaking, with the firelight behind me? There's no way I can hide.

I thought I saw movement, and fell into a crouch.

I ducked and moved to the right, and hurried down the slope.

Something was down there.

Another crack sounded in the darkness.

That's a branch being stepped on.

I crept closer to the shadow I thought was the intruder.

My eyes went wide when I saw the shadow closer.

It was a unicorn.

That explains the clouded-over stars.

I glanced around and saw darkness had unnaturally blanketed the hillside we were on.

Something wasn't right.

Why would the unicorn step on a branch to make a sound I could hear?

The animals were used to this land. This was their home, their territory. They should be able to move about soundlessly here.

Unless it was trying to draw you away from camp.

My face went icy cold. A sinking feeling entered my stomach. I glanced up at the camp. The firelight silhouetted several figures against the light, as they crept up to the campsite.

More unicorns!

I glanced back downhill and saw the unicorn that had drawn me away from camp was advancing on me.

No need for sneaking now.

I stood up, my scimitar held easily in my hand, watching as the unicorn approached.

Behind me, I heard Tam's exclamation.

He can handle himself.

I felt a quick wave of thankfulness he'd woken up early, so he could help defend the camp against this nighttime attack.

The trick is to stop the blanketing darkness before it gets overwhelming.

We'd all discussed it after the unicorn attack in the forest, and agreed that the darkness spell the beasts made had been worsened by the trees and the close quarters of the branches.

Out here in the open, the sky was darkened, and far off, it was hard to see the bushes, but I had a clear view of this attacking beast.

It was running now, its head lowered, the deadly sharp horn pointed directly at me.

Fifteen feet.

Ten feet.

Five.

I stepped swiftly to the side and brought my sword down heavily, slicing at the neck of the unicorn as it ran past me.

It seemed to realize at the last minute that I had moved to the side, and swerved at the last minute to catch me with its horn.

But it was too slow.

My hand came down hard, the sharp scimitar slicing through flesh, down to the bone.

The unicorn went down, crashing into the dirt and rock, its head half severed; it slid several feet before coming to a stop.

Before the body was still, I was racing back up to the camp to lend aid.

Tam had cut down one unicorn, and was sparring with another.

Darkness blanketed the camp, and even the firelight was dimmed.

An unnatural silence dampened all sound, and my ears were ringing with the faint noise of Tam's sword hitting unicorn horn.

I ran up to three other unicorns that had crept up to attack the camp.

The element of surprise was on my side, so I dispatched the first one quickly, striking it as I ran past, my sword cleaving its neck clean off. The body fell heavily.

Next I faced a large male, he'd lowered his head and pointed his horn at me, and pawed the ground as a prelude.

Was it trying to intimidate me? Not working, unicorn.

I waved my scimitar, twirling it in my hand, moving it back and forth across the front of my body, tempting the beast to charge.

It took the bait.

Running forward, its hooves pounding the ground, it came at me fast.

I waited, in a slight crouch, as it approached. I would use the same move as I had before: the sideswipe move, I liked to call it.

The unicorn's eye was focused on me, its steely gaze seemed evil.

Of course it's evil: It's attacking me.

Well, yeah.

It was time.

The huge unicorn, head down, sharp horn extended in front of it, was here.

I jumped to the side quickly, and attempted to bring my sword down on its neck.

Except this unicorn was faster. And bigger. And there was firelight, so it could see me better.

Keep telling yourself these things, Charlotte.

As I brought my sword arm down, the thing turned and its horn scraped my shoulder.

My sword met flesh, but slid down the side of the neck as it turned away from me.

Ugh.

I brought my left hand up from where I'd ducked to grabbed the long dagger out of my boot holster, thrusting it deep into the beast's side and slicing its belly wide open.

It ran on, guts spilling out onto the ground as it galloped.

It knew it had been fatally wounded.

The thing galloped forward and down the slope, and disappeared into the darkness below.

I turned.

Tam had dispatched the second unicorn and was busy with a third.

I faced the last beast.

I bared my teeth and exhaled a challenge as I faced it.

This one looked smaller, and I wondered if it was fully grown.

It stared at me for a few moments, then turned and ran down the slope.

I chased it a few dozen yards, waving my scimitar as I ran, trying to scare it away.

It worked.

I hiked back up to camp, cleaning my sword as I went.

Tam was dragging unicorn bodies to the edge of the slope. They tumbled down as he released them, hooves flying as the corpses fell to the forest below.

"Don't know why they tried that," Tam said, brushing his hands together.

I waved my hand in the air, scattering what remained of the unicorns' unnatural darkness, and walked back to the fire.

Plopping down to my seat, I reached for my cup and took a sip.

Smiling, I raised the drink in a toast. "Still warm!" I chuckled.

Tam looked over the sleeping forms of the troupe.

"They didn't even stir," he said in approval.

"The darkness spell the beasts exude dampens the sound." I waved my hand vaguely. "Very useful."

Tam sat back beside me. "I think we make a good team."

"We all do. Together we're quite formidable." I smiled.

"How's your arm?" he asked.

I glanced down at it. A red streak stretched from my shoulder halfway down to my elbow.

"Awww, that'll take some sewing. This poor shirt has already been patched once on this adventure," I put my finger through the hole in the cloth.

Tam chuckled. "If that's all they were able to do to you, you're lucky."

I glanced at him, a serious look on my face. "Not lucky. Fast."

He nodded. "You're very fast on your feet, Princess. It serves you well."

"There you go again, calling me 'Princess'." I said.

"Sorry," he smiled.

"It's okay."

We sat in contented silence for a while. Tam put the water to heat again.

"Tam?"

"Yes," he answered.

"Tell me about your homeland. I understand you're from the eastern shores of Alkebulan?" I said.

He shrugged. "Not much to tell, really. Left home when I was ten. Father beat me, and I got big enough to fight back. He threw me out. I made my way to the sea, and signed on as a cabin boy to the first captain who would take me." He stared into the campfire's flames.

I remained silent, listening to the crackle of the fire, hoping he'd say more.

A few minutes later, he spoke again.

"I learned a lot those first few years. We traveled all over the Mare Internum, and I stayed mostly in the crow's nest during the day. I had good eyesight, and I was little, so my weight didn't pull much at the mast." He turned to me. "That first ship only had two mantas pulling it, so it was slow as heck." He turned back to face the fire. "It was smaller than Pride. But I was still fond of it. You never forget your first ship." He smiled with the memory.

"What happened to it?" I asked, enchanted with the story.

"Oh, it was bought by a sheikh who fired everyone and put his own staff on board, then sailed away for good. I never saw that ship again." He reached over and dropped a few tea leaves into my cup, then a few into his.

"Was this near Tambibo?" I asked.

"Nah, this was farther east, and down the coast a bit. I haven't been back to that area in years." He poured steaming water into my mug. "Made my way north after that, spent a little time in Tambibo, then moved west, searching for work. It was a lean time," he made a face somewhere between a grin and a grimace.

"It must've been hard," I said, taking a sip of the steaming liquid. "Mmmm, this is good."

Tam sipped from his own cup and nodded.

"It was a hard time, but I survived. Even spent a few months as a pickpocket," he chuckled.

"I'm shocked!" I said in mock horror. "Such a wholesome man as yourself!"

"I know, I know. Incredible, isn't it! My mother would not have been pleased." He smiled into his cup.

"Is she still alive?" I asked.

"No, she died years ago. My uncle came to tell me." Tam sniffed. "We got drunk the night he came, toasting Mama. She was a tough old bird," he raised his cup to the flickering fire. "Here's to you, Mama, wherever you are!"

I raised my cup, joining him in his toast. "To Mama!"

"To Mama!"

I brought my cup back to my lips and swallowed the rest of my tea, then I stood up.

"Well, my friend, I should hit the sack. Dawn comes early on this mountain, and I have yet to sleep."

Tam rose to his feet, drinking the last dregs of his cup. "Goodnight, Princess."

I stared at him, smiling. "Good night, Tam."

Chapter Eighteen
Harassed

The next morning found us hiking up the mountain in the dawn air, our breath visible in the chilly morning. I was out front, Caroline and Tam alongside me. Then came Khepri and Christianne.

Jim and Kym brought up the rear.

"Carrie, weren't you telling me just yesterday about the time Greta got lost and you headed a search party to go find her?" I said.

"Yes, Miss. It was a long night, full of worry," Caroline said.

"I was just mentioning it to Tam this morning," I said.

"Oh." Caroline glanced at Tam, smiling.

"She was explaining how fierce and headstrong you are, Caroline. How you led the search party and pushed them to search all night?" Tam said.

"Oh, goodness," said Caroline. "Well, when your little girl is lost, nothing can stop you finding her. I was deeply determined and refused to quit. She was only three, you know."

"Only three years old?" Tam said.

Caroline nodded. "We searched and I did not let anyone quit or sleep or anything."

"Where did you find her finally?" Tam asked.

"Well, and this is funny, because we started our search down on the outer ground of the castle, then on the moors. Goodness, it was so foggy that night ..." Caroline said.

"I think that's part of what scared us, if I remember," I said. "The thought of a three-year-old little girl, out on the misty moors, all alone ..."

"Goodness, yes, lordie, my heart is racing just remembering that night. Anyway," Caroline patted Tam's arm and continued, "you will never guess where we finally found her." She paused for effect. "Deep in the straw in the kitchen wagon, right outside the castle side door, fast asleep! Ha ha ha! Can you believe it?" Caroline shook with laughter.

Tam laughed.

"Charlotte!" Khepri's sharp call stopped me in my tracks. I looked and followed her pointing arm.

It was the weather faerie, flying in the sky toward us.

"Oh, man," mumbled Tam.

We stopped and waited for his approach.

"You! You humans!" he screamed as he came closer. "You have angered the gods of this land! You should leave, immediately!"

I sighed. For some reason, this little old man did not frighten me today.

He hovered there in the air above us, the mountain to his side, his old raggedy coat flapping in the wind.

"Humans are not welcome here!" he screeched.

"This guy was so calm and quiet when we first met him," Caroline said quietly. "What happened?"

"I don't know, but he sure looks mad today," I murmured.

"I have seen the evil that you do! The violence you have brought to this land!" the faerie screamed.

I shook my head.

"Listen, old man," I began ...

He cut me off.

"No! No, you listen TO ME! I know what devilment you did last night! I have examined the corpses of my brothers! You are evil!" The weather faerie spat.

"What is he talking about?" Khepri asked.

"Probably the dead unicorns. They attacked last night, and Tam and I dispatched them." I turned to the floating old man.

"Faerie, those beasts attacked US! We just defended our camp!"

"Lies! False speech! The unicorns are noble beasts! They have roamed this land for millennia and have never caused harm to the denizens of the forest!" it screeched.

This was getting old.

"Listen, old man, we have brought no violence to you or any of the other creatures of this land, unless attacked first! We are defensive! Not offensive!"

"Yeah, not offensive," Christianne called. "Like you and that coat of yours!" I looked over at Christianne. She was holding her nose in an exaggerated gesture.

I laughed.

Jim walked up and stood next to me, his arms crossed in front of his chest.

"YOU LYING MURDERERS! I have watched you for DAYS! You've killed rabbits! And a snake!" the faerie screamed.

"Hey! That snake was coming up behind Christianne and was about to strike at her!" Khepri yelled at the weather faerie hovering in the sky.

"It doesn't matter one bit! THIS MOUNTAIN WAS THAT SNAKE'S HOME!!! And you KILLED IT!" he screamed, spittle flying from his mouth.

"This is ridiculous," Caroline turned away.

"You humans need to LEAVE THIS LAND!" the faerie screamed.

My patience was running out. "Listen, you little ... I ..." my internal censor was making me sound stupid. I stomped my foot angrily.

"Charlotte," Jim said quietly next to me. "Don't let him get under your skin."

I took a deep breath.

The faerie hovered above us and seemed to be waiting.

Hmmm.

I waited as well, my hands on my hips.

The weather faerie did not say anything.

I shrugged, turned to my troupe and waved them forward. "Come on, everyone, let's move on."

We began hiking again, leaving the faerie behind.

I walked, trying to cool down. I stopped for a minute and took my waterskin out; I sipped a few swallows, then repacked it and kept going.

I ran up a few dozen steps to catch up to the others. Jim was in the lead. I looked back, and there was no sign of the irritating faerie.

"Hey," I said, stepping up next to Jim.

He glanced at me, eyebrows raised.

I continued, "Jim, what do you know about weather faeries?"

He thought for a moment, then spoke. "Not much, actually. I assume they are indigenous to this land, but I could be wrong." He glanced up at the sky and behind us.

Then continued in a lower voice. "They seem to like eavesdropping, for one thing."

I smiled.

"I may not know much about weather faeries specifically, but I do know a thing or two about faeries in general," he said quietly.

"Oh?" I said, my ears perking up.

He leaned over. "They like goading people."

"Ohhh. That totally makes sense, actually," I said.

"I wonder why he was so polite when we first met him," said Caroline on my other side.

"He was probably lonely. Plus, he didn't know what we were about. I think he started following us in earnest after we left his cave," said Jim.

"Why didn't he confront us after our first battle with the unicorns?"

"Maybe he isn't as all-seeing as he wants us to think. Or maybe he's just wacked. Unstable."

We hiked on, rounding another curve.

A new stone shrine came into sight.

I had my flint and steel ready. As we walked up to it, I lifted my arms and stepped up to the oil lamp atop the shrine.

Flicking the steel against the flint, I had sparks flying and the oil lit in seconds.

I turned around to look down on my troupe.

"HEYYYYY!"

I jump a foot, grabbing onto the side of the stone shrine to steady myself.

"My goodness, don't do that!" I breathed hard.

"I will do WHATEVER I want, human!" the weather faerie screamed.

I looked up. The faerie was hovering in the air above the shrine.

He leaned over and put his thumbs in his ears and waggled his fingers. "NYAHHH!"

I took a few more deep breaths, then stepped down onto the path and gave Jim a look.

Jim nodded, rolling his eyes.

Yeah. Wacked.

We started up the path again.

The faerie followed us, screaming as it floated along. "You cannot proceed any farther, humans! It has been decreed by the gods! We have decided that you may GO NO FARTHER!!!"

Jim jumped up and spoke loudly. "You! Faerie! You are no god!"

"YES, I AM! I am the god of the shrines! We built these shrines, and you have NO RIGHT to light the oil!" the old man turned upside down and around, and bent over, and made a rude gesture at us.

I scowled.

"I say again: You are no god! You did not build these shrines!" Jim called out.

"I doubt that a faerie could build a fire, let alone carve a stone shrine," Khepri mumbled.

Kym giggled.

I smiled at her. "Are you amused by all this?" I asked.

She laughed out loud. "HA HA HA! He's funny!"

This seemed to anger the little faerie, all five foot two of him, and he drifted lower in the sky. "YOU EVIL THINGS! BEGONE FROM MY LAND!" He waggled a finger at us.

I saw movement out of the corner of my eye, and, keeping my face forward, turned my eyes to see what it was.

Jim was surreptitiously ducking behind the stone shrine, putting it between him and the hovering weather faerie. I caught on that Jim had some plan up his sleeve, and walked forward, drawing the faerie's attention.

"Listen! You were amusing at first! And that cake wasn't half bad, but enough is enough! Please leave us alone!" I turned away from the old faerie. I wasn't sure why I had said *'please'* to the rude little man. I guess it was my nature to default to politeness.

Even when he's trying to goad me with rude gestures.

I nodded to myself. Even then.

"HA! YOU ATE MY CAKE! THIEVES! I want it BACK!" the faerie screamed.

"You *shared* it with us! You mean old faerie!" Christianne yelled back.

I gestured to the others to move toward the mountainside, across the path from the shrine.

"Hey! Weather faerie! Do you have any tricks up your sleeve? Telling us you're a god is pretty lame! Ha ha ha!" I called out, trying to goad the goading faerie closer.

It worked, and the hovering old man dropped closer.

"I AM a god! I AM!" he gestured at the mountain. "I made this whole LAND myself!" He floated lower.

Suddenly, the djinn flew out from behind the shrine, moving so fast he appeared as a blue-green blur.

He grabbed the weather faerie with both arms, and held him there, about ten feet above the trail.

"LET ME GO!" the old man screamed. "LET ME GO AT ONCE!"

"Not a chance," the djinn said quietly.

I smiled.

My friends are the best.

I walked out across the path, my arms crossed in front of my chest. The others followed me.

The djinn drifted down to the ground and stood there, his arms tightly wrapped around the weather faerie, who was held fast, his arms in his old brown coat held against his side. He struggled for a moment, watching me as I approached.

"Well, well, well. What do we have here?" I stopped a few feet from the old faerie.

"Let me go!" The faerie squirmed in the djinn's arms.

"What?" My eyes widened in mock surprise, and I spread my arms wide. "I thought you were a god!" I pointed at the stone shrine beside us. "I thought you had carved this shrine!" I looked at the creature expectantly.

He remained silent, his mouth turned downward into a pout.

I waved all around me. "I thought you had made this whole mountain! I thought you were all-powerful!"

The faerie remained quiet, but began to struggle against his living bonds.

I turned my head to the side.

"Are you not the massively wonderful god who rules this land?" I stepped closer. "Aren't you?" I brought my nose right up the old faerie's face, stopping an inch away.

He scowled fiercely.

I stepped back and looked at him, considering the situation. I stood there, not speaking any more, just breathing hard.

This old faerie had made a lot of accusations, and some of them had stung.

A minute passed while I collected my thoughts.

"Sure," I said, "we have killed in this land, but it was in self-defense! And we have won every fight!" I pointed at the faerie, stabbing my finger at his face.

Calm down, Charlotte. Hold it together. Be cool.

I took a deep breath. Then another.

"You killed rabbits!" The faerie said in a small voice.

"And I saw cured meat hanging from the ceiling of your cave home, way in the back!" Tam said.

"Nice one, Tam!" Khepri said.

Tam grinned.

"Listen, old man," I said to the rumpled figure the djinn held tightly. "You're no god, you're not all-powerful ..."

"Yes, I am!" he sputtered.

"Really? Really?!" I took a few steps back. "If you're all powerful, get free of that djinn holding you. Go on!" I waited a minute, staring at the faerie.

He slumped in the djinn's embrace and fell silent.

I took a deep breath and waited.

"What are we going to do with this guy?" Tam whispered in my ear.

I actually wasn't sure. I was starting to feel sorry for the thing.

Do not weaken, Charlotte. Not now.

"Old man," I walked back up to the djinn and the old man. The faerie looked up at me expectantly, his eyes sad. "Leave us alone. Stop taunting us. Go fly away somewhere." I waved my arm. "Go bother somebody else for a change."

The faerie looked at me, his expression inscrutable.

"You're an obnoxious little faerie, and we have important things to do, so go away and leave us alone!"

I stepped back and nodded at the djinn, who turned to face outward from the mountain and open his arms.

The weather faerie flew out, faster than we'd seen him flying before. He zinged away through the sky, not looking back, and disappeared over the horizon.

The djinn transformed back into his human form and brushed his hands together.

I looked at the sun, it was slowly starting its descent into the western sky.

"We still have a few more hours of daylight, let's try to at least get up to the next shrine, okay?

The others nodded.

"Hey, Charlotte," Kym called from the back of the stone shrine. "Come see this."

"What's up?" I walked over.

Kym was standing on tiptoes on the upper base of the stone, and pointing to some marking high up on the back of the top arch, behind the oil lamp.

"Look at this. These look kind of familiar," she said.

I followed her small, dark finger and stared at the stone.

"Khepri, Caroline, Christianne," I said slowly, "You're not going to believe this."

I shaded my eyes, peering closer.

The small marks carved onto the back of the shrine were very weathered, but still quite distinctive.

They came close.

Kym and I pointed.

The marks carved into the stone, looking for all the world like maker's marks, were clear as day.

They showed two centaurs, facing each other, and the stars and moon above them. Off to the side of the carving, was the distinctive mark of a double sun, with rays shining down on the centaurs. The curved line the centaurs were standing on was like a half-circle, and on the edge was waving lines, that I would bet my favorite sword, were depicting water.

"Quamernats. Quamernats built this shrine." I turned to smile at the others.

"Oh, my god!"

"Can you believe it?"

"I believe it."

"Makes sense."

"Those quamernats get around, huh?"

"They make all the cool things!"

"I should've known."

I smiled.

What an interesting afternoon.

We hiked up farther, and reached the next shrine, lit it, and decided to hurry up to the next one. By the time we reached it, we were getting tired.

Climbing steps was exhausting.

"Hey Caroline, do you have any more blackroot?" I asked. "I'm all out."

I plopped down to the ground, dropping my pack behind me, and yawned.

"Sure, Miss, here you go," Caroline handed me a fat, black twig, which I immediately stuck in my mouth and began to chew.

"I've got a large bundle of it here somewhere," said Khepri, looking in her pack. "Here you go," she lifted out a tied bundle of twigs, pulled out a handful, and handed them to me.

"Thanks," I stuffed them into my pack.

Tam built up a fire and we unrolled our bedding and tried to relax. Caroline started a pot bubbling on the fire, and added herbs Khepri handed her.

Jim then took Tam off hunting, and they returned ten minutes later with two fat rabbits.

"This mountain is teeming with game," Tam said, handing the rabbits to Khepri, who soon had them skinned and cleaned and sliced into long strips of meat.

I watched as the long sticks Christianne had gathered, and Khepri had slid the meat on, bubbled and sizzled against the fire.

The sun sank lower in the sky.

I was relaxed.

I closed my eyes.

"Hello."

I jumped in my bedroll at the voice an inch from my ear. "WHAAAA?" I swung around. It had been a small, squeaky sort of a voice.

I looked closer, next to where I'd been lying.

A small sprite stood there.

She was about ten or eleven inches tall, and wore a dress fashioned out of leaves. I looked closer. The dress looked like it was sewn together with grasses, and purple flowers adorned her hair.

"Uh, hello."

The others came closer.

"Um, hello," the high squeaky voice of the sprite said. "I would just like to say, there are many of us here." She waved her hand around her.

I blinked.

"Many of us," she continued. "And, and that mean old tripkin, he doesn't speak for all of us," she squeaked out.

Jim came closer, and got down on his hands and knees to get a better look at the little fae.

"Anyway, I would just like to say, welcome!" she bowed and waved her arm. "Don't listen to that mean tripkin, you are welcome on our mountain." she smiled.

I had no words.

"Well, bye-bye!" she waved, and was gone with a flip of a leaf.

Chapter Nineteen

A Wall of Ice and a Loss of Strength

It got rockier and colder as we climbed the mountain steps. We wrapped ourselves in our bedding, tying the blankets around ourselves, as the wind whistled around us. Snow flurries fell, alighting on our eyelashes and the scrub bushes that lined the trail.

Around midday, we rounded a turn in the trail and came upon ...

"An ice sheet," Khepri stated.

"But why?" Kym whispered, dropping her head.

The stone steps that wound clockwise around the mountain, flanked by a few stunted bushes here and there, stopped abruptly. Our destination lay somewhere beyond the thick sheet of ice that covered the sheer granite of the mountain.

I walked up to it and touched it.

"It's just ice: cold and," I pressed my fingers a bit, "wet once it melts." I sniffed the ice.

Jim transformed into his djinn form and began to drift upwards. "Be back in a bit," he called down with a wave and a smile.

"Okay then," I walked to the side. Beyond the outer edge of the trail, to the left, lay a steep drop over a jagged, rocky cliff. As I stepped close to it, my boot dislodged a few pebbles which tumbled downward, gathering more debris, in a waterfall of rocks and dirt. It was a long way down.

"Looks like this is impassable," called Caroline from the opposite end of the trail. She stood by the high vertical wall of mountain, which looked just as forbidding as the ice wall that blocked our path.

"He's coming back," said Christianne. I glanced up and saw the djinn descending slowly. His face looked grim.

His feet met the earth on the path beside us.

"Well," he rubbed his neck. "It's not good news."

Ugh.

"The ice goes up for over a thousand feet," said Jim, transformed back into human form. "The wall is sheer, icy and slick. There are no overhangs or ledges or anything. I think it was man made."

I looked up at the looming blue-black ice, then back down at Jim.

"Is there any way around it?"

"No, the trail continues at the top. It's as if the path was broken in two, and some of it dropped part way down the mountain." He shrugged. "Might've been an earthquake. Hard to tell."

"Jim, can you lift us up?" Tam asked.

Jim looked at the sailor. "Yes," he said slowly. "You should know that the ice wall goes up past where the trail starts again, it follows the slope of the mountain. It covers this side of the mountain. On the part above where the trail starts again, I saw a huge cave."

I looked at him sharply. *A cave?*

"It did not look like the other caves we've encountered. This one is huge and covered in ice. I did not investigate, but the interior is dark and looks like it goes in quite a way." Jim looked at me, his eyebrows raised.

"A place to camp for the night?" I asked.

He nodded.

Caroline spoke then. "This wind is freezing." She glanced up the ice cliff. "It's probably even colder up at the top." She looked back down and met my eyes. "Shelter would be a very good thing. We could build a fire."

Turning to Jim, I put a hand on his arm. "Jim, do you think you could lift all of us up there without sustaining injury?" I mentally crossed my fingers. I didn't see an easy way to get up this ice cliff. Even if we had rappelling equipment, it was sheer, with no shelves or places to rest, and we were not mountain climbers.

Jim turned to me and spoke quietly. "I can get us up there, but it's so far that I will be weak as a kitten for the rest of the day, maybe two." He looked at me meaningfully.

I understood. If any emergency came up while Jim was weak, we would be on our own.

There was a sound from behind me and I turned to look. *Oh dear.*

Kym had transformed into her chimera form and was trying to climb the ice wall.

She reared back and leaped up, her massive lion paws scrabbling to find purchase on the sheer ice. Sliding back down, she bunched her hind quarters, her snake tail and goat legs crouched. She leaped again, and went higher, but with the same result. Her front claws made a screeching sound as she slid back down.

The chimera then sat back and her haunches and proceeded to groom herself.

She looks so much like an embarrassed cat, of all things.

"Does anyone have any other ideas?" I said to the group at large.

"I could try climbing it. I'm good at climbing the ship ropes," Tam said.

"It's over a thousand feet high. If you fell, you'd be toast," Jim said.

Tam fell silent, and looked thoughtful.

"Could Jim take a rope up there, and tie it, and we could all climb the rope?" Christianne suggested.

"I suppose," I said slowly, thinking of a dozen things that could go wrong with that.

"I think we should have Jim take us up, one by one," Caroline said.

"But what if we needed him right afterward?" Khepri said.

"It's a chance we have to take," Caroline said.

"There is a lot of risk in going up any other way," Tam said. "I think Caroline is right."

I thought for a few minutes.

"Jim, could we rig a rope ladder?" I asked.

"I don't think we have enough rope for a thousand-foot ladder," he replied. "Plus, it's more like thirteen-hundred feet."

There was no easy way up this monster of a mountain, was there?

"Charlotte, maybe there's a trail around the other side of the mountain?"

"I think we would have seen it."

"Do we have to go straight over the top? Is there a way around the side?"

"No, it's just sheer cliff up and a drop off below."

"We're stuck."

Jim looked at me, waiting for a decision.

I thought of the giant carnivorous vine that Jim had rescued Christianne from. He was indispensable.

Maybe we could just camp at the top and wait for his strength to return?

I shook my head, hoping a great answer would drop out of my ears.

Sometimes I hate this responsibility.

But would you want your life in the hands of another making the decisions? A voice in my head answered.

I sighed.

"I'll just bring you all up to the top of the ice cliff, where the trail begins again, okay? To conserve my strength," Jim said.

I nodded. Lifting us all the way up to the ice cave would be wasting his stamina, which was very soon going to become quite a precious commodity.

"Okay, well, might as well start." I looked up at Jim and nodded.

He closed his eyes and began to transform into the djinn. Blue-green-purple. Three meters tall, nearly ten feet high. And muscular, my goodness, those muscles bulged out and gave an immense sense of strength. He was amazing.

He nodded to me and turned to the others. "Everyone, gather your packs and belongings, I'm going to carry *you*, everything else you want to bring up has to be tied on." He turned to me. "You want to come up first? Or last?"

"First. I need to explore what's up there." I nodded, indicating the others. "You going to be okay with all of them?"

"Oh, Pffttt, yeah. I'll be fine."

I smiled. I had noticed the djinn fidgeting slightly, and wondered if he was nervous. The message was clear: not that he was willing to express.

Gotcha.

I winked at Tam, behind the others. He had his sword out, ready to defend the troupe against anything that might threaten them while I was a quarter mile straight up.

Kym was back to her human form, and approached me.

"Be careful, Charlotte." She gave me a hug, a solemn look on her face.

"I will." I turned to the djinn. "Bring Kym up second, I want her up with me, in case anything bad is up there." He nodded.

I turned to the troupe. "Everyone, this might take a while, but I think it's the best course of action if we are to ascend the mountain. Be ready for anything."

I turned to the djinn, looking into his eyes. "I'm ready."

The huge, powerful djinn smiled and winked at me, then bent over nearly double and gathered me in his arms, one arm under my shoulders, the other under my legs. I was surprisingly comfortable.

"Ready?" he asked quietly. I nodded. He began to rise slowly into the air. It was very weird. I focused on his chest; the swirling tattoos were mesmerizing. His upper arms had an intricate design around them.

I glanced over at the ice wall. It was zipping by faster and faster. I closed my eyes.

Ah, so much more calming and restful.

The wind was blowing harder up here.

Another good reason not to have the troupe come up on ropes.

I turned my glance outward and was met by a swirling white blast of sleet. I quickly turned my head into the djinn's chest and wiped my eyes.

Something told me we were heading into harsh weather.

The rise up the ice wall was steadily slowing. Then I felt him turn in toward the cliff and stop.

"Here you go, Charlotte." He deposited me gently on my feet.

I turned to look around. The world was white. Bushes and low pine trees grew sideways among brush and small plants. The rocks and the ice wall led up even higher on the inside of the mountain, and everything was covered in white.

"If you're okay, I'll just go bring Kym up ..." the djinn said.

I nodded. "Thank you for lifting us up. Thank you so much."

He nodded and was gone over the edge.

I turned and walked to the side of the trail, looking up at the ice cave. The trail continued, curving up and around the mountain in a gradual ascension up to the top. The steps were still carved in the stone. On the inside of the trail, the mountain reared up, and the ice wall continued, too, but it was more slanted and not sheer. There was bushes and hand- and footholds here and there. I squinted and walked closer.

Was that an animal trail going up to the cave?

I couldn't see clearly. The ice cave was really very high. It did not reach where the trail curled around again, though. I could see the trail if I looked far along up, and it was a distant darkness along the gleaming white.

I heard a sound and turned. The djinn was back, carrying Kym. She had a wide grin on her face and seemed to have had an easier time of the ascent than I had.

I smiled and walked over to them.

"How was it?" I asked.

"Oh, that was SO MUCH FUN!" Kym clapped her hands and jumped a few times. She turned to the djinn and gave him a hug. "Thank you!"

He nodded tiredly, smiled and floated back over the side.

This is harder for him than he's letting on.

I looked out over the edge long after the djinn had disappeared to get the next of us, lost in thought.

All in all, it took almost three hours to bring the whole troupe up. The djinn was moving slower than he had when he'd brought me up. Tam was the last one up, his feet hit the ground, and he came trotting over to me.

"How's everything look?" He glanced around the snowy trail.

I pointed to the ice cave above us.

He looked up. "Oh, wow." He scouted around, staring up at the side of the mountain. "Well, it looks like we'll be able to make it up there no problem."

I noticed Kym and Christianne wandered off a few dozen feet to explore the snowy new trail.

Our most adventurous explorers.

"Miss, here is some blackroot, Khepri's handing it out. She says it will help warm you," Caroline handed me a black twig.

I took it gratefully and stuck it in the corner of my mouth and bit down. I was rewarded with a warm licorice taste flooding my cheek. The warmth continued, flooding my entire body. It was subtle on most days, but up here on the icy trail, the warmth was very welcome.

I turned to the rest of my friends. "How's everyone doing? Shall we head on up to the ice cave?"

"Charlotte," Khepri said quietly.

I turned to her. She was sitting on a rock next to Jim, who had transformed back to human form, and was bent over, his hands on his knees, the picture of exhaustion.

"Oh, Jim." I knelt in front of him, hugging him.

"I'll be fine," he gasped in a weak voice.

Chapter Twenty
The Ice Cave

I glanced around, looking for Kym. She caught my eye, standing just a dozen feet away. I gestured for her, and she hurried over.

"Kym," I whispered. "Can you carry him up to the ice cave? He so weak he can barely stand."

Kym looked at Jim, her eyes softening. "Sure," she murmured.

I rose to my feet.

"Everyone," I called. They looked up from their exploring, and I gestured them over. "Let's head on up this animal trail to the ice cave just above. We need to get out of this wind and make camp."

They nodded, and Tam took the lead, starting up the side of the mountain.

I turned back to Jim. He looked awful.

"Khepri, maybe you should ride with him, to hold him on?" I said.

"Good idea," she replied.

I nodded at Kym, who began to transform into the chimera.

As she came fully into her form, she crouched next to Jim. Khepri and I wrestled the big man onto the chimera's back. Khepri got on behind him, holding him firmly with her arms even as her legs gripped the chimera's sides.

"Grab on to her fur in front, this is going to be a bumpy ascent," I advised.

She nodded and grabbed a large tuft of fur.

The chimera looked back. "Ready?" she asked.

"As ready as I'll ever be," said Khepri.

The large chimera, climbing very carefully, started up the steep slope.

It's good there's a small trail.

I followed everyone else up.

It was not too bad. I stepped between mountain flotsam, small plants, and a few rocks. The wind had scrubbed the side of the mountain nearly clean of snow and, as I climbed, I could feel the harsh breeze whipping around my head. I'd tied my blanket around myself, taking special care to wrap my neck and head tightly in the cloth.

Otherwise I'm sure my ear would freeze and break off.

White puffs of warm breath obscured my sight as I climbed, and I had to pause while they cleared.

I glanced up at the chimera. Khepri was struggling to keep Jim from falling.

I took a deep breath and ran up a dozen feet, my boots pounding the animal trail, springing forward on my toes. I slowed as I came alongside the pair.

"Having trouble?" I asked.

I put my hands up to steady Jim, and his head flopped to the side.

"He's lost consciousness," Khepri said in a small and worried voice.

"Oh, dear. Should I climb up?" I asked.

"Just keep your hand on him from that side, I'll grip him from this side," she replied.

It was hard going, keeping Jim on the chimera's back while we climbed the trail, but we finally reached the cave.

Hands reached down to grab Jim off the chimera's back as we leveled off. I looked up and saw Tam and Caroline help ease the unconscious Jim to the ground.

"Christianne is checking out the ice cave," Caroline said. I glanced over at the looming cave entrance.

It was much larger than it looked from below. The entrance was massive, at least a hundred feet high, I estimated.

The wind whipped over us viciously and I hurried to cover Jim's face with his blanket, which had worked its way loose during the ascent on the chimera's back.

"Let's get him inside so I can settle him out of this wind," Khepri said.

We all carried the big man in, and found the ice cave to be cleared of rocks and debris, its dirt floor flat and leveled off.

A little too perfect.

I shook my head.

Stop being so paranoid, Charlotte.

As we carried Jim into the cave, at a certain point, the wind was cut off. The silence was so sudden and complete it felt almost tangible.

"Wow, this is ..." Tam's voice trailed off, his eyes surveying the cave walls as we carried Jim in.

Christianne hurried up. "Charlotte, um ..."

I glanced at her.

"Let's put him down over here," Khepri indicated a side recess in the curved cave wall.

We lowered Jim onto the ground gently. I looked into his face and saw how pale he was, and felt a curl of worry wrap around my stomach.

I straightened and was suddenly overwhelmed by a sense of foreboding.

Something ...

I looked around.

Christianne was there, behind me, trying to get my attention.

"Charlotte," she said in a low voice.

"What is it?" I asked, matching her tone. The hairs on the back of my neck rose at the look in her eyes.

"There's a stash of game in the back," she said.

I blinked.

"... and a place that definitely looks like something has slept there." She finished, a significant look in her eyes.

"Charlotte," Tam said. I turned. He was indicating the cave walls near the entrance.

I looked up.

Ohhhh...

The walls of the cave were covered with lines and swirls and large primitive pictures of elephants and unicorns and some large humanoid with a spear, hunting them. They looked like they'd been drawn with a red clay or something similar.

The prickling feeling on the back of my neck doubled.

I took a deep breath.

"Okay, well, let's just make sure the cave is empty and then figure things out. Those look kind of old ..." I trailed off.

"Oh, the cave is empty, I've already checked," said Christianne. "Come look over here."

She led Tam and me to the rear of the cave and pointed. Sure enough, there was a grubby half-eaten unicorn carcass, stuffed into the corner. I pressed against it with my toe. It was frozen. I sniffed. No odor.

Makes sense. Frozen meat doesn't smell.

I looked over at the rest of the "camp," or whatever this thing had made.

Huh?

The flattened area was large. Really large.

"Do you think this is a sleeping spot?" I whispered?

"Most assuredly," Tam whispered back.

It was a whispering kind of a situation.

I turned back to the mouth of the ice cave, about a hundred or so yards away. White swirling snow and a dying light greeted my eyes. The light was still strong enough so that I could plainly see that nothing except us was currently in the giant cave.

"I think we need to get out of here, Charlotte," Christianne whispered.

I stared at the cave mouth, mesmerized by the swirling white snow. Then, realizing the situation, I ran back to Khepri and Caroline and Jim. Kym was lying beside the inert form of the djinn-turned-man, presumably to warm him.

"Khepri, everyone, we need to get out of this cave," I whispered hurriedly.

Khepri raised her face. "What's wrong?"

My eyes dropped to Jim's still form. "Is he going to be okay?"

"He's simply exhausted. Completely out of energy. He'll be all right, but he needs to sleep." Khepri tucked the man's blanket around him tighter.

"Well, listen, it looks like this cave is occupied," I said rapidly. Khepri glanced up at me sharply. I continued, "I don't know where the thing is that lives here, or when it's coming back, but by the looks of things, whatever it is, it's large. Really large." I stared at them, my eyes wide.

Khepri stood up. "Let's get the torches out of our packs and light those, first of all. Then I want a look at what you found."

I nodded.

Makes sense.

Ten minutes later, the sunlight had all but faded to twilight, and we were making our way back to the rear of the cave, each of us carrying a large, lit torch. The flames were bright in the ice cave, and made the cave drawings flicker and jump on the wall.

Khepri, the oldest among us, not counting the djinn and the chimera, was also the most pragmatic. She led the way, alongside Christianne, a firm no-nonsense manner about her.

We'd left Kym to guard Jim, who was sound asleep.

As we approached, Khepri glanced at the cave drawings dancing in the torchlight.

"I see why those may have made you worry a little, but truthfully, they look old. Possible even ancient."

I stared at the pictures painted with clay onto the rock walls. I stepped closer and extended my torch upward. The figures were on the wall starting about fifteen feet high, then reached upward about fifty feet.

Someone would've needed a ladder to reach that high, or be incredibly tall...

I glanced around. No ladder in sight. I looked at the ground. No ladder marks, nothing at all, except our own boot prints. I looked up again and examined the cave wall paintings. I tried to see them in a different light.

Hmmm.

I looked closer and saw ice layered over the red clay figures. I looked at the edges and saw they indeed looked old. Very old.

I took a deep breath and could feel myself beginning to relax.

"Okay," I murmured to myself as I walked to join the others near the back of the cave.

Christianne walked up to the frozen unicorn carcass and pointed. Khepri bent down to examine it. She touched it with her torch, sniffed at it, and looked it over thoroughly, then rose.

"This is old. Months old," she said. "Possibly years old. It's hard to tell. Freezing preserves organic matter." She pointed out the edges of the carcass. "There are signs small creatures have been nibbling at this, even though it's frozen. I doubt the predator that killed it is anywhere nearby, I expect they'd've eaten the rest of it by now, if they were."

"What about that," Christianne pointed at the bed spot. Khepri turned and walked over.

She knelt and placed her hand gently over it.

"There are ice crystals covering the ground, and a few small pebbles here and there." She rose and brushed the dirt off her hands. "In my estimation, whatever slept here last did so a long time ago. Possibly months. Ice crystals are disturbed when laid on. These are undisturbed."

We made a camp fire next to Jim and arranged our bedding around it. If there'd been anything outside, they would have seen the firelight, and smelled the food we roasted over the fire.

Seriously, I have to calm down. I'm way, way too paranoid.

Christianne had expressed her apologies for the false alert and her own paranoia.

"Don't you dare, it's that kind of caution that keeps us alive," Khepri had said. "Better safe than sorry."

Christianne had rewarded her with a small smile, and we all felt relieved.

Still, we talked in low tones, and the howling wind outside kept us just a bit on edge.

It was a long night.

I took first watch, and I made myself a small spot near the ice cave entrance. I built a small fire, ringed by rocks, and sat with my back to the cave wall, my senses alert. It was an uneventful few hours. The snow kept swirling outside the entrance, and the wind's howling whistle was a haunting sound.

Probably makes my nerves worse.

I walked a complete circuit of the inner cave's perimeter, noticing everything, smelling everything, and finally, upon returning to my little fire and settling down for the watch, mentally agreeing with Khepri. This cave had been abandoned for some time.

I passed the time making drawings on the dirt floor, glancing up every minute or so to check the cave entrance. Every single time, my eyes were met with the same snow flurries tossed about by the wind.

Around two in the morning Tam came to relieve me.

"Hi," he said quietly, settling down next to me. "Anything going on?"

"Nope, it's been utterly quiet." I glanced out at the wind-tossed snow. "I don't think anything is out in this weather, to tell you the truth." I got up, grabbed my pack, and gave him a salute , then walked back to the troupe.

I checked on Jim before I bedded down for the night. He was sleeping soundly on his side, having turned over in the night. *That's a good sign.* I patted his shoulder and got in my blankets, and was asleep within minutes.

Morning came early. I sat up, yawning, awakened by the smell of Caroline frying rabbit meat over the fire.

"Where'd that come from? I thought we ran out?" I asked.

"Tam set his traps last night and caught three huge jackrabbits," Caroline indicated a pile of fur: the source of the meat. Snowy white and grey rabbit fur fluttered in the air. I smiled.

"Goodness, it smells like heaven." I reached into my pack for my waterskin and washed my hands and face.

I looked over at where Jim had slept, and saw his bedroll was empty. Farther on, I saw Tam snoring in a blanket. I looked over at the cave mouth.

Jim sat at the small watchfire, Khepri beside him. They were talking.

I wonder how he's feeling, I thought as I settled back down onto my bedroll.

As if she could read my mind, Caroline spoke.

"Jim woke up about a half hour ago, declared himself fit, and went to relieve Tam. Tam's been asleep now for about two minutes shy of half an hour.

We'd trained to fall asleep fast, which came in very handy when taking watch shifts. I smiled. "Sounds like everything is going well," I looked over at her. "How are you doing, Caroline?"

"Oh, I'm just fine, Miss." She handed me a plate of food, then settled down with one herself.

We ate in companionable silence.

After I ate my fill of fried rabbit and wild carrots, I washed my hands and then walked over to talk to Jim.

Khepri looked up as I approached, and smiled.

"Hey, how is everyone doing this fine morning?" I patted Jim on the shoulder and looked into his face.

Hmmm.

Khepri spoke before Jim could. "He's still weak. It'll probably be another day before he's fully recuperated."

Oh, dear.

I looked closer at Jim and noticed dark smudges under his eyes. Some of the brightness was still absent, but he looked better than he had last night.

He sputtered at Khepri's words and rose to his feet. "I am fine, Charlotte. Fine." He looked pointedly at Khepri, who met his gaze with raised eyebrows.

She said nothing, but gave me a significant look as she walked back to the cooking fire.

I turned to Jim, putting a hand on his arm. "Jim," I said softly. "It's okay to still be recuperating."

"Charlotte, I am fine. I swear."

I looked at him silently and waited.

"Okay, I may not be one hundred percent but I am ninety percent or more." He raised his eyebrows and gave me a 'so what' look.

I made a mental note. *Jim still needs rest.*

"Perhaps we should stay here another day," I said.

"That's not necessary, really," Jim replied.

I hugged him. "I'm glad you're feeling better, Jim." I looked up at his face as he sat back down. "Have you eaten?"

In answer, he burped and patted his stomach, winking at me. I laughed and headed back to the large fire.

Jim may think he's recovered, but I don't want to start out on our hike up the mountain without each of us in tip-top condition. Anything could happen. My thoughts flickered back to the ogre. To the huge plant attacking Christianne.

Nope, I think we'll camp here one more day.

I returned to the others.

"Troupe, I think we'll stay camped here for one more day," I glanced back at Jim, then forward again. "I want us all to be in the best shape possible for the next leg of our journey. Remember what the merman elder said about this mountain."

They all nodded. We remembered.

I busied myself by tidying our camp area. This took maybe a half hour. We were getting to be a clean camping crew.

I approached Caroline. "Carrie, did you cook all the rabbit meat already?"

"No, Miss, I cooked half of it," she replied.

"I wonder if I should go hunting?" I looked out the cave mouth.

"Did someone say 'hunting'?" Tam said, walking up to me.

"I'll go too!" said Christianne.

In the end, there were four of us who set out that midday to see what we could capture.

"If we don't cook it, we can salt it and preserve it," Caroline told me. "So, don't hold back."

We walked out of the cave mouth. The wind had died down, and the snow had stopped. The icy glittering whiteness was beautiful.

A rabbit ran across our path, completely unafraid. Then another.

This land is full of game. We're going to have an easy time.

Tam took out his bow and started shooting game. I wandered off with Christianne and Kym and set a few traps. The day was shaping up to be beautiful.

Chapter Twenty-One
A Great and Terrible Loss

"I can't believe we found this spring," Christianne said as she sat on the edge of the hot spring.

The water was warm and had steam rising from it in a cloudy, mystical sight.

Christianne and Kym had taken their boots off and were dangling their feet in the water, their faces blissful.

I sat nearby, trying to rig up a way to capture the huge crawfish we'd seen.

We'd noticed the steam rising from beyond some bushes; stepping through them, we'd seen the spring. Then the crawfish. At least eight or ten of the fat crustaceans were half out of the water, just resting there.

Waiting.

Waiting for my hook and line. Waiting to be boiled for lunch. Waiting to be dipped in butter and eaten.

My mouth watered as I stood there, the hook firmly tied on the thin, strong line. I hadn't been sure if I would find anything to capture when we'd first set out on this adventure, but the fishing gear was a part of my pack, something I always carried, and I was grateful for it. *Especially since those delicious morsels had flipped back into the water so fast after seeing us that they'd created a huge ripple on the surface, and even the steam rising from the spring had been disturbed.*

I searched along the edge of the water for anything ... *AHA!* I lifted the fat insect up to my eyes. Right under the loamy ground surrounding the hot spring. I stuck the unhappy bug onto my hook, wrapping it tightly, and dropped the line into the water with a soft *plop.*

I sat to wait.

Tam walked up then, his hands gripping two snowshoes rabbits. "How are you ladies doing? Ooh! A hot spring!" He winked at us. "I'm going back to drop these off, but when I return, I just might join you."

"Okay!" Christianne waved.

I dipped my hand in the water. It was deliciously warm.

My eyes closed in contentment.

I was roused by the tug on my fishing line. *OH!* I'd dozed off, but I'd curled the line around my fingers. Sitting up, I flipped the crawfish out of the water, and it plopped onto the ground at my feet. It flipped and flopped. I grabbed it. It struggled. It pinched me.

"Oh, no you don't!" I was determined.

The thing was a good eight inches long, and I had it tied and hanging from my belt in five minutes.

Tam clapped, smiling.

A half hour later, six more of its brethren had joined it, and I was baiting the hook again.

"Those look really good. They're so fat!" Tam said from his position next to Kym. His boots were off and his feet were in the water, and the little hot springs was starting to resemble the royal baths I'd visited in Kemet.

I stared at his long legs, bare in the warm water. The tanned lengths of each, with softly curling hair ...

Stop staring, Charlotte.

I shook my head and looked at the swirling hot spring water, then looked up at Christianne. She was braiding Kym's hair.

Tam was leaning back on his elbows, his face lifted toward the sun, his eyes closed. Long, dark lashes rested against the suntanned cheeks. His beard looked ...

I shook my head again. *Lord Almighty, woman ...*

I held up the string of crawfish.

"A few more, and it'll be enough for dinner for all of us," I smiled.

"They're so easy to catch!" said Christianne.

"I think humans might be new to this area; they're not used to predators like us," Tam said, opening his eyes.

I winked. "Not used to a baited hook," I laughed. "They just think they're getting lucky." The line tugged against my hand. "Oh, got another one!"

In the end, after two hours fishing, I'd caught ten of the crustaceans. We all decided to head back and have a hearty lunch.

"Caroline will be so surprised," I said.

"Surprised? At what?" said Caroline, meeting us at the edge of the cave mouth. "Ooh! Miss, what have we here?"

I handed the heavy load of crawfish over, and she hurried away to clean and prepare them.

"I can't wait." My stomach grumbled and I patted its flat surface. "I ate a full breakfast, I swear."

Kym laughed. "Those huge crawfish looked so enticing, my stomach was grumbling, too."

I looked up at the sky. It was a deep blue. The wind that had been such an onslaught during the night was nowhere to be seen. I closed my eyes and took a deep breath.

Christianne, Kym, Tam and I stood there in the sunshine, the cold air icy on our skin after the warm air above the hot spring.

"Do you want to go exploring?" asked Tam.

"Sure."

"That sounds nice."

"Anything to stay in the sunshine."

We walked to the right, along the animal path, in the opposite direction we'd gone that morning. About fifty yards up the side of the mountain, I noticed the ground was firmer here, and the bushes thicker.

"It's getting colder the higher we go," said Tam. He had his bow out again, in case he spied any game.

"I think ..." I stopped in my tracks and put a hand out to stop Christianne, who was walking beside me. I put my finger to my lips and looked forward again.

Tam had halted and was nocking an arrow to his bowstring.

Kym looked on, speechless.

We'd rounded a corner and nearly fallen into a small recess in the ground that was the mouth of a small cave, much smaller than the cave where we'd taken refuge. It was maybe twenty feet tall and twice as wide. We couldn't see how far deep into the mountain it went, because it was obscured by a slumbering monster.

I held my breath.

It was huge. Curled up in the cave recess, it barely fit. It had to be at least forty feet tall when it stood upright.

Probably taller.

I watched it for a minute as we stood still and tried not to make a sound.

The thing was only eight feet from us, and it was facing out of the mountain, toward us.

I tried to take a step back, and the monster's face twitched.

It looked humanoid, but massive. Its coloring was a plain grey, with grey hair the same shade as its skin sitting sparse atop its head. A raggedy bearskin, sewn together haphazardly, was tied around its waist.

It slept curled up like a bear, its two palms clutched together, obscuring half its face. A bulbous nose snored quietly, set between thin, ruddy cheeks.

I looked closer. In fact, the monster's whole body looked a little thin.

It must take a lot of food to sustain a creature that large.

It shifted in its sleep, its head moving slightly, and I saw that it had only one eye.

What?

Oh, no. No no no no no. Not a cyclops. Ohhhhh, my god ...

Cyclops were known to be vicious, strong and violent. And fast. A monster you did not want to meet, especially on a lonely, frozen mountain path.

My eyes grew so wide they began to ache.

Tam tapped my arm, and I looked at him. He gestured that we should move back. I saw Kym and Christianne frozen in place behind me. I looked at Tam and nodded.

I carefully tried again to take a step back. My foot landed quietly. I took another.

Tam moved beside me, trying to place his boot on the path without making a sound.

Christianne and Kym stepped away, moving fast.

The problem was, everything was quiet around us. So, a noise, any noise, would sound loud in the cyclops' ears. My stomach clenched in fear. I took another step. Then another. Christianne was already more than twelve feet away from me.

I heard a loud snore, then a grumble.

I turned back to look. I couldn't help myself. Tam, beside me, looked as well.

My eyes fell on the face of the cyclops.

And its eye.

It was open. It was staring at us.

I knew I was groggy when I first woke up, maybe this monster will be, too.

Tam's hand was on my arm, squeezing.

The cyclops seemed to focus.

Its mouth opened and a roar of indignation bellowed out.

"RUN!" Tam yelled, pushing me up the mountain trail.

I heard Christianne scream. Glancing up, I saw she had stumbled. Kym was grabbing her, trying to pull her along.

I sprinted up to them and helped Christianne to her feet, and together we glanced back.

The cyclops was coming to its feet. It was even bigger than I'd thought: As it rose upright, I could tell it was over fifty feet tall. And its legs were half of that height.

The blood drained out of my face. I could feel it go.

"RUN!" Tam screamed a second time.

I needed no further encouragement.

Christianne, Kym, and I ran up the mountain trail as if one of those evil demon spirits from the Tomb of Ancients was on our tail.

No, this is worse than a demon spirit. This thing is worse. Much worse.

The animal trail was a thin path through the brush, made by rabbits, deer, elk, goats, and whatever else lived on this mountain. We ran as fast as we could, our boots pounding the uphill trail with skill, our eyes searching for every foothold.

Tam was right behind me, his hand pushed against my back every now and then. We ran up the trail so fast. *Were we free? Had the cyclops stopped chasing us?*

I glanced back over my shoulder. "Is it gone?"

I was rewarded by a new push from Tam, a quick shaking of his head, and a roar from the monster gaining on us.

It's gaining on us?

This mountainside was the cyclops' home. It lived here. It knew the trails, the rocks, and the ice. It knew every inch.

I ran, right behind Kym, who was right behind Christianne. I ran and my breath came in gasps, and my heart pounded in my chest, and I still ran. We did not slow down.

The cyclops climbed up after us, barely gaining, but we were smaller and seemed to be able to flit across the trail more easily than the lumbering, humongous beast that was chasing us.

My breath puffed out of me in white clouds, hot and furious, and we ran.

We ran hard.

Thank god for adrenaline.

I am not sure if the sound the cyclops made next was in frustration, or what, but there was a tremendous roar, and it lunged at us, I saw it out of the corner of my eye. It jumped, nearly horizontal, its arm outstretched, its hand trying to grab ...

Everything happened at once.

Christianne screamed, and stumbled. Kym flipped over in the air and transformed instantly into the chimera, and I felt myself choking. Some piece of trail flotsam had flown into my mouth, and suddenly I couldn't breathe.

The chimera was next to us, roaring ferociously, growing to her extended height of thirty feet tall

But ...

Where was Tam?

I coughed, and coughed again, spitting, my eyes on the chimera. She was roaring and pawing the air, and I saw the cyclops' arm come up against her. It was huge, much larger than the chimera.

All this was happening just a few feet from me.

The cyclops arm swung and missed the chimera and slammed into the ground.

I turned and looked.

Oh, no! NO!!!

The cyclops had Tam in its other arm. It had the sailor curled up against its side, and gripped Tam's middle tightly. I saw Tam had his sword out, and was trying to stab the giant creature. But the cyclops was shaking him in such a rage that he couldn't aim straight. I saw it was squeezing him. Tight. It was squeezing the strength ... the breath out of him.

The chimera launched itself at the cyclops, landing on its shoulder. The locked fighters tumbled down the mountain a dozen feet.

"TAM!!!" I screamed.

The air was filled with the roar of the chimera, fierce and chilling. The cyclops had its hands full fighting my friend, and the chimera, even though much smaller than the monster, used her massive claws to draw blood over and over again, swiping at the cyclops in a desperate attempt to save Tam.

The chimera roared and jumped again, landing on the cyclops' head. I saw her bite down, and heard the cyclops scream out in pain. It jumped to its feet, moving faster than such a huge monster should move, and swung an arm against the chimera.

The blow landed squarely against the chimera's head, and she went down.

I screamed again.

The cyclops turned toward me and roared viciously, then stopped and turned away, Tam's now-limp form still clutched to its side. It jumped down the mountain slope, landing twenty to thirty feet away, then jumped again. I watched it go. It leapt down the mountain without slowing, sure of foot, and was gone.

I raced down the path to the chimera, bent to be sure she was still alive, then raced after the monster, hurrying down the path after the cyclops, after Tam, leaving Christianne cradling the chimera in her lap, hot tears running down her face in thick streams.

I went after the monster, my scimitar drawn, my boots sure on the animal path, following him all the way. Caroline and Khepri had heard the screams and raced out of the ice cave, and I pointed behind me, up the mountain, toward Christianne and the wounded chimera.

I raced after the beast. I could no longer hear it, but the running cyclops had made a clear path down the mountain. I followed it all the way back to the top of the ice cliff.

Where had it gone?

I raced desperately along the top of the ice wall, trying to find where it had run.

I ran down to the sheer drop, then up again toward the mountain path that led to the ice cave. It was nowhere to be found. I raced and retraced my path, searching over and over, for over an hour.

I called out, crying for Tam, hoping he was still alive.

Khepri can heal him. Khepri can heal anything. She was an amazing and miraculous healer.

I searched and searched.

I finally found them. I'd climbed far off to the right, nearly falling several times, out over the ice cliff, back toward the side of the cliff we'd come up and over. I finally spotted a ledge, far, far out, halfway down to the ice cliff base.

Khepri can fix anything.

The cyclops had a second camp. It was huddled there, at least two hundred yards away, halfway down the mountain. It had a fire going, and it was crouched over it.

I knelt behind some bushes, staying hidden, and took out my brass sight.

I focused. I saw what the cyclops was doing. Then I turned and vomited into the bushes, tears streaming down my face.

The cyclops had ripped Tam's arm off, and was roasting it over the fire.

Chapter Twenty-Two
Of Butterflies and Dragonflies

It took me a long time to walk back up to the ice cave. Mostly because I was crying so hard, but also because I kept vomiting, until all I could do was dry heave. And still my stomach contorted, stopping me, bending me over to spit green bile into the bushes.

I finally made it to camp.

Caroline met me at the mouth of the cave, her face frantic with worry. She took one look at me and knew.

"MISS! Oh, Miss! Oh, my God. I ..." She came and folded me into her arms.

I stumbled as a fresh course of tears made their way out of my eyes. Sobs wracked my body as I staggered to the fire, and fell to the ground next to Khepri, Kym, and Christianne.

Jim came over and enfolded me in his arms, and held me as I sobbed. Caroline wiped my face with a cool, wet cloth.

Kym lay there crying, as Khepri doctoring her wounds, which had been too severe to disappear entirely when she'd transformed.

Christianne was face down on her bedding, her moans audible as she wept into her pack, her back heaving with sobs.

We all cried.

My chest convulsed with sobs, and I clutched at Jim; Caroline lay next to me, and we all held each other as we mourned Tam.

They next day, we set out at dawn. None of us spoke much as we hiked up the icy stone steps.

We did not encounter the cyclops again. I had never battled such a fierce monster, not even when I had faced the manticore two years ago in the deserts of northern Alkebulan.

What little we spoke was in quiet tones. Tam's death warranted deep respect for the warrior he had been.

The stone steps carved into the mountain were covered in a layer of ice. We stayed to the sides, where the snow was still fresh and not blown away, to avoid slipping. The middle steps were icy and slick. I nearly fell twice when I wasn't paying attention and strayed too far off the crunchy snow.

Jim walked with his head hung. He looked miserable.

I kept assuring him that it hadn't been his fault, that the cyclops was the fiercest monster we'd fought in years, and that the terrain had been impossible, and steep. The cyclops had come upon us too quickly, and had moved too fast. It had been an unwinnable fight.

I had a sick feeling in my stomach as I hiked up the steps, and my chest felt tight. And something else. A sorrow in my heart that would not abate.

We stopped for rest and a short meal when the sun was high.

The shrines every thousand feet had been a welcome sight, and we'd dutifully lit every one we'd come across. Fresh flowers had been placed at the base of these higher-elevation shrines; the petals were nearly frozen, but they looked as if someone or something had visited there in the past day.

We scouted around, looking for any sign of life, but despite the flowers, no one appeared.

"Charlotte, I think the ice is melting," Kym said, pointing.

She was right. The steps were wet. I looked up and saw strange clouds in the sky.

"Those clouds ..."

"I don't think those are clouds."

We ran up the steps, and as we ran, curving to the right with the steps, the snow disappeared.

"It's just ..."

"It melted, look at how it's raining."

"It's raining?"

"Look."

"Oh, yeah. Huh."

The steps were wet and it was drizzling. Two hundred feet down the stairs it was snowing.

"I think the air is a little less freezing, too."

"But the wind is kicking up, making it seem colder again."

I looked up once again. Thick, white smoke was rising from something on the mountain, something higher up. I guessed it was about a mile away.

"Let's run."

"Race you!"

We pounded up the steps, and I felt my heart race with the renewed purpose. I was glad to feel alive.

Tam would have wanted me to remain strong and vibrant and alive, not wallow in sadness.

Kym and I raced, side by side, and found myself gritting my teeth and running up the stairs faster than I thought possible. My long legs carried me forward, and I was three steps ahead of Kym when I made it to a plateau.

"WOOP!" I thrust my arms in the air in triumph as Kym landed beside me, laughing.

"This is nuts ..."

"God, that felt great."

"Did you see the clouds?"

"Whoa."

I turned around and was amazed at what I saw.

The stone path we'd been following wound across a short meadow, maybe fifty yards across, full of grass and flowers. After that, it continued its ascent. The steps on the far side of the grass looked inviting, and something inside me wanted to run across quickly and get to the other side.

"Let's proceed with caution," Khepri said.

"Awww."

"Khepri is right, these grasses could hide anything. A swamp creature, a giant snake. Alligators ..." Caroline's voice trailed off.

I glanced at her. "Alligators?"

"Well ..." She smiled.

"Let's just cross, but Khepri is right, no running. Swords out," I drew my scimitar.

We marched deliberately across the strange meadow, and our boots sank into the ground so far that the grasses reached well past our thighs by the time we were halfway across it. My eyes searched in the tall grass and flowers for anything that might be a threat.

"Look!" I turned and saw Christianne had stopped, and several butterflies were perched on her arm. They were flexing their wings back and forth. They were beautiful.

"Oh look!" Kym held out her hand, a brilliant blue dragonfly, about two inches long, sat on the end of her finger.

We were more than halfway across the meadow.

I smiled and closed my eyes, taking a deep breath of this beautiful place. The scent of flowers filled my senses. A cloying, sweet, spicy scent entered my nostrils.

Suddenly, a scream rang out.

My eyes sprang open, and I turned, trying to pinpoint its source.

Behind me, at the back of our straggling line of wanderers, was Christianne.

Butterflies and dragonflies, as well as moths, honeybees, and a few strange fluttery insects I had never seen, were converging on her face.

Jim sprang into action, racing back and grabbing at the things that had landed on Christianne. They were so thick I couldn't even see her face.

She screamed again, pawing at her cheeks.

Jim gave up trying to get them off, picked her up bodily, and turned, racing with her in his arms toward the steps that continued upward. He transformed as he ran, growing taller and bigger before our eyes.

I followed him with my shocked stare, as I stood in the tall grass. All of this happened within fifteen or twenty seconds.

Another scream.

It was Caroline. Butterflies and other winged insects were clustered on her face, growing thicker as the seconds passed.

I dove for her hand, grabbed it, and yanked her forward, running after Jim.

The butterflies were now attacking me as I ran. A half dozen lit on my face, and somehow hooked themselves there, unmoving. Where they touched my face, I felt a stinging sensation. On every point of every insect leg. More insects converged. More stinging. My face felt like it was on fire.

My run became a sprint. I was still dragging Caroline, who somehow remained upright and was still running beside me.

"AHHHH!" I heard. I did not glance behind me to see who it was.

Khepri ran beside me, on my other side. Then she passed me. Dragonflies and moths covered her entire head. She batted at them as she ran.

I finally felt the grasses part and stone beneath my feet, as I pelted across the rock expanse and on up the stairs. I grabbed at my face with one hand, ripping butterflies from my skin as I ran. My other hand kept a firm grip on Caroline.

We stumbled up the stairs after the djinn, who was bounding ahead so fast I was close to losing sight of him.

If we don't hurry, we're going to get separated.

That hadn't turned out well the last time. I thought back to our quest for *The Book of Mysteries* and how we'd gotten split up while running from a threat.

"Wait!" I called out. "Find a safe spot and stop!"

The djinn seemed to slow a little. He was at least fifty yards ahead of us.

Well, I hope he stops soon.

I heard footsteps pounding up the stone behind us.

I tore the last butterfly off my face and slowed down.

A dragonfly lit on my cheek.

Dagnabbit! I reached up and tore at it ferociously, flinging it away. This was getting old.

I was now puffing along, running but slower than I had at the beginning. I still pulled Caroline up after me.

"Charlotte, Charlotte," the voice of the djinn was close. I looked up from my concentrated stare at the steps I was mounting.

He was up about ten feet, off to the side, standing at another shrine, with Christianne.

I raced up to him with renewed vigor, dragging Caroline along with me.

"Miss, I'm okay ..."

I still didn't let go of her hand.

We reached the landing, and I allowed myself to bend over, hands on knees, puffing slightly to catch my breath. Kym ran up and stood beside us, followed by Khepri.

Oh, god, she still had some insects on her face.

"You're bleeding," I said to Khepri, as I picked the things off and threw them down to the stone ground, where I smashed them with my boot sole.

"Oh, man, oh yuck ..."

Jim was back to human form, and he was looking us all over. The insects hadn't touched him.

Lucky duck.

Oh, I take that back. They'd nailed him on his left side. I reached over and brushed his ponytail back.

"They got you, I think. It looks like stings, but there's very little blood.

Christianne was the worst off. Her face was a mass of tiny droplets of blood.

We made camp behind the shrine, lighting it and some brush nearby ablaze to ward off any more carnivorous insects.

A small spring bubbled up not far away, with a stream that led downward and through the meadow. I looked back on the wide expanse of grass and flowers, and shook my head. It looked so beautiful and peaceful. So safe.

I looked closer. I could see butterflies and dragonflies dipping and flitting over the grasses, looking innocent and sweet.

Probably looking for more prey.

I was washing my face and hands in the spring when Khepri came over.

"Those things left a venom," she said, handing me a towel and some salve.

She looked my face over.

"Hmmm … a little redness: The blood has stopped flowing. Not as bad as Christianne, thank goodness. She's a mess." She indicated the girl a few yards away. Caroline was applying salve to her face, which was red and slightly puffy.

"What were those things?" I asked as Khepri took the salve from me and began applying it to my face. "And why didn't they go for my hands, too?" I looked over the exposed skin on my wrists and fingers. There wasn't a mark on them.

Khepri put one hand under my chin and tilted my face upward, reaching up with the other to treat a spot near my ear. "They were apparently attracted to the carbon dioxide coming from your mouth."

"You mean when I exhale? My breath?"

"Exactly. They're bloodsuckers, like mosquitoes, only bigger. How they evolved this way here, when, back home, butterflies and dragonflies, and moths for that matter, generally feed on the nectar from flowers, I don't know." She capped the bottle of salve and nodded.

"Okay, you're set." She looked over at the others, then back to me.

"I think it would be good if we moved to the next shrine, a thousand steps farther, just to make sure." She looked at me, her eyebrows raised.

For a second, I imagined those things besetting us as we slept, and shuddered.

"Good idea."

That night, so far up the mountain that the bit of meadow we could see was a small square of green far below us, we feasted and talked.

Khepri set to the task of boiling more herbs in a small iron pot on the side of the fire, collecting the sticky substance as it accumulated on the top inside edge of the pot. She kept adding more herbs, and the process continued for several hours.

"Most of you have had good results from the salve, and I want to have plenty on hand," she explained, stoppering another jar of the medicine and placing it carefully into her medical bag.

Christianne groaned from the blankets she was settled in. She had experienced a bad reaction from the butterfly and dragonfly venom and had a fever.

Caroline gently touched a cool, wet cloth to her forehead, and the teenager mumbled in her sleep.

"Here, rub this on her feet." Khepri handed Caroline a bottle.

Caroline unstopped it and took a whiff; wrinkling her nose, she withdrew it from her face, and examined it closer.

"Potent stuff," she said.

"It's medicinal alcohol. It will draw the fever down," Khepri said.

Caroline nodded and lifted the blanket from Christianne's feet.

I reached over to the fire and turned the spit a quarter of the way around. Two rabbits were skewered there, fat and sizzling. Jim and I had shot them as we hiked up to the second shrine.

I glanced at the oil lamp atop the shrine. The flame flickered merrily in the dying light. I lifted my face higher, to the deepening indigo blue of the darkening sky. Stars were beginning to appear.

A shooting star flamed a wide arc across the sky. Then another.

"Oh, something auspicious is going to happen soon," Khepri said. She reached down and scraped the salve off the inside of the pot.

I hoped it will be a good event, we could use some good luck.

Chapter Twenty-Three

Midnight Watch

I took first watch, as usual, and found myself staring moodily into the coals of the crackling fire. I'd developed the habit of using my time on watch to go back over the events of the day, and consider how we might have reacted better to the challenges we'd faced.

My troupe had responded well to the insects. Our reaction time and strength in the face of sudden danger were improving. I flexed my arm out beside me, watching as the bicep rose to a strong mound. I looked down at my legs and flexed the muscle, watching as the top of my thigh rose above my knee and grew firm. I rapped my knuckles against the bulging muscle, and it made a satisfying *thump*.

I'd grown tough and muscled since my arrival in Alkebulan two and a half years ago. I felt older than my twenty years, more mature and seasoned as a warrior.

A firefly lit up briefly, then another. They stayed back from the fire, and flittered here and there in the darkness on the other side of the shrine.

"Charlotte..."

I turned around.

"Hello?" I said.

No answer.

I must've imagined it...

I stared back into the fire, feeling unsettled. The fireflies flickered just beyond the firelight.

I sat up, senses alert. I had seen something other than fireflies in the darkness. I stared unblinkingly past the camp and to the trail, where the stone steps formed a plateau, a recess in the path where the stone steps curved. The stone was flattened out there, where the huge shrine had been built. The oil lamp atop the shrine was still lit from where we'd touched our torch to it the previous day, as we'd hiked up to the stone structure.

I surveyed the entire area from where I sat.

A firefly lit briefly and flickered across my field of vision. The trail of light from the insect made it harder to see beyond it, and the landscape farther on looked even darker.

"Charlotte..."

There it was again.

"Okay, whoever you are, show yourself," I said, shivering as I scrambled to my feet.

I decided to make a circuit of the camp, and check everything.

I unsheathed my scimitar and balanced it easily in my right hand.

Familiar. Comfortable.

I swished the sword back and forth through the night air. The weight was right for my height and strength, and it felt natural in my hand.

We'd spent much of the voyage time sailing west in training. I had sparred at least three to four hours a day, practicing moves and experimenting with different actions and motions, adding them to my repertoire.

I thought back to those days, when the ocean breeze sprayed fresh in my face, and I'd laughed easily with my sparring partner.

More often than not, lately, that had been Tam.

Tam.

A lump formed in my throat, and the memory threw me off balance.

I still couldn't believe what had happened. And it had happened so quickly.

I shook my head, tears forming in my eyes.

I have to get over this. At least enough to proceed with the task at hand.

I stepped forward, determined to complete my rounds of the camp. Walking the perimeter of the small circle, glancing down at my sleeping troupe, I felt my balance returning.

I gazed out at the darkness surrounding us. Crickets chirped, and everything was calm. The stars twinkled in a clear sky.

The air and ground had grown warmer since we'd reached the meadow.

Khepri had guessed that there might be volcanic activity inside the mountain, warming everything, melting snow as it approached the ground, allowing the grasses and bushes to grow alongside the trail again.

Khepri also guessed that the strange magical quality of the land, and the volcano inside the mountain itself, might also be the cause of the carnivorous butterfly and dragonfly insect life.

We'll probably never know.

I wanted to proceed up the mountain, find the treasure with the poisonous coins so we could keep them from infecting the oceans, and then leave.

So much sadness.

I was already sick of this mountain, but what had happened to Tam was a large part of that.

I finished my round of the camp, and stood next to the fire once again, staring out into the dark night.

"Charlotte..."

I turned my head, trying to sense where the voice was coming from. It was a whisper, and it was hard to tell if the voice was female or male, human or otherworldly, real or imagined by my tired brain.

"Charlotte..."

I swung around, then jumped to the side, staring.

What was that?

I thought I'd seen something on the other side of the fire again. Gripping my scimitar, I grimaced and rushed forward, leaping over the fire and landing on the other side, next to the stone shrine.

A mist was forming. There, just beyond the trail. I walked forward, trying to see what it was.

"Charlotte..."

I walked forward a step, then another. A shape was coming out of the mist ...

It was Tam.

My eyes opened wide, and my throat constricted.

He was there, walking forward, whispering my name ...

"Charlotte..."

But he was covered in blood. The side of his neck was bloody, and his leg dragged.

I could not stop staring.

The bloody stump of his arm reached forward, reaching for me ...

"Charlotte..."

"AHHH!"

I sat up, my heart racing, my eyes wide.

Kym looked over at me from her spot by the fire, where she was on second watch.

"You okay, Charlotte?" She asked.

I looked around wildly, trying to calm my breathing.

Had it been a dream? It had seemed so real ...

I took a deep breath.

"Yeah, I'm okay. Just had a bad dream," I looked at her. "How is everything going?"

"All quiet since I relieved you."

"Which was ...?"

"About an hour ago, Charlotte." Kym stood and stretched. "Thinking of heating some coffee, want some?"

"Nah," I replied. I'm going to try to get back to sleep."

"Good idea," she looked east, over the mountainside. "Dawn will come early this high up."

I nodded and turned over, punching my bag, which served as my pillow, and settling back down.

It seemed just a few minutes later that my eyes opened once more, but this time the sun was up. Khepri had a pot bubbling, Kym was walking the perimeter of the camp, and Caroline was rousing Christianne awake.

I sat up, rubbing my eyes.

Well, that was a horrible night's sleep.

I pulled my boots on and stood up.

"Charlotte?" Kym called from the path. I walked over, grabbing my waterskin on the way.

"What's up?" I asked.

Kym just pointed. I looked down. My eyes focused.

There, on the stone, by the shrine, was a spot of blood. Fresh blood.

I looked closer.

Now there were three spots of blood. Thick drops that looked as if they'd been dripped from a wound just at that moment.

My heartbeat quickened.

I knelt down and touched my fingers to the blood; there were now eight or nine fat drops.

Fresh. Not even dried at the edges.

I brought my fingers up to my eyes, smearing the blood on them with my thumb, mesmerized.

What is going on?

I felt two drops fall onto my outstretched hand. Blood. I looked up and ...

"AHHH!"

Tam stood above me, the stump of his arm extended out over me.

It was pitch dark again.

"Charlotte ... why ... did you let me die ..."

"AHHHHHHHH!"

I looked around wildly, jumping to my feet.

It was still night, everyone was asleep, the fire had died down to just one log, barely flickering.

I swung around to look at Tam, but he was gone.

I looked at the stone ground.

The blood was gone, too.

I looked at my fingers, and they were free of blood.

I am losing my mind.

My breathing was fast and shallow in my chest, my heart raced, and my ears rang, as I threw a couple of more branches onto the fire, poking it until they caught and the flames flickered higher. Then I stood to make another pass around the camp perimeter.

I walked swiftly, scanning the darkness for anything, anything at all. I threw a few rocks into the dark bushes, and surprised a bat; it fluttered away, squeaking its complaint at having been roused from its nighttime search for food.

By the time I sat back down to complete my watch, I was talking to myself.

"Well, Charlotte," I said aloud. "I don't know if you're just tired, feeling survivor's guilt, or actually being haunted." I looked around at the night that surrounded the camp. "But I cannot wait to get the heck off this mountain."

I shivered, completely creeped out.

The rest of my watch proceeded uneventfully, for which I was immeasurably grateful.

The moon was overhead when I heard Kym yawn and sit up.

She looked over at me and smiled sleepily.

"Hey, Charlotte, everything okay?"

"Yep," I answered. "Everything's been quiet. No bugs trying to eat my face, no cyclops trying to rip me to shreds, no nothing." I smiled. "All quiet on the western front."

I stood and stretched.

I had decided to keep my experiences to myself, especially since I didn't know if they had been in my imagination. I was betting Tam's ghost had been all in my head, since there were no outward indications that he'd actually been here. I'd done a few more sweeps of the camp, walking the perimeter, searching for anything odd, and had found nothing. Nothing at all.

Keep telling yourself that, Charlotte.

Kym stepped up to me, patted me on the shoulder, and looked up into my eyes.

She was a child, and yet thousands of years old, so it was an odd situation. I appeared older than she did, more mature, and all that. But Kym had an ancient wisdom that accompanied her childlike traits, that often gave her the ability to voice sage advice and wisdom.

She patted my shoulder again, then gave me a hug.

"It'll be all right. It'll take time, but it'll be all right," she said, nodded quietly.

I nodded, unable to speak past the sudden lump in my throat.

I walked back to my bedroll and settled down, lying there, facing Kym as began the second watch.

I felt content knowing there was a chimera watching over us as we slept.

My eyes closed, and I fell into a deep sleep almost immediately.

Chapter Twenty-Four
Infection

I had noticed that Christianne was tossing and turning in the night, and moaning in her sleep. Right before dawn, Khepri got up and went to her, soothing her, and brewed a tea for her, which she made Christianne drink, lifting her shoulders so she could sip the medicinal drink. Shortly after that, Christianne fell back asleep and lay still, deep in slumber.

In the morning, I checked the teenager's forehead.

"Khepri, she's burning up." I sat up and bent over Christianne. Her face was bathed in sweat, and very pale.

Khepri came over with a cup of her medicinal tea.

"I know, I checked her just a little while ago." She lifted Christianne's shoulders. "Okay, come on, let's drink this down, little lady. You'll feel better soon ..." Khepri tipped the cup into Christianne's mouth and the groggy teen swallowed. "There we go, that wasn't too hard, was it?" Khepri gently laid the girl's shoulders back down.

I was worried.

"It's those butterfly bites, isn't it?" I said.

Khepri nodded. "I think so." She gestured around Christianne's neck and jaw. "See how the bites have disappeared, but there's now redness all around here? I fear whatever was in that venom has infected her." She looked around the camp. "No one else seems to have been affected."

I looked down at Christianne. "How can I help?"

"Bring back some fresh water, we need to keep her cool and bring that fever down," Khepri said.

I pulled on my boots, rushed off, and was back in a few minutes.

"There's a creek nearby," I said to Khepri as I set the waterskin down next to her.

"Yes, I think the shrines are built near them on purpose." She poured some of the fresh water onto a cloth, and began dabbing at Christianne's forehead.

I wandered off to see what was cooking over the fire.

"Miss." Caroline smiled as she stirred the cooking pot. "How are you this morning?"

"Fine, except I'm a bit worried about Christianne," I glanced back at the sleeping young lady.

"Yes, I spoke with Khepri earlier. I feel confident that our healer will be able to help her, though."

"I hope so."

I bent and inhaled the fragrance of the food. "What's for breakfast?"

"Oh, nothing special, just reheated rabbit stew, but I found some new herbs this morning down by the creek. Khepri said to check with Jim, who said they were okay. So, I added them in." She shrugged happily.

"May I?" I asked.

"Sure!" Caroline reached and handed me a spoon. "Here you go."

I dipped the spoon into the pot and lifted out a fragrant, steaming bite of food. Sniffing it, I confirmed it was going to be good.

It's hot.

I blew on the delicious-smelling morsel, then popped it past my lips. A delicious flavor filled my mouth, and I closed my eyes in pleasure.

"Mmmm!"

Caroline grinned.

"It should be ready in about ten minutes." She gestured at some wrapped leaves on the coals. "And look, I've cooked lammas bread!"

"How did you manage lammas bread, Carrie?" I was astonished.

"I found some grain growing down by the creek yesterday, and I gathered a bag of it. Not sure exactly how it'll taste, but we'll see." She winked at me conspiratorially.

I laughed.

"I can't wait," I told her.

Jim came walking into camp, and handed Caroline a bag. "Lots of berries out there this morning." He smiled.

"Ooh, thanks. These will be great with lunch." She took the bag from him and began humming to herself.

I walked over to Jim, to speak to him quietly.

"See anything out there?" I whispered out of the corner of my mouth, looking the other direction.

"No, everything is quiet and normal." He gripped my arm for a second, then rubbed it and gave me an understanding look.

I knew it would take a long time to get over Tam's death. I just wished for no more nightmares. Those I could do without.

I walked down by the creek a second time, taking extra time to wash up this time.

It was a beautiful morning. I was able to see quite far down the mountain, as the sun slowly rose in the sky.

"AIEEEEE!"

Having bent over to wash my face, I jerked upright.

That sounded like Christianne.

I raced up the slope and into camp. Everyone was crowded around the teenager.

I pushed my way through.

"What's up ...?" My voice died and I stared in surprise.

Christianne was sitting up in her blankets, her eyes wide with fear. Khepri was leaning over behind her, examining what appeared to be multiple hives on her back.

Raised angry red bumps covered a large portion of Christianne's flesh, from her shoulders down to her waist.

"AHHH! Khepri, STOP!" the girl cried out.

I winced.

"I'm not really touching much, sweetheart, I'm just trying to see what these wounds are doing," Khepri said.

She patted Christianne's shoulder and sat back, looking at her worriedly. "There's several dozen wounds; they look mostly like hives of some sort. Almost as if you were allergic to something." She glanced at the blankets.

"Is there something in the bedding? Or inside her tunic?" I asked.

"Not that I can see," Caroline said from behind Christianne. She flipped the blanket over again and looked thoroughly, then looked up at me. "Nothing." She seemed at a loss for words.

"It hurts," Christianne wailed. She started to weep quietly.

"Well," Khepri said, standing up. "Let's get the wounds cleaned up. There's blood seeping out of some of them. I'll get my special salve. I'm sure we can have them healed in no time. Will that be okay?"

Christianne nodded and wiped her eyes.

"There we go. That's the spirit," Khepri said.

"I'll clean her back," said Caroline.

"I can help, too," Kym said.

"I'll get more water and boil it," I said.

An hour later, Christianne was bathed with water I had boiled over the fire, and her wounds were dressed with salve and wrapped carefully in clean cloth. She lay back and looked happier, although worried.

I was worried, too.

"Khepri," I whispered, drawing the healer aside to speak privately with her. "What really happened to Christianne?"

We walked some distance away.

"I'm not sure," Khepri said in a low tone. "I thought she had a bad reaction from the insect bites. Those dragonfly and butterfly bites on her face were very worrisome. This morning, the marks on her face are nearly gone, and these wounds have appeared all over her back. But the insects did not bite her anywhere near that area." Khepri looked truly puzzled, something that rarely happened.

"Do you think it's some kind of poisoning or pathogen or something?" I asked. "Do you think she's contagious at all?"

"No, I highly doubt that." Khepri looked back in the direction of camp. "I still think this is from the insect venom. How it may manifest in the coming days, I can only speculate. I'll continue to treat her symptoms, and just hope for the best, I guess." She shrugged her shoulders.

And THAT was worrying, too. Khepri was normally a very decisive healer, she always had a plan to bring a patient back to complete health.

"Let me know if there's anything you need," I said.

She nodded.

"Or anything I can do," I added.

"Keep Christianne's mind off of her pain. Read to her. Sing to her. Anything to distract her. It can only help," Khepri said.

We walked back.

We spent the day trying to cheer the teenager up.

Kym bounced around and acted like a clown, much to everyone's amusement.

I read to her from a story I'd started writing, the pages fluttered in the breeze as I held them and read aloud.

Jim made a small flute out of some reeds he found down by the creek and played a lively tune to lift her spirits.

That night, Caroline and I played out a small skit in front of the fire for everyone's amusement. It told the tragic story of a moon who fell in love with a star, and how they could never be together. Jim played his flute while we recited our lines. It was very maudlin.

Christianne loved it.

Chapter Twenty-Five

A Surprise

The next morning, Christianne was worse.

"Let me see, Christianne," Khepri pleaded.

"Nooo, it hurts. It itches. I can't move ..." Christianne groaned and curled into a ball. Her face was flushed and sweaty.

"You've got a fever. Here, let me ..." Khepri tried again.

"Nooo! Everything aches! Ohhhhh ..." Christianne moaned.

Khepri stood up and moved to the other side of the fire.

Christianne pulled the blanket over her head and rocked back and forth, groaning.

"Jim, can you pick her up? Take her down by the creek to wash her off. Maybe I can examine her there while she's in the water. It will help bring her fever down." Khepri whispered to Jim, "You've always had a way with her." Khepri pleaded with her eyes.

"Of course," answered Jim.

"I'll help. Let's go," I said, walking back over to the ill teenager.

Jim bent over his friend, and laid his hand on her shoulder. "Christianne, sweetheart, let me take you down to the creek. We can get you washed up," Jim whispered.

She pulled the blanket off her head and turned to look at him.

Jim nodded, smiling gently.

"I will help you, too, Sweetie," I said beside Jim.

"Okay," she said in a small voice.

The big man bent and gathered Christianne up, blanket and all, and lifted her up into his arms.

She groaned as he lifted her.

Her bodyaches must be terrible.

We all made our way down to the creek, and Jim got right into the water and held her there as she looked around.

"Let me get this blanket off, honey," Khepri said gently.

"Okay," she said.

We peeled the sweaty cloth off of her. Underneath she wore her sleeping tunic over her underwear. The short, loose, blousy nightshirt came to her knees.

"Do you want to put your feet into the water?" Jim asked.

"Okay," Christianne's voice was small and quiet.

"Can I look at the hives, Christianne? To see how well they've healed with the salve?"

"Okay," Christianne said.

Khepri and I lifted her shift in the back so we could examine the welts on her back.

Jim held her arms and shoulders up, and turned his head.

Always the gentleman.

"Do they hurt, sweetie?" asked Khepri. "Do they itch at all?"

"N ... no, they ... they don't hurt really ... it just feels weird ..." Christianne said.

Khepri lifted the cloth up off her back and shoulders.

"Hmmm," I said.

Khepri didn't say anything, but took a long time examining Christianne's back.

The welts were gone. In their places were two raised red vertical lines reaching from high on Christianne's shoulders, down to mid-waist level.

Huh. That's weird.

Khepri finally spoke. "Christianne, would it be okay to splash water on your back a bit? Just to clean it? I think you must be sweaty, dear."

"Okay."

"And feel free to wash your face, too," Khepri said.

Jim turned to the side to allow the girl to splash her face and rub some water in her eyes.

"I'll bet that feels good, huh?" I asked.

Khepri dipped a cloth in the creek and drew it across Christianne's back, then repeated the motion several more times.

"It's cool," Christianne said, sounding calmer.

"Water is always nice," said Jim. "I bet you'll be feeling better in no time."

We finished up with the examination and water application, and Christianne was settled back into the fresh blankets Caroline had arranged for her, new salve applied and cloth wrapped around her. None of us said much. It was clear that Christianne wasn't getting better, but that her infection was changing.

How it was changing, we had no way to know.

Christianne had a rough night.

I took first watch, as usual.

I'd never needed much sleep, and I was a natural night owl.

I watched as Christianne tossed and turned for hours, groaning and talking in her sleep.

Maybe her bodyaches are subsiding, since she's moving around so much.

Khepri got up several times during the night to check on her and reapply the cool, wet washcloth across Christianne's forehead.

When Kym came to relieve me for second watch, we didn't say a word, just gave each other significant looks after glancing at the sick teenager.

I settled down to sleep shortly before two in the morning, and the sound of Christianne moaning in her sleep followed me into my dreams ...

A low, heavy fog rolled in, thick and moist, on the morning of the third day of Christianne's illness.

"Wow, this is ridiculous." Kym's voice reached out and penetrated my sleepy mind.

I opened my eyes and saw what she was referring to.

"Khepri?" I mumbled sleepily.

"I'm here." The healer's voice came from my other side.

She must be tending Christianne.

"How's she doing?" I asked.

"Well, better, I think. Her aches seem to have abated. She's sleeping now," Khepri said.

I pulled my boots on and stood up.

"When did she finally settle down?" I asked.

"About an hour after you fell asleep. I stayed here beside her; seemed to be a time saver," Khepri answered.

"Did you get any sleep?" I asked, rubbing my eyes.

"About four hours, give or take."

"Oh, wow, so she slept that long, too?"

"Yes."

"That's good." I stretched, yawning.

Khepri turned and walked toward the creek.

We settled down for an easy morning, waiting for Christianne to wake up.

"Ssssssss," came the sound.

"What is that?" I turned my head trying to located it.

"I didn't hear anything," Kym said.

"You're kidding," I said.

"I heard it," said Jim.

"What's up?" Caroline asked, walking up with a bucket of fresh water.

"Charlotte heard a sound." Kym said.

"What did it ..." Caroline's eyes opened wider.

"Sssssss."

"I heard it then," Kym said.

"Me, too," Caroline said.

Khepri walked up from the creek.

"Khepri," I whispered. "Listen."

We all fell silent, trying to hear the odd noise again.

"What?" Khepri said.

"Shhhh," said Kym.

Jim knelt by Christianne.

"Sssssss."

"It's over here," Jim said.

We gathered around Christianne.

"Should we wake her?" Caroline whispered.

"I'd rather not," said Khepri. "She had a rough night. She needs all the sleep ..." Khepri fell silent as the odd noise began again.

"Sssssss."

"That's coming from Christianne," I said, kneeling down and putting my hand on her shoulder.

"Christianne?" I said softly.

The teen murmured in her sleep and sighed.

I put my head down low and waited.

"Sssssss."

Hmmmm.

"Where's it coming from, Charlotte?" Kym whispered.

"Not sure," I put my finger to my lips and turned back to Christianne.

"Sssssssss."

That time, my hand on her shoulder felt a vibration.

What the ...?

I gently turned her over onto her stomach, and pulled down the blanket wrapped around her.

OH!

"Oh, my God!" Khepri whispered, kneeling down and examining Christianne's back.

"What are those?" Jim said.

Wings. They're wings.

"Ssssssss."

The sound was a rustling coming from the two cracks going down Christianne's back. Two wings were peeking halfway out of the cracks, vibrating with almost a buzzing noise as they fought to emerge from the long, red fissures on her back.

"Ssssszzzzz."

Suddenly, the two cracks broke all the way open, a sticky residue parting, to allow four wings to break through the skin completely.

The damp, curled translucent wings dropped out of the fissures and fluttered there, expanding slowly.

Christianne was stirring.

The sight before me rendered me speechless, but Khepri was examining the wings and the cracks, careful not to touch the wings themselves.

Kym knelt on Christianne's other side.

"Hey," she whispered, bending low to her friend's face. "Wake up."

"Nnnnnn," Christianne said, then opened her eyes a crack.

Seeing all of us bent over her, her eyes opened more.

"Hey," she said, yawning. "What's going on, you guys?"

"Umm ..." Caroline said.

"Lie still, honey," Khepri said.

"You, um ..." I said.

Jim remained silent, his eyebrows raised so high they threatened to disappear over his head.

"You have wings!" Kym said.

Christianne blinked. "Be serious," she said.

"I am being serious, Christianne. You. Have. Wings." Kym reached behind Christianne and ran a finger along one expanding appendage.

"Hey! That tickles!" Christianne said, shrugging her shoulder away.

The wings, perhaps aided by the movement, inflated even more and shifted downward.

"See here," Khepri said in a low tone, pointing, "the blood vessels coming from her back are flowing into the wings, helping to inflate them.

"Huh?" Christianne turned her head to the side.

She saw the edge of the wings coming from her back.

She stared at them, speechless.

"Well, I've completed my examination, Khepri said. "The infection from the dragonfly bites triggered an allergic reaction in Christianne; the wings are like huge dragonfly wings. I suppose it's a good thing they aren't butterfly wings; those would've probably been bigger. Although Christianne disagrees, she loves her new appendage. And they look to be permanent. The wings are real: They are a now part of Christianne's body, and she can move them," Khepri said, sitting by the fire. "And I'm beat." She blew air out of her mouth and rubbed her eyes.

"Here," Caroline handed her a bowl of stew.

"Is there any lammas bread left?" Khepri asked.

Caroline reached into a bag and withdrew a flat square. "Here you go."

"Khepri, did you say that she can move the wings?" I asked.

"That's what I said, yes." Khepri looked at me with a smile.

"Are they dangerous?" Caroline asked.

"Only if she tries something hazardous with them?" Khepri said.

"What do you mean?" Jim asked.

As an answer, Khepri pointed down the slope that led to the creek.

We all went to look.

"Oh, my God," I said.

Halfway down the slope, Kym and Christianne were running a race. Christianne was winning, mainly because the wings on her back were whirling and propelling her forward.

"Um ..." Caroline said.

Christianne got to the creek and fell in, face-first.

We could hear Kym laughing as she ran up to her friend.

"So much for avoiding hazards," I mumbled, smiling.

"Khepri, can they lift her?" Jim asked, curious.

Perhaps there'll be two of our party who'll be able to fly?

"Oh, no. No, the wings push her along a bit, as you saw, but she's still human, albeit a human with wings. Her bones are far too dense and heavy for the wings to lift her." Khepri glanced at Jim. "And before you ask, the djinn can fly through his use of magic. Yes, that's right. Surprise! Djinns are magical creatures." She looked back at Christianne, now splashing and laughing with Kym, her wings fluttering in the air. "Humans? Are not."

"Well," I looked out at the laughing teenager. "I guess we can start hiking again."

Chapter Twenty-Six
Lake of Fire

"I guess this is why everything got so warm," said Christianne. She turned to me, "What do we do now, Charlotte?"

I looked out over a short valley on the side of the mountain and my mouth set into a grimace.

It was a lake of fire.

Lava, to be exact.

The stone path we'd continued to follow, which curved up gently and around the left side of the mountain, had led us to several more stone shrines – which we'd dutifully lit – and then, after about three hours of hiking, to this.

We'd come around a corner in the path and had seen the white smoke again. This smoke had been hidden on the other side of the mountain as we'd slept, affording us a nice view of the starry sky. But seeing the white plumes of gently rising smoke, we had hastened our step, and the last half mile had been hiked at a jog.

Up more steps, then a stone dip, then more steps and the curve around the side, some large boulders, and ...

A lake of lava.

"Seriously, how do we get across this?" Christianne asked.

We both were standing closest to the edge, the others behind us, resting and drinking from waterskins.

I idly chewed a twig of blackroot while I thought.

"Well ..." I fell silent.

I did not want to ask Jim to transform and fly us across; that had delayed us several days while he recuperated, and had left us with a serious gap in our defenses.

Don't think of it. That path leads only to sadness.

Ugh.

I looked down at the rocks. The stone had changed to the distinct rough red igneous rock that formed when lava cooled. The shores of the lava lake were littered with tens of thousands of fist-sized rocks, nearly black, and tumbled together. It would be easy to lose your footing here.

I picked my way through them, back to the stone walkway.

"Okay," I sucked on the blackroot, thinking furiously.

How are we going to get across?

"Charlotte?" Jim walked up to me just then.

"Hmmm?" I looked over at him.

He pointed.

Oh, duh.

The stone path continued around the lake, and disappeared out of sight. Maybe there was a way around the lake that way. I grinned at Jim, and he winked at me.

Too many rocks, too many blocked lines of sight.

A half hour later we were hiking the stone path again. It indeed led us on a curve around the lake, and we could see a bridge in the distance.

"That's crazy," said Caroline. "It's like walking out onto a spit over a fire."

"Well, it might work," Christianne said.

"It had better work," said Khepri. "Otherwise, it looks like it would take several days to walk around this lava lake."

Yeah.

"Why would anyone build a bridge over a lake of lava if it wasn't easily traversed?" asked Khepri.

"Hmmm," answered Jim amicably. "The lava could've come afterward."

"Then why make a bridge at all?"

"You'd just walk over the land."

"Well, let's go see."

I was beginning to trust the stone path. It was mostly steps carved into the mountain, out of the stone granite, but sometimes it went forward in a straight path, like now. *And it had never led us wrong.*

The stone path led right up to the bridge.

We stopped at the first step.

"Well, this is it."

"It's now or never."

"Everyone ready?"

"Ready to become a crispy critter?"

"We're either going to become tonight's supper, or we'll make it across with just scorch marks."

"We could become toast."

"Toasted troupe?"

"A toasted bunch of explorers!"

"Toasted adventurers!"

"Toasted marshmallows!"

"All right you two," I said, "Cut it out."

I stepped onto the bridge. The stone was warm.

I looked down. The edge of the lava lake was maybe a dozen feet away, but the bridge arched high over it. The angle at first was more than ten percent – significant, but manageable. I took another step.

It's fine, Charlotte. Look over there.

I looked toward where my subconscious was directing me.

Oh, brother.

I glanced back at the others, grinned, and took off running.

The bridge over the lava was made of the same granite stone as the path up the mountain. A mottled grey, it was smooth – but not too smooth. When it had rained the other day, it had not become slick.

My boots gripped the surface as I ran, and my arms pumped, my heart quickening at the exhilarating experience.

The bridge was hundreds of yards across. I ran fast, not wanting to know if the stone was hot, yet waiting for my boots to heat up. I soon reached the apex of the expanse, and stopped there, breathing hard, waiting for the others to catch up.

The view was magnificent.

Bubbling lava in reds, purples and blacks, stretched away all around me.

I had no idea lava could be so iridescent.

Jim and Christianne jogged up to me. Then Caroline, Khepri and Kym.

I turned to grin at them. They laughed in delight.

The bridge was not hot at all. If anything, it was just mildly warm. A breeze blew briskly through my hair as I looked out onto the lava lake's expanse.

It was beautiful.

Okay, enough of this. Onward.

We turned to race each other down the other side, and it was So. Much. Fun.

For the first twenty yards.

As we reached the apex where it began to arch downward again, something came into view.

Something big. And alive.

Oh, no.

I heard Kym transform behind me. The chimera appeared, and stood at my shoulder, waiting.

Waiting.

The creature was blocking our path.

The bridge was about ten feet across, from side to side. The railing on the edge was stone as well, and measured about two feet high – high enough to guard against accidental falls, yet low enough that it still made me slightly nervous.

I'd been running right in the middle.

But now, this creature was in the middle.

It sat on the ground, its hands on its knees, looking at us. It looked to be about fifteen feet tall, and covered in stone-colored, rough-looking flesh.

As the last of the troupe came running up, and we stood together as a united force.

Then, the creature began to speak.

"I am the troll of the Mountain Lava Bridge, and I am compelled to ask all travelers a question before I allow them to pass," it said. Its voice was deep and sonorous, with an almost gravelly quality to it.

I stepped forward, putting my hand down, palm face back, to indicate to the chimera that she should remain where she was.

"Hello, I am Charlotte, and this is my troupe." I indicated the others with a sweep of my hand. "We are on a mission, and we need to get to the top of this mountain. Please let us pass."

Hey, sometimes polite respect works. You never know.

"Hello, Charlotte, and welcome. You may pass if you answer my question," the troll said.

I heard the chimera growl, and I saw the troll's eyes flicker behind me.

It looked like an expression of resignation.

"Charlotte, here is the question: ..." the troll began.

It never had the chance to finish.

The chimera roared, jumped forward, and pounced.

The troll let out a high-pitched squeal and fell to the side.

The chimera put a paw on its chest and held it down.

The troll began to talk rapidly, from its position on the ground.

"I never wanted this job in the first place. Hey, I was just going to ask you an easy question. And there's no real wrong answers, if you think about it. I've thought about it, you know, long and hard. Because no one wants to be bothered by a troll on a bridge, I'm aware of that. You don't have to tell me that. I was just going to ask you something easy, like 'what's your favorite color?' or something like that. You were going to answer right, no matter what, I can see that, heck, anyone can see that. I'm actually all out of riddles so you never had to worry, anyway. I actually had lots of things to do this afternoon, so you can just walk over the bridge and leave, and I can get to my list of chores. I'm really a very busy troll, one of the busier ones in these parts, you know, so I should actually be on my way. Feel free to pass, just pass. And don't mind me, I'm actually quite non-confrontational, my mother raised me to be this way. She always told me, 'Sonny Boy, confrontational trolls get stuck with swords and knocked off their bridges, so listen up and heed my words: do not be that confrontational troll!' And I always told her, 'No, Mama Troll, I will never be that way, that's why Great Uncle Troll died so young. I promise to heed your words.' And I have ever since. So, really you are all free to pass, be my guest, and have a heart and happy day traveling up the mountain. There are some really nice views up there, too. My favorite color was always blue, you know. The color of the sky. It's so pretty, don't you think? Hey, have a great time! Um, do you think you could ask your friend here to get her paw off my chest? I'm actually a bit claustrophobic, and she's pressing down pretty hard, and I was just wondering..."

The troll finally fell silent.

I had stood next to it, and the chimera, as my troupe passed by, and now it was just the three of us.

"Kym, enough." I patted the chimera's massive lion's paw as it pressed on the troll's chest.

The chimera looked at me and I swear she winked. She lifted her paw and turned and walked away.

I offered my hand, and the troll accepted it. I help it to its feet. It remained speechless, with a grateful look on its face.

Just before I turned and walked after my troupe, I leaned over to the troll and spoke in a low voice. "My favorite color is green," I said with a wink.

I patted its arm and left it there on its bridge. I hoped it didn't get in trouble with whoever had assigned it to stand guard there.

The stone path continued, and we trotted forward, reinvigorated. The path curled around, and we left the lava lake behind as we started up more stone steps.

The steps were becoming shallower and curving more than usual, and just as I was going to say something, we hiked around another shrine, lit the oil lamp at its top, and came around the bend to see a new sight.

"Well, this looks really promising, if I'm honest," said Khepri.

Rising out of the mountain, having been obscured from sight until just now, was a ...

I actually had no word for it.

"It's a sanctuary," said Jim helpfully.

"Thank you," I patted his arm, smiling.

The sanctuary rising out of the side of the mountain, was pitch black, and rose many stories high, the apex of its highest tower coming close to the height of the mountain, which curled around it in a peculiar way.

"It's almost as if the mountain is protecting the sanctuary," Khepri mused, her head tilted to the side.

"Miss," asked Caroline, "Are we going to go in now, or wait for sunup?"

I looked around and realized the sun was setting.

"Well, actually, I think we can hike over to the entrance, it might take us a while and bring us to sunset." I indicated the long stone path to the front steps of the sanctuary.

It was an optical illusion. The sanctuary was black and huge, and the path was winding, and the building actually looked at least a half mile away.

I started walking, the others following me.

My heart beat in excitement.

This is it. This is what we've been waiting for.

I didn't run, in case anyone was watching. I wanted to be smooth about it. But I have never walked so fast in my life.

Chapter Twenty-Seven
The Sanctuary

The sanctuary was made of polished obsidian stone, the edges of which were almost sharp enough to cut the flesh, I found out. We reached the black walkway that began a dozen feet outside of the door. I put my hand out as I walked past, and jerked it away as it passed over the corner of the stone.

I looked at my palm. The streak of faint red there would have been a line of blood in a few more seconds, I was sure, if I hadn't jerked my hand away.

"Ouch," I said.

I called over my shoulder, "Don't touch the edges of the stone. It's sharp obsidian, and I almost got cut." I lifted my hand, palm facing behind me, to show them.

I shook my head and continued to the door of the sanctuary, which rose to more than twice my height. It was intricately carved in a beautiful design depicting a garden: Roses crowded around leaves and butterflies carved there, on the flowers.

I placed my hand on the door and knocked, then held my breath as it opened slowly inward.

The interior of the sanctuary seemed almost pitch dark to our eyes, accustomed to bright sunlight. We all filed in and stood there, our eyes adjusting to the shadows.

Sconces were mounted on the walls, and oil lamps stood, flames flickering, on the many tables. Slowly, my eyes adjusted.

An old man, or what appeared to be an old man, approached.

I held my nose as he drew near.

Ugh.

He stank.

Pull it together, Charlotte.

My hand dropped, and I smiled.

The old man – although it was clear he was not human – came to a stop in front of us, and stood waiting.

He was a few inches shorter than I, covered in old robes that looked like they hadn't been washed in a decade, and long nails grew from his fingertips. His hands were mottled brown and wrinkled.

Eyebrows grew in bristly white hairs reaching out of his face as if searching for something. A large nose turned downward between cheeks that were wrinkled except in the middle; his mouth was ringed with lips the color of old wine. The eyes were...

Unseeing.

Behind lids just slightly open, I could see hints of the clouded eyeballs.

He carried a cane, as it were. The massive wooden stick was blacked with age and encrusted with things I didn't want to examine too closely.

His robes fell to about a foot off the ground.

Behind him, extending out from the robe, was a tail.

Again, it was clear he was not human.

"Greetings, children," the old man's voice rang out surprisingly strong. "Follow me, please."

He turned and walked into the sanctuary.

The floors inside were made of dark slate, and were cool to the touch. My boots had become used to the heated path across the bridge, and I could feel the coolness come through the soles now, in contrast.

We were quiet as we walked, and our eyes took in everything. Very high ceilings, oil lamps and torches everywhere, and the smooth slate floor.

We passed several other old men as we walked after the first one, and these others turned and walked with us, falling in behind us one by one, until we were a procession of more than twenty.

We were led to a room with a long table, with wooden chairs arranged around it, and the old man indicated we should be seated.

I glanced at Caroline and Khepri and shrugged, and we sat.

The other old men moved to sit at the table as well, and they moved slowly. It was a while before everyone was situated and waiting expectantly for the first old man, who sat at the head of the table, to speak.

But finally, speak he did.

"Greeting, children, and welcome. We," he waved his arms to encompass the other old men, "are the anchorites of the lu'um's mountain sanctuary. We guard the otoch treasure. This sanctuary is our Chúunul, our home."

He stopped and took several deep breaths, then retrieved a small bell from within his robes, and rang it.

The tinkling sound traveled far in the obsidian halls, and I heard some far-off scrabbling sound, then several voices.

I could not make out the words they spoke, but their tone was one of surprise and mild panic.

The old man waited.

I looked to the side and saw his tail lying flat on the floor beside him.

No, wait.

I saw the end of the tail twitch, then fall still again.

The voices died down, and then we heard feet pattering quickly, getting closer.

Several more old men appeared, carrying what appeared to be cups and several pots.

They dispersed the cups out among those of us seated at the table, and men holding the pots proceeded to pour out a steaming hot liquid into each cup.

"Ahh, that is better," the old man said as he lifted his cup to his lips and took a sip.

I glanced at the other old men and saw they were drinking from their cups as well, so I gave a mental shrug and lifted the cup to my lips to taste it.

It was tea.

I took a drink and swallowed, then took another drink. It was delicious.

"Now then, as I was saying," the old man continued in a clearer voice, "We guard the otoch treasure of this land." He waved his hand to encompass a wide arc.

"The outside world knows the treasure we guard as the treasure of El Dorado."

We had found the right place.

YAY!

"We have come from a faraway land, to the east, because gold coins have been dropped into the ocean at regular intervals, in a line from the coast of this land, all the way to the coast of Alkebulan. And the coins are poisoning the water. We've found dozens of sirens poisoned, and they died in agony, their insides cramping so badly that some of them tore their abdomens in their death throes. The poison inside them then spread outward into to sea, from their blood."

I sat back. *Long speech.*

Khepri spoke then. "Sirs, we have come to find the source of these gold coins and to stop them being dropped into the sea. We are worried the poison in the waters will spread, and the delicate ecosystem of the oceans will be forever affected."

The old man nodded, his hands held together in front of him, fingertips touching in an arch.

"What is the source of the coins?" asked Caroline. "Do you know?"

The old man looked thoughtful, then nodded again. "We know of these coins. They are part of the treasure of El Dorado."

"Great!" said Christianne. "Then we can stop them being dropped into the ocean?"

The old man shook his head.

My heart sank.

The whole reason we'd come all this way was to stop the oceans from being poisoned. As long as these coins kept falling into the sea, the devastation would only spread further.

"We need to stop this poisoning of the seas, somehow, some way. There is no other option." I said, my voice firm.

The old man held up his hand. "My child, it is not that we want to stop you from healing the oceans, it's that ... how do I explain ..."

Khepri leaned forward. "We figured the coins were somehow forged with a poison, imbued with it. We can smell the poison; we can see the discoloration of it. It's real!"

"We know it is real," the old man said.

"Well then what's the problem?" Caroline said in frustration.

"Let us have the treasure; we will throw it into the lava!" said Christianne.

"That's not a bad idea."

"But won't the lava get poisoned too?"

"You can't poison lava, silly."

"How do you know?"

"I just know."

"Lava is really hot. It's molten rock. It'll burn anything up that you throw in, right?"

"Well, yeah."

"You don't know what'll happen, though."

"We've got to do something!"

"SHHHHHHHH," I spread my hands out, calming my troupe.

"People, people, listen." I turned to the old man.

He studied me silently.

I raised my eyebrows.

"You can control them," he said.

"Welllll, I lead them, if that's what you mean. And that's only because I'm the ... the bossiest," I finished.

"You are not," said Kym.

I turned to her, "Yes, I am, Kym."

"SHHHHHH," Khepri's voice rang out. We turned to her. "Listen," she said. "Let's trying to figure this out."

"Okay."

Khepri turned to address the old man. "Sir, how are the coins escaping into the sea?" She raised her eyebrows and waited for him to answer.

The old men all seemed to be taken aback by us, and it was a while before the old man at the head of the table spoke.

But after a few minutes of calming silence, he spoke.

"Children, hear me. I will give you all the explanations you ask for."

He gestured for more tea, and the acolytes came forward and refilled everyone's cups.

We sat, sipping tea, for another minute.

"Now, as to your question," he nodded to Khepri. "The coins were spilled into the ocean because thieves came last year, looted the treasure, and ran off with a sack of the coins. They escaped in their ship, which was hounded with bad luck their whole way back, and death followed them the entire way. Each sailor on their ship had their share on their person, and died in one fashion or the other, all violently, and fell overboard. The bodies decayed rather quickly, as bodies do in the open ocean, and the coins were left behind. The coins' essence bled into the ocean waters, and poisoned them. They are already out there, in the seas."

He took another drink out of his cup.

We held our breath.

He continued. "The coins are slowly being called back to the treasure, and will return to it, by magic, but it will take a long time. Meanwhile," he spread his hands in a 'what can we do?' manner.

I leaned forward.

"Are you controlling the retrieval of the coins?"

"No" he answered.

"Who controls the retrieval?" I asked.

He shrugged.

I raised my eyebrows in question.

He explained. "We guard the otoch treasure. We guard it, in a manner of speaking."

What.

"What do you mean, 'in a manner of speaking'?" I asked, and I could not keep the demanding tone out of my speech.

"We guard the passage to the treasure," he said. "We guard it from ... interlopers who would ..."

"Would what?" I asked.

"Who would perish in the retrieving," he finished.

"But you said that thieves had stolen part of it."

"Yes ... they had snuck in and taken a small part of the treasure of El Dorado."

"Well, then, if thieves could get at it to steal it, it must be easy to reach."

"But most of them died getting to it, and in stealing it, they doomed their entire ship.

Oh, dear.

I rubbed my eyes.

"Okay," I tried a different tack. "How, HOW do we hasten the retrieval of the poisoned coins?"

"That you would have to take up with the creature who guards the actual treasure, up in the tower." He waved his hand vaguely behind him.

Okay, right. Now we're getting somewhere.

"Will you let us pass through to it?"

I tensed up. These old men said they guarded the treasure, would they let us pass? I mentally crossed my fingers. I did not want to have to sneak, like the thieves.

"They did not sneak, we let them pass as well, even knowing they were thieves."

What?

"How did you know what I was thinking just then?" I asked, amazed.

"We are Anchorites. We can read minds." The old man twitches his tail.

This was new.

332

I leaned forward. "If you let them through, then WHY do you refer to them as 'thieves'?"

"Because of their intent," the old man answered, sipping more tea. "They wanted the treasure of El Dorado so they could possess it, and grow rich from that possession."

Huh?

"But ..." I thought for a second. "Okay, well, how do you know we do not wish to also possess it? Well?"

The old man smiled. "Because you've told us you wish to stop the poisoning of the seas, and the deaths of the sirens. They told us they wanted to grow rich from it." He leaned forward, still smiling. "Your shipmates have witnessed the death the coins have brought to the oceans, they've witnessed it firsthand. We trust your sincerity." He sat back. "Plus, your auras are bright, while theirs were dull. Bright auras are bright because the person is not engaging in subterfuge. Dulled auras mean they are hiding something and not being honest. Your auras are so bright, they are nearly blinding."

Okay.

Kym giggled beside me.

I scowled at her, then smiled.

I turned back to the old man. "Okay, then, would it be okay for my troupe to spend the night here in your sanctuary? And then, will you allow passage to the treasure of El Dorado to us in the morning?"

The old man thought for a minute.

"Yes, I think we can do that. If you will dine with us and visit with us. We've been in here, alone, for a very long time. We're lonely."

They showed us to our quarters, and we each had a small alcove and a bed. We washed the dust of travel off, and then met them for the evening meal.

As we sat at the same table as before, more Anchorites brought us more tea, and then a meal of stew. It was delicious.

"Sir, I have questions," said Caroline after we'd been eating for a few minutes.

"Ask away, child." The old man smiled. The rest of the old men never spoke, they just smiled and nodded and ate their stew and dank their tea.

"Well," Caroline said, "you said you've all been here a very long time. How long, may I ask?"

"The current set of Anchorites have been here well over seven hundred years," he nodded. The other old men nodded in unison, I noticed out of the corner of my eye.

"Wow. So, you're immortal?"

"Well, child, after a fashion, after a fashion."

"How do you mean?" asked Caroline.

"Well, child, this tea we are drinking," he gestured at his cup, and we had the same tea in our cups, "this tea greatly increases our longevity."

You're kidding.

"Oh, my goodness!" Khepri burst out, looking into her cup.

"The tea is delicious, sir," I said, and I was telling the truth. It was slightly sweet and tasted faintly of grass and sunshine.

Hmmm.

"Sir," I said, "What is the tea made of?"

"Well, child, there is a meadow, down the mountain, you might have passed it. Once a year, on the longest day, we take a pilgrimage down there and gather the grasses, at their peak, when they are loaded with butterfly cocoons, and ..."

Oh, no.

Oh, yuck.

I looked down into my mug.

But it tastes so good ...

"... and we make the tea from the steeped grasses, and the butterfly cocoons mashed up ..."

I spat out the tea.

I looked into their faces.

Those old men were silently laughing, every single one of them.

Oh, my God.

The old man held up a hand, still shaking with laughter. "Okay, okay, my child, I am kidding, I am kidding." He put his hand on his belly and laughed silently some more, his mouth open in amusement.

I scowled.

The old man gestured for more tea, and our cups were refilled.

"My child, we collect the grasses on the longest day of the year, because that is when the butterflies and dragonflies are under the sun spell, and dormant for that one day."

He chuckled silently, smiled broadly, then said, "You should see your face," and continued to silently laugh.

I sipped more tea and smiled.

I guess I might try the same, if I was super lonely and hadn't had hardly any visitors in seven hundred years.

Khepri spoke then. "Sir, may I have a sample of the dried tea?"

"Of course, of course, my child. We will have it ready tomorrow morning, before you leave."

"I also have questions!" Kym raised her hand.

"Yes, my child?" the old man answered.

Kym sat taller in her chair, happy to speak. "What do you Anchorites do with all the time you have?"

The old man smiled. "That is a wonderful question, child. We are skilled in the arts of Harmony and

Understanding. We meditate and discuss philosophy. We create art." He gestured at the sanctuary around us.

"We sculpted this sanctuary out of the volcanic obsidian ourselves. We spend much of the day polishing it with smooth stones, which we, in turned polished long ago, to use as tools. This is how the walls of our sanctuary became so smooth. It took our order ten thousand years." He winked at us, a finger on the side of his nose. "It used to be rough."

I legitimately could not tell if he was putting us on.

The obsidian walls looked like they had been cut with a large plane, not smoothed over with little rocks.

Oh, well, who knows?

I turned to Caroline beside me and yawned. She smiled. "Long day, eh, Miss?"

I nodded.

Chapter Twenty-Eight
Dark Passageway

The next morning found us gathered in Khepri's room, checking over our packs.

"I slept really well, how about you?" I asked Caroline.

"Oh, yes, I did as well, Miss."

Khepri had double-checked that her healing sack had all its herbs and salves and ointments. She had her surgical kit as well, and was rechecking the implements.

There was a knock at the door, and a bell sounded.

Khepri went to open the entrance and found one of the Anchorites. He handed Khepri a large packet wrapped in brown paper and tied with a black string, then bowed and retreated, all without saying a word.

Khepri brought it to the table.

"This is the tea they spoke of," she said excitedly.

She carefully untied the string and unwrapped the packet. The paper was medium brown, looked somewhat waxy, and was definitely homemade. It was thicker and smelled faintly of nuts, and it crinkled as it opened.

Layer upon layer unfolded until, finally, she opened the last flap to reveal a large cache of dark green tea leaves, ground almost into powder, glittering in the sunlight coming from the window.

"This is marvelous. The old man said the tea greatly increases their longevity," Khepri said.

"Well, yes, but also remember, they are of a different species," I said. "Kym here is of very long life, and she doesn't need to drink any tea." I looked over at Kym, and she beamed at me happily.

Khepri chuckled.

"Yes, Charlotte, but I wish to study this tea to learn *why* it helps the old men to live linger. It no doubt has to do with its chemical properties and configuration. There might even be magic involved. You never know," she said happily, carefully wrapping the tea back in its packet and stowing it deep within her healing bag.

I smiled. Khepri was happiest when performing her scientific studies.

We soon gathered in the central room. The Anchorites were waiting for us.

The old man who had greeted us first led us down a passageway, through several doors, and down a long, dark corridor, to a stone archway.

Two lit torches sat in sconces on either side.

The whole effect was very serious and dramatic.

There was a sense of impending action.

We all held our breath.

He waited until we were all gathered there before the archway, then the old man began to speak.

"We are in the very back of the sanctuary here." He gestured beyond the archway. "If you follow this corridor, you will find another door, and beyond is a passage that leads into the mountain, and deep into the ground." He stopped and took several deep breaths. "The passageway is long, and heads far back and slopes downward, into the rock."

He looked at me, his eyes opened as far as he'd ever opened them in our presence. The rheumy, cloudy orbs studied me for a minute, then continued. "At the end of this passage into the mountain is a vault guarded by a beast of such terrible power mere words cannot describe it."

"Before the thieves last year, no one had ever seen the beast and lived to tell the tale."

I held up my hand with a question, and he stopped and looked at me expectantly.

"Why," I asked, "have they never been seen again? How do you know?"

He replied, "Because they never came back, and we never saw them again."

I made a face but said nothing. I saw Christianne open her mouth, then close it again.

"So how do you know what happened to the thieves last year?" I asked.

"Well, my child," the old man answered, "The gold treasure of El Dorado is enchanted. We can see everywhere it goes, and what happens there."

He held up his finger.

"One last thing," he said.

I waited expectantly.

I sensed the other old men gathered were holding their breaths.

What was he going to say?

"My child, you spoke of your belief that the gold coins of the treasure of El Dorado were somehow poisoned. That you wondered if they had been forged with some chemical, that was poisonous." He took a deep breath, wheezing. "It is not anything as simple as that, my child. There is magic involved. These coins, this treasure, was once held by a king of this land, who guarded it jealously, and wanted no other to possess it. He used to bathe in the coins every day. He had some of the gold ground into powder, and every time he returned victorious from battle, he would have his servants cover him with it. He would then go out to speak to his people, covered in gold powder, looking like a living god.

Now, he was not a god, but he did have several powerful magicians working in his court for him. They imbued the gold with special properties. For instance, the treasure was said to grow larger. Even though the king had some of the coins ground into powder to cover himself with, at least every year or so, the treasure never diminished in size. The coins expanded in number, instead. The chest they were kept in grew so full the lid could no longer be closed.

The king grew in his avarice, until one day, returning triumphant from a particularly fantastic battle against an enemy kingdom that sought the gold itself, he was so overwhelmed, and became so drunk, that when his servants came with the ground-up gold powder to cover the king, he grabbed the powder for himself, banished the servants, and proceeded to cover himself with it. And he was so drunk that he got the powder into his eyes, and his lungs, and it suffocated him."

I was speechless.

"And so, I caution you, my children. Because of its history, the gold of El Dorado is alive, it is imbued with magic. IT IS CURSED."

Oh, great.

I stared at the old man. He had finished speaking and he stared at us, and it did not seem as though he looked with blind eyes, but with his soul.

Then he and the other old Anchorites slowly retreated, down the corridor back the way we had come, and we heard the door close in the distance, and we were alone.

"Well, that was cheerful," Christianne said, breaking the awkward silence.

I swallowed hard. "Okay, listen," I looked at them all. "Let's just go, and somehow get the coins retrieval sped up, so that the cursed things are taken out of the ocean much faster. Then we leave." I looked at them. "Deal?"

"Deal," they said, almost in unison.

I think the old man's story freaked us all out. It sure freaked me out.

We turned and looked down the passageway.

"Well, I'm taking these torches," Jim said, grabbing the large wooden torches out of the sconces. He handed them out. They were bigger than ours, and it always paid to gather supplies as you went, when on an adventure.

The passageway was about four or five feet wide, and about ten or eleven feet tall.

Plenty of room, right? Right ...

Jim and I led the way. The torchlight cast spooky shapes onto the stone walls.

"I guess the Anchorites didn't get inside here with their polishing stones, huh?" Christianne joked.

"Ha ha!"

"Nope."

I put my hand out and felt the rough stone surface. "It's rough-hewn granite, I think," I said, walking forward.

"Keep a lookout for anything odd."

"Absolutely."

"After what happened on the centaur island inside that volcano, I always 'keep a lookout for anything odd' ha ha!"

I smiled.

We were a brave lot, and when we were in spooky circumstances, we liked to whistle in the dark. It made us less jumpy. *Right? Right?*

Khepri let out a scream behind me. "AHHH!!!"

"What WHAT?

"Oh, GOD."

Khepri, what is it? What happened?"

"Are you okay?"

"Khepri?

"KHEPRI!"

"Where'd she go?"

We all turned around, and backtracked. Khepri was not there.

Where had she gone?

"What is that?"

"Listen, LISTEN!" I said. "Let's listen!"

We fell silent.

I could hear a small, faraway knocking.

"Where is that coming from?" I asked no one in particular.

Jim swung around, silent. searching. I got on my hands and knees, and began searching as well.

Caroline, Kym and Christianne followed suit.

"Khepri?" I called out, then fell silent again.

I listened.

There it was again.

Knock ... knock ...

"I've found it," Jim said. He was far back in the passageway, kneeling at something on the side of the wall.

We gathered around, our torches extended.

It was some kind of doorway, in the wall, you could barely make out the seam.

Jim tried to pry it with his fingers.

"Hold on, I've got a small pick in my pack," Caroline said, taking her pack off and rummaging around inside.

A minute later, she handed me a small T-shaped pick, excellent for chopping at rocks ...

Or getting into a small seam.

I stuck the smaller point into the crack between the door and the wall, and pried ...

If this can even be called a door ...

There was a screeching sound of metal on metal, then the edge came loose.

"I think it's latched on the other side," I said.

"BY WHOM??" asked Jim.

I looked back at him. *Yeah.*

Someone didn't want us to get to the vault.

I worked at the latched door for a while, and finally got a corner of it up enough so that Jim, transformed into djinn form, could grab it with his huge hands.

He leaned back and pulled, and the metal door curled outward as he bent it. The latch on the other side popped with a snap, and the door sprang open.

I peered inside.

"Khepri?" I called.

Very, very faintly, as if from a long way away, came Khepri's voice.

"Here, I'm here!"

The djinn stuck his torch in. We could not see the end of the side passageway, but it was clear that it went down, and looked as if it curled back around to the sanctuary.

"Dagnabbit, if those Arthropods, or whatever they are, didn't want us to seek the treasure, then why on earth did they point the way for us?" I groused, and sat back on my heels.

"Maybe this is part of the challenge," said Kym.

I turned to her. "What?"

"Well, the Anchorite," she looked at me pointedly, "said that they guard people from getting to the treasure. Maybe this is part of that." She raised her eyebrows.

"Not a bad guess," The djinn said. "She could be right."

"Hello?" Khepri's voice came from far away again.

"She's probably stuck. We need to go get her," Christianne said.

"Do you think it's a trap?"

"What?"

"If we try to get her this way, it might be a trap?"

"Well, of course it's a trap. That's the whole point."

"Well, okay. I was just checking what everyone thought."

"I'm going in," said Kym.

"What? Why you?" Christianne asked.

"Because I'm the smallest, and it looks like she's in tight quarters."

"Okay. but let's tie a rope around you. It'll make it easier to get back up, for both of you," The djinn said.

"Okay."

"Not a bad idea," I winked at the djinn and patted him on the back.

We had a rope tied around Kym, and she was down the chute in few minutes.

"Don't lose the torch, Kym."

"I won't!"

It took her ten minutes to get all the way down.

"Got her!" We heard Kym's voice come up from far away. Then ...

"It's really quite filthy down here."

I turned to the djinn. "Our friend the chimera is hilarious," I laughed.

He smiled broadly.

Christianne laughed, "Ha ha ha!"

Then we waited ...

And waited ...

"Everything okay?" I called down.

"Yes," Kym's voice came up from not as far down as it had before. "We're coming up."

The djinn began to pull on the rope, hauling it up hand-over-hand.

Finally, Kym's head peeped over the top. "Hello," she said.

"Hello. Give me your hand," I said.

She extended a dirty hand, and I grabbed it with both of mine and pulled.

We soon had both of them out.

We gathered on the floor of the passageway.

"Charlotte, something grabbed me and pulled me down that chute," Khepri said.

I looked back at the open door of the chute.

"Was it one of the Anchorites?" I asked.

"I don't know. They got me from behind," she sounded worried.

"Okay, new plan. We walk together. Tie the rope around each of us, and walk hand-in-hand." I looked back the way we'd come, and raised my voice to echo down the passageway. "Whoever's playing these games, it's not funny, I don't like it, and if they continue, I'll settle things with my sword."

Kym, Caroline and Christianne all nodded.

Khepri looked satisfied.

Jim, who had transformed back from his djinn form, looked resolute.

Me? I was hoping they tried something again. I was itching for a real, honest-to-gosh swordfight. I was tired of all this sneaking around.

I scowled and glowered down both sides of the passageway.

"Now," I said, getting to my feet. "Let's get going, shall we?"

We were tied and holding hands, and marching down the passageway within five minutes. Nothing was going to stop us.

Chapter Twenty-Nine

Hyperventilating

W_e had walked for what seemed like miles, down the passageway, down into the mountain, down the dark, dark wide tunnel toward the unknown.

Nothing else tried to nab us, and we saw no more side doors, but then again, we weren't looking for them. In fact, we rather hurried, eager to get to the end and get on with the task.

"Do you think it'll be some ferocious beast?"

"I don't know."

"Do you think it's another troll?"

"Not sure."

"This isn't a bridge, so it's probably not a troll."

"What if we get to the end of this passageway and it's a bridge?"

"Well, then it might be a troll."

"You don't know."

"I know I don't know, I'm just wondering. Just making small talk."

"…"

"Do you think it's a weather faerie?"

"Kym, I don't know. None of us know. It'll be a surprise."

"I like surprises."

"Not bad ones you don't."

"Well, no. Not bad ones."

"Hey, I was wondering."

"What?"

"Do you think those Anchorites were the ones who put the troll on the bridge? As a barrier?"

"I don't know. Maybe."

"I liked the troll."

"Yeah, he was actually not too bad."

"Hey, do you see that?"

"What?"

"That light?"

"Hmmm."

"There's a faint light up ahead."

"Thank goodness, I was getting tired of this passageway."

"It's supposed to be a vault, right?"

"Yes, guarded by some kind of powerful beast."

"Hmmm."

"What?"

"Do you think it's going to be ferocious?"

Sigh

We could all see something there, up ahead. We could see it long before we got to it. In the end, I was running forward, eager.

Anything to get away from that banter.

Jim and Caroline pounded after me. Then came Khepri, running. We pulled Christianne and Kym after us.

We all came to the end of the passageway and stopped, staring.

"It's a corridor," I said, stating the obvious.

The dank passageway we'd come down, which had been angled downward and then flattened out, had ended in a corridor that split it like a "T."

This was extremely strange, because the corridor was nothing like the dark passageway. We no longer needed our torches, for one thing.

"Let's just set them down here, okay?" I put my torch on the ground just inside the passageway, and walked forward.

The corridor was brightly lit, and its sides were white.

"I think this is some kind of marble," Khepri said, touching the smooth white surface of the walls.

"Probably," I murmured, distracted. I thought I saw something up ahead.

The long, white marble corridor led to the right and left, but on the left it ended in a dead end about fifty feet in.

So, we followed the thing to the right. It curved around and slanted upward, and then around the other way, and ended at a corner, which we walked around.

I blinked. At the far end, about a hundred feet away, was something ...

"Is that the beast that guards the vault?" Kym whispered.

I nodded at her, and put a finger to my lips, then slowly walked forward.

I could not make out what the beast was, but it was covered in feathers, from what we could see as we approached.

As we got closer, we could see it was asleep.

We were fifty feet away, then forty, then thirty, then ...

"Oh, no." Jim said.

Huh?

I stopped.

I turned to Jim behind me. "Jim," I whispered, "what?"

He beckoned me back, and we all retreated down the corridor until we'd gone back around the corner and out of sight of the sleeping beast.

I turned to Jim.

"What?" I looked at him expectantly.

"That," he whispered, "looks an awful lot like a sphinx." He fell silent.

"A sphinx?" I said, matching his volume.

"Yes," he looked at me significantly.

I thought back to my time in Swerighe, under the tutors that had taught me.

Magical beasts ... Magical beasts ...

I tried to remember.

I remembered that a sphinx had the body of a lion, the head of a human, and wings.

Oh.

"So, it wasn't covered in feathers, it's just wrapped its wings around itself?" I asked.

"Looks that way," Jim answered.

"Okay, but ... Jim: why did you react that way?" I asked. "We've encountered magical beasts in the past. Heck, YOU'RE a magical beast!"

I ducked my head and apologized. "Sorry, I didn't mean to call you a beast. I meant, you're a magical creature, and we've met lots of magical creatures before ..." I trailed off, looking into his face.

Jim took a deep breath. "Look, Charlotte," he glanced around at the whole troupe. "All of you, I only mean for you to use CAUTION. The sphinx ..." At this he turned and glanced around the corner to check on the sphinx, then ducked back over.

I glanced with him. The creature, if it was a sphinx, was still fast asleep.

I looked at Jim again.

"The sphinx has the power to teleport others away, to wherever she wants."

He looked at us significantly.

I looked back.

"So? So, we'll be polite. What's the issue?" I asked, whispering.

"The issue is, they are guided by their own rules. I mean ... okay, I once had a really bad encounter with a sphinx. Just be careful." Jim looked sick.

I thought for a minute.

Khepri whispered to Jim, "Sweetie, what did the sphinx do to you?"

Khepri understood.

Jim looked down at his hands, which he was wringing, then up again. Then he spoke.

"My old master once forced me to act as a go-between between him and a sphinx, to gain access into a certain cave system that you are all somewhat familiar with."

I blinked.

"Jim, what happened?" I asked.

"Okay," he sighed and looked around, then continued. "My masters, about a thousand or so years ago, they wanted the treasure in the Tomb of Ancients. Remember that place?" He looked at me pointedly.

I nodded.

"Well, have you ever wondered how my lamp ended up inside that room?" he asked.

We waited.

"The sphinx banished me there. Took the lamp right out of my old master's hands, smacked him back and tossed my lamp over her shoulder, flung it back into some kind of vortex behind her, which flipped me far away, because we were nowhere near the Tomb when we encountered this sphinx. Anyway, she flung me into the Tomb. I actually had no idea how far it was, how she did it, or anything." He took a deep breath, which was a good thing, because he had been nearly hyperventilating. "Listen, sphinxes are tricky, and the one I encountered gave no second chances, and they can transport you far away. THEY CAN TRANSPORT YOU FAR AWAY. Do you understand?" He shuddered. "I mean, I was in that haunted Tomb for over a thousand years. A THOUSAND YEARS."

I put my hand on his shoulder. "Okay, calm down, it's going to be okay."

Jim glanced at me, his eyes full of fear.

This sphinx has really triggered him.

"Okay, let's just back up. Let's back all the way up and regroup, okay? Jim, breathe, my friend. Just breathe."

We decided to fall back past the passageway junction and regroup.

"Come on, Jim," I grabbed his arm and pulled him back.

He didn't want to move; he was so upset.

"Come on, Jim!" I pulled his arm again. "Hey, we don't want to wake that thing up, do we? Let's move back a bit."

He reluctantly got up and allowed himself to be pulled back to the end of the corridor.

"Let's just take a breather, shall we?" I sat down and unpacked some blackroot, handing it out.

We needed to calm down.

"Sit," I directed Jim, pulling on his arm. He sat down next to me. "Chew this." I handed him a twig of blackroot. He slowly put the end in his mouth and bit down.

I waited, staring at him with my eyebrows raised.

He chewed the stick.

I could see him visibly relaxing, the blackroot calming him, his shoulders dropping as the tension drained out of them.

"Feeling better?" I asked him.

He nodded.

I retrieved the waterskin from his pack. "Here. Drink."

He sipped water as I waited.

"Okay." I took a deep breath and glanced at Jim. "So, let's assess our situation." I put my hand up, and pulled down fingers as I made each point.

"First, we have a powerful magical creature. Right?" I looked at everyone. They nodded. "Second, we have information about this creature. She is powerful and has the ability to get rid of us all at the blink of an eye," I glanced at Jim.

He nodded, dipping his chin toward his chest, then raising it again slowly.

"Third, we have information that creatures like this are very mercurial. They act without warning, to the deep detriment of the person or persons they are judging, correct?"

Jim nodded again.

"Okay, everyone, give me your ideas," I said.

"I think we should go back into the sanctuary. This might end badly for us."

"We can't do that. We must stop the poisonous coins from infecting the ocean."

"They said the coins were being pulled back."

"They also said it's been over a year and the process is very slow."

"Yeah, how many sirens will die while the cleanup continues at a snail's pace?"

"If the sirens die, that will upset the entire ecosystem."

"Really? How? They're just one species. Just. One."

"Oh, don't get me started. We studied this back in Swerighe. Ecosystems are actually very delicate. Every animal serves a purpose."

"Caroline is correct. Remove the sirens from their niche, and you could affect multiple other niches. For instance: what do the sirens eat? And what eats the sirens?"

"And don't forget the rest of the sea life poisoned by the coins. You saw how they were affecting the mantas. And we don't know everything that's been affected."

"She's right. Remove the micro-organisms from an ecosystem, and you affect everything that eats them, and everything that eats what eats them, and on up."

"Okay, okay," I put my hands up. "It's agreed that we need to get past this sphinx to get to the treasure. We need to get the poisoned coins out of the oceans fast. This is not in dispute."

"But the sphinx is ..." Jim started.

"I know," I put my hand on his arm to calm him. "Listen, we've dealt with magical creatures before. I feel confident that ..."

"And if you're wrong?" asked Jim quietly. "If she waves her hand and transports you to the bottom of the sea?"

I took a deep breath.

"Then we will deal with it as it happens." I looked at him. "Look, we have never hesitated before. Even when faced with overwhelming odds."

Jim started to speak. I stopped him with a wave of my hand.

"I know you're worried. I've heard your warning. I think we still have to try." I looked toward the rest of the troupe. "What does everyone think?"

There was thoughtful silence.

Then, Christianne spoke. "I think we should try."

"Every time we go on an adventure, be it quest or assault on a fortress, we risk life and limb," said Khepri.

"We have the skills. I think we should proceed," said Caroline.

"I want to meet the sphinx," said Kym.

"Jim?" I looked at the man sitting next to me. He had an expression on his face I could not read. "Jim?"

He looked up.

"Do you want to stay here while we go and meet the sphinx?" I asked.

He looked appalled. "I think I've been absent from enough emergencies on this adventure already. I will not let you all go without me, whatever happens." He took a deep breath. "And since I can't stop you from going, I will come, too." He stood and hefted his scimitar in hand, his face resolute.

I could see he was still afraid, but we all knew that bravery was not the absence of fear, it was going forth into danger even though you were afraid.

We all stood and took deep breaths.

I nodded at my troupe. "Okay. Let's go."

We all walked down the white corridor, and to the corner. I glanced around the corner and then pulled back.

"It's still sleeping."

"Let's go anyway."

I nodded to everyone, and we turned the corner and walked down toward the sphinx.

Chapter Thirty
The Sphinx

The feathers surrounding the animal ruffled as we walked up. Then its head poked up out of them, the eyes opened, and the sphinx stood up.

The sphinx was magnificent. Her head was that of an old woman. Very wrinkled and looking very wise. Grey hair with silver highlights had been brushed out and curled down her back, reaching all the way to the floor.

Her eyes were a piercing blue, and opened wide, surveying the troupe gathered before her.

The body of the sphinx was of a lioness, different from the chimera, who had a mane that flowed down to her legs and back, where the goat hind end took over.

This was a lioness, lighter in color and sleek.

Two wings sprouted from her back, and the feathers were shades of cream and white. I tried to count how many variations I beheld and lost count.

The sight was disconcerting, the human head of the old woman atop the lioness body, and the wings, all served to present an intensely alien sight.

Her feathers ruffled as she arranged herself. Although she had just awoken, she did not yawn, nor appear sleepy at all; her eyes were bright and alert, and I wondered if she had truly been asleep at all, or just resting.

I thought about why a creature so grand might want to appear asleep, and realized she might have wanted to appear vulnerable.

We knew the sphinx was anything but vulnerable.

She was large: Her head brushed the tall ceiling above us, and seemed at least fifteen feet high. I looked down at her lioness paws and saw they were huge, a good foot in diameter.

This creature could kill us easily, but she doesn't have to: She has great magic.

She looked down on us expectantly.

I took a deep breath and stepped forward.

"Greetings, great sphinx." I bowed. "We have traveled far across the ocean, and up the mountain, to reach the treasure of El Dorado. The coins spirited away from the treasure last year have been dropped into the ocean, dribbled from this land, across a vast distance, all the way to the western and northern shores of Alkebulan, a faraway land to the east." I waved my arm waved in the direction I hoped the old continent lay.

"The Anchorites told us there might be a way to hasten the removal of the coins, which are poisoning the oceans, and we have come here to try to achieve that goal."

I took a deep breath and waited a minute.

The sphinx didn't move, didn't speak.

Caroline leaned and whispered in my ear. "Perhaps you need to ask her a question before she can answer, Miss?"

I nodded, not taking my eyes off the sphinx.

That would be hard to, she fills my whole field of vision.

I cleared my throat.

"Please can you let us pass, mighty sphinx?"

The sphinx finally moved. She bowed her head in acknowledgement and cleared her throat.

"I hear your request. I am compelled to ask you a riddle before I can grant it." She dropped her forequarters to the ground, and her head came almost level with ours.

"Adventurers, answer this riddle: What creature walks on four legs in the morning, on two legs during midday, and on three legs in the evening?"

I blinked.

Surely it cannot be as easy as this?

I glanced back at Khepri, then further back at Caroline, Jim, and the others.

They all looked at me with confidence.

Jim had said the sphinx he had encountered had flung him far away, into the Tomb of Ancients, after he had asked to gain access to it. It was possible he had already answered the sphinx's question.

Perhaps the danger lies not in giving the answer, but in what comes afterward.

Regardless, I realized the sphinx was waiting for my answer.

I straightened my back and spoke with confidence.

"The answer to your riddle, 'What creature walks on four legs in the morning, on two legs during midday, and on three legs in the evening?' is: Man — Man crawls on all fours as a baby, then walks on two feet as an adult, and then uses a walking stick in old age."

The sphinx blinked, then spoke. "You are correct. You may pass and you may ask one wish of me."

Behind me, Jim grabbed my arm and squeezed.

I remembered back to last year, when I had been enjoying an evening meal with Jim and the troupe, and we'd all been curious about how it worked, being a djinn.

Jim had invited us to ask all the questions we wanted, and had assured us he'd try to answer them.

One of my questions had been: "Can a djinn do anything? Anything at all?"

Jim had answered that, no, obviously a djinn could not free him or herself, but further, that a djinn was powerless against certain enchantments. And that the Tomb of

Ancients had been enchanted against any entry, even from a djinn.

I wondered now if Jim had been punished because, as his master's djinn, he had asked the sphinx to give his master all the treasure from that enchanted place – even though he had already known entry was forbidden.

I remembered the key the sheikh of Abdü had given me, or, more exactly, had asked me to try to retrieve.

The key in the box.

I had been able to lift it from the box, and therefore use it to gain entrance to the Tomb of Ancients.

But the djinn, asking on his master's behalf, had been unable to do so.

I looked back at the sphinx, who stared at me unblinking, inscrutable, judging.

I took a deep breath.

"Oh, mighty sphinx. Please grant us the power to remove the poisoned coins from the oceans."

Maybe we could solve our problem right here and now, huh?

The sphinx blinked and did not move. Did not twitch at all.

I asked again. "Sphinx, you said you would grant us one wish. We wish for the power to remove the poisoned coins from the oceans."

The sphinx looked away, then closed her eyes.

Huh?

"Maybe that wasn't a good wish," Jim whispered in my ear. "Watch out, she might ..."

The sphinx turned back to me, her eyes open again, and then ...

"I will grant one wish, but the wish you have asked for is not possible."

My heart sank.

Why not?

As if she could read my mind, the sphinx spoke again.

"You already possess this power," the sphinx said.

Whatttt???

"Ask a wish that you do not already possess," she said, her blue eyes blinking again.

Jim whispered in my ear, "I don't think the blinking is a positive thing. Watch out, she might ..."

The sphinx blew out a blast of hot air and looked over my shoulder. "Djinn, please stop warning the adventurer. I can hear everything you are saying. I could hear everything you were saying when you were back in the other corridor. I can hear everything the Anchorites are saying back in their dusty sanctuary. I can hear everything that is said on this mountain." She stopped and took in a deep breath, then exhaled loudly in frustration.

My jaw dropped open.

I stared at the sphinx.

She had heard us discussing her? Oh, no ...

Kym came forward then; she walked past me and right up to the sphinx, where she stopped.

I held my breath in shock.

She looked up at the grand old woman's face of the sphinx, and she seemed to look deeply into her eyes.

Then she nodded and turned and sat down between the sphinx's great lioness paws, and smiled.

"Charlotte, this sphinx is friendly."

I should have known Kym could make contact with the sphinx. Both were not only magical creatures, but leonine. Related, in some manner, to the great king of the jungle, the lion.

I watched, amazed, as Kym transformed into the chimera and sat against the sphinx, leaning into the magical creature with her great lion's head, her mane ruffle nearly obscuring the sphinx's face.

We all watched, speechless.

We all just stood there, watching as the chimera and the sphinx cuddled.

The chimera began licking the sphinx's foreleg, and the sphinx closed her eyes in contentment.

We waited.

After a few minutes I spoke.

"Kym?"

I cleared my throat.

"Kymmie? Sweetie?"

The chimera stopped grooming the sphinx, and turned her eyes on me.

"Don't call me 'Kymmie,' Charlotte."

"Sorry. Kym." I looked down.

Now what happens?

The voice of the sphinx rang out. "Charlotte."

I looked up and into the eyes of the sphinx.

"Charlotte, you do not have to make a wish if you do not want to," the sphinx said.

Khepri put her hand up.

I glanced back.

"Charlotte, how about wishing for successful passage ... um ..." Khepri nodded above her.

Oh!

I winked at Khepri, who smiled back.

"Great sphinx, I have decided on a wish," I said.

The sphinx looked at me expectantly.

"I wish for our troupe to be victorious in our quest today," I held my breath, looking into the old woman eyes of the sphinx.

She looked surprised and then amused. The sphinx turned to the chimera, her eyebrows raised in question.

The chimera closed her eyes briefly and dropped her leonine chin, then raised it again.

The sphinx nodded and turned back to me.

"Granted."

Then the sphinx looked back at the chimera and whispered, "Stay with me, child."

The chimera purred and snuggled the sphinx for a few long minutes, but then rose and, with one last touch of her paw to the sphinx's paw, she walked back to stand beside me.

Shimmering, the chimera transformed back into the six-year-old girl I knew and loved.

"Kym." I put my arm around her and hugged her, and she hugged me back.

The sphinx got to her feet and walked to the side, revealing a huge round metal door behind her. The wall around it marked the end of the corridor. This was it. This was the vault the sphinx guarded.

The door looked intricate, as if it had been forged long ago. It was grey, and there was a scene depicted on it that could only have come from the sphinx: a scene depicting an adventurer passing through a doorway into a vast meadow.

With a creak, the huge round door began to open.

It swung open completely and we saw there was a staircase rising from it.

The sphinx bowed her head and gestured with her paw that we should proceed.

I took a step past the door, and my foot was suddenly on stone.

The staircase was made of slate, dark grey, with lit torches set in sconces at regular intervals.

Looks familiar.

We all stepped through and took several steps onto the staircase.

"Ohh!" I looked back and saw Christianne had gasped, and why: the door we'd just come through was no longer there. A blank wall greeted our eyes.

There was no way back.

"Well, I guess we go onward," I said, and turned and began walking up the stairs.

Why does this look familiar?

It was Jim who said, "Hey, does this look like the steps up from the Tomb of Ancients to anyone else?"

"Me."

"Me, too."

"I see it, these are nearly identical."

"Oh, brother," I mumbled.

I started running up the stairs, pumping my arms and hopping up fast. I took the stairs two at a time. My heart was racing, and my head was buzzing.

We got past the sphinx? HA!

As I got to the top, there was a hatch. The ceiling extended across the stairwell, and the only way out was to go through ...

"Charlotte, wait."

I looked back. Khepri was straggling behind. Jim reached down and took her hand, pulling her all the way up.

We gathered there, on the stairs, and looked at the latched trapdoor above us.

I looked down at the troupe. "Ready?"

They all nodded, and I reached my hand up and grabbed the handle.

It turned easily, and a circle of metal opened upward. I had to step up to push it all the way back.

I poked my head through.

We were in a tower. I lifted myself up and swung my legs over, and stood up, brushing myself off.

We were in a narrow, circular staircase, with narrow windows looking out on the mountain.

I looked out the window and saw the lava lake and the bridge. The troll was back, sitting on the side of the bridge.

We were pretty high up, so I couldn't be sure, but he looked bored.

"Is that the troll?" Kym asked.

I turned and smiled. "Yep, ha ha!"

We were all up out of the trapdoor, so we closed it.

"Okay, this looks like it's pretty narrow, so be careful. Let's start up it." I glanced at Jim. "Might be extra tight quarters for you, Jim."

He shrugged. "I'll make it."

I turned and touching my hand to the sides, took a few steps up.

The stairs were narrow and steep, and reminded me of the stairs at the highest towers of the queen's castle back in Swerighe.

The narrowness was almost an aid, if you stumbled, you fell against the stone sides. But stone can hurt, so I was careful.

I struggled, squeezing around and up, mounting the stairs as they came, one at a time.

Luckily, the curved ascent ended after a few hundred feet or so. I sat on the top stairs, and waited for everyone else to catch up.

"Okay," I whispered. "It's another trap door." I glanced outside a narrow window beside me. "I think we're high up on the mountain, possibly at the top."

Khepri looked out and muttered, "Wouldn't want to fall from this tower; it looks like we're on top of the world."

I reached up and unlatched the door above me, swung it open and climbed through.

We were in a tower room, large and bright.

The trapdoor has opened onto the middle of the room, and after we'd all climbed through, we got a good look around us.

The room was circular, and about ten feet in diameter. There was an old wooden door at one end, with narrow windows at another.

The ceiling rose to a point, and there were bats roosting up at the very top.

I glanced at the floor and saw mounds of dried guano, with small bits of wet guano on top.

"Ugh." I sidestepped the mound and walked to the side, looking out the window. I thought I could see the ship, far off in the distance, but I couldn't be sure.

Turning to the door, I waited until everyone was out of the stairway and into the room.

"I think this is the final room."

"Let's hope it is."

"Okay, let's go!"

I nodded at them, reached out and turned the old oak door's latch.

Chapter Thirty-One
Sapientia

This final room was three times as big as the one behind us, and circular. We were still in the high mountain tower.

On one side of the room was the treasure. A huge chest full to the brim with gold coins. They spilled out onto the floor around the chest, and the gold winked bright in the sunlight that flooded in from through stained-glass windows. Colorful and bright, and beautiful, they depicted various scenes in nature.

My eyes returned to the gold.

A dragon slept comfortably atop the treasure. A lazy spiral of white smoke drifted up from its nostrils. It was snoring.

As everyone entered the room, and the door was shut behind us, the dragon stirred.

We'd seen dragons before, diving for fish off the coast of Alkebulan. Those had been larger than this one; blue and green in color, with some of them quite dark. They'd looked to be the sizes of large dogs. Perhaps fifty pounds.

This dragon was small, about the size of a cat. Maybe ten or eleven pounds. And it was gold, like the coins themselves. Its wings had been folded carefully against its back as it slept, and when it woke up it yawned, lifting the wings out and stretching them, as it arched its back and stretched its legs as well, looking very cat-like in attitude.

It glanced at us briefly, and turned around twice. Then, with a leap that reminded me of our foxes back in Swerighe, it jumped up in the air, made an arc downward, dove into the pile of gold coins ... and disappeared.

I blinked.

As we watched, we saw a coin drop from a swirl of mist near the ceiling. Plink! Down it fell onto the pile of coins that were already there in the overflowing chest.

I looked closer at the treasure mound. A few gold coins tumbled off the top and on to the floor with the movement of the burrowing dragon. Then, a moment later, all was still.

Looking around, I could see that a fine layer of gold dust covered everything. The coins, the walls, the floor, everything was lightly dusted in it.

The treasure of El Dorado ...

I took a deep breath.

A ruffling sound came from above us, and as I glanced up, my mouth fell open in surprise.

A brilliant orange-, yellow- and red-plumaged bird sat perched on a thick wooden stick that extended from above on of the stained-glass windows about fifteen feet into the room.

Its long tail dripped with thick feathers and fluttered in the air.

Kym clapped her hands in delight.

It regarded us with deep eyes.

"Well, hello there," I said.

The bird squawked and spread its wings, then extended one foot to the side, stretching it out.

"It's about time you got here," the bird said.

I blinked in surprise. I hadn't really expected it to answer me.

"Um, well, we hurried as fast as we could," I answered.

"That can be debated," the bird replied.

"Well, anyway, hello. Are you the guardian of the treasure of El Dorado?" I asked.

"I am," the bird said proudly. It preened its feathers proudly. "I am the phoenix that guards this treasure."

A phoenix!

Kym walked over to the bird, reaching her hands up to it, and groaned, "Ohhhh ..."

I looked at the bird, amazed.

The phoenix was fabled to be completely immortal, dying in flames every five hundred years, rising again anew from the ashes. We'd encountered one in the Aoudaghost oasis, where the chimera had come from.

The phoenix in Aoudaghost had not spoken. I hadn't realized they could.

I guess this one can.

"Phoenix, we have come to ask ..." I began.

"Sapientia." The phoenix said.

"What?" I asked.

"My name," the huge bird said. "Please call me by my name. Sapientia. It means 'wisdom'." The phoenix proudly preened its feathers.

"Er, oh. Sorry," I cleared my throat and tried again.

The bird asked, "What do you seek? What do you want? Do you want the gold? You can't have the gold. It is laced with a poison, drawn from its enchantment." The bird made a snorting sound through its beak. "Well, I use the word 'enchantment' lightly. It's more of a curse."

I blinked.

"I'm sorry, please, speak, speak." It fell silent, waiting.

"Sapientia, greetings," I bowed deeply at the waist. "We have traveled far, from across the sea, to this tower, to stop the ocean from being poisoned further by the treasure of El Dorado," I gestured toward the chest of gold coins, where the dragon had disappeared.

The phoenix ruffled its feathers again.

"I know why you've come. It's as plain as the nose on your face." The phoenix leaned down, its dark, piercing eyes unblinking, staring into mine. "The question is, do *you* know why you've come?"

"I've come to hasten the removal of the coins from the ocean," I repeated.

The bird shook its head.

Was it rejecting my explanation?

"What do you mean?" I asked, in spite of myself.

"I know why you have come," the phoenix repeated.

"Okay, tell me why you think I've come," I said, feeling a little frustrated.

"You have come to clear your worries. Yes, the cursed coins are part of that. But you want the treasure back. You want to possess it."

This last sentence was delivered with a knowing look.

What on earth is it talking about?

"Okay, I have questions, Sapientia," I said.

The phoenix sat back on its perch and waited.

"The treasure of El Dorado is cursed, correct?"

Sapientia nodded.

"And the coins from this treasure that were spilled into the ocean have poisoned, sorry, cursed the waters, correct?"

Sapientia nodded again, then spoke, "Well, the coins are cursed, but the poison they are leaching into the ocean is chemical. That is the curse."

"Okay. Whatever. We need to get the coins out," I said.

"Working on it," Sapientia said.

"Okay, but: not fast enough," I replied.

The bird seemed to sigh. "Each coin has to be located and retrieved. It takes a long time."

"The Anchorites and the sphinx seemed to think we could speed that up," I said.

"After a fashion," answered Sapientia.

"What do you mean?" I asked.

The phoenix seemed to ruminate on something, then: "I don't know how to explain it, really. If you pick up the coins here, the process can be sped up there." Sapientia pointed one wing in the direction of the window.

"This is getting us nowhere, Sapientia," I said, exasperated.

"Tell me about it," the bird replied.

I tried a different tack.

"Can you get the coins back faster?"

"No."

I blinked.

"Look, human, I have nothing to do with pulling the coins back from the ocean. The curse does that all by itself. That's what the curse is – besides the poison. If anyone takes the coins from the chest, they slowly return, so that no one can ever truly possess the treasure. Do you see?" Sapientia

"Okay. How do we hasten this process?"

"Now you're asking the right questions." Sapientia pointed at the chest of coins. "Remove a handful, and the rest are pulled back more quickly. Remove the whole thing, and the coins are immediately brought back together."

"Miss," Caroline whispered in my ear, "I think I understand."

I turned to her.

"We must pick up the treasure and take it away," Caroline said.

"I wouldn't advise that," Khepri said. "The poison on the coins," she glanced at the phoenix, "Or the curse, or whatever, it burns the skin. It's like an acid, remember?"

I turned to Sapientia, "We don't want to touch the coins. They will burn us."

"It was entirely unnecessary for you to repeat what she said." The bird nodded at Caroline while looking at me. "I heard her, you know."

"Sorry." I gestured for Caroline to come forward, then for the whole troupe to come forward.

They all began talking at once.

"Sapientia, do you really rise from the ashes like a newborn phoenix chick?"

"I do!"

"And can you help us move the coins so they zing back here faster?"

"I guess I can."

"And why didn't you say that in the first place?"

"If you'd been sitting here for thousands of years, bored out of your skull, you'd have some fun with your first visitors in a hundred years too, you know."

"No, I wouldn't."

"Yes, you would."

"No, I wouldn't."

"Well, you *might*. It's hard to say."

"Sapientia, tell me about the golden dragon buried in the gold coins."

"That's no dragon."

"What?"

"Are you serious?"

"I am entirely serious."

I decided to sit down while the troupe got all their questions out.

Who knows? It might speed things along…

"Sapientia, can you read our minds?"

"No."

"Are you sure? What am I thinking right now?"

I stood up. "Okay, that's enough." I walked to the treasure chest and studied it, my hands on my hips.

I turned back to the phoenix. "How do we move it?"

Sapientia flapped its wings and squawked, "I'll do it."

Caroline spoke then, as if reciting a textbook. "Phoenixes can carry immense weights, I remember!"

Sapientia pointed a wing at her. "That's right." The magical bird flew down from its perch, landing atop the gold coins. It slid down the side and grabbed the handle on the side of the chest. The phoenix flapped its wings again, and, effortlessly, it seemed, rose into the air with the chest, ascending toward the top of the room.

Coins spilled out as it went, some landing near us.

We ducked aside, trying not to get hit by the falling gold.

This is stupid.

"Sapientia! Come down!" I called.

The phoenix flew back, plopping the chest of gold back where it had been.

The dragon poked its head up out of the gold coins and made a questioning sound.

I sat down, putting my head in my hands.

The troupe fell silent.

I waited.

The phoenix finally flew to my side, and sat there beside me.

I waited a few more minutes, then spoke.

"You're putting us on, aren't you?" I asked.

There were a few seconds of silence. Then, ...

"Yes, I guess I am."

"You must've been really lonely, huh?"

"Yes, I was," said the bird.

I turned to the phoenix again. "Well, that's no reason to play games with us! Really, this is getting old."

The Anchorites had made sport of us in similar fashion. Loneliness seemed to give the inhabitants of this place a sense of humor.

At least that's something. But it does get tedious always being on the receiving end.

The phoenix hung its head.

I breathed, trying to calm my irritation.

A few minutes passed.

"Look," I said to the bird. "We've come a long way to fix this problem."

The phoenix nodded.

"One of our friends was killed on the mountain." I'd been containing my sorrow over the loss of Tam pretty well ... by trying not to think about it. But the minute I allowed the thought of him to return, the lump in my throat and the pain in my chest were back, as strong as ever.

Ugh.

Sapientia hung its head lower. "I know," it whispered.

I gathered my composure again and spoke firmly. "We need you to remove the coins from the ocean. Right now. All of them." I held my breath.

The bird was silent for a long time.

Then it rose, sighed, and gestured with its wings.

Suddenly, gold coins started pouring out of thin air, from a spot directly over the treasure chest, about six inches from the rest of the mound of coins.

They were wet. Oh, my god, they weren't only wet, they were slimy.

"Ewww," Christianne said, stepping back.

Some of the coins had seaweed stuck to them.

They started coming down faster.

"Back up, BACK UP!" I said, scooting my rear back hurriedly, until I hit the wall behind me.

The phoenix hopped back to the edge of the room.

It took a long time for all of them to drop back down onto the pile, where they belonged.

I noticed that as soon as the coins had hit the rest of the pile, the slime and wetness began to evaporate, until, a few minutes later, the gunk had vanished.

Finally, the dribble of coins came to a stop.

We had watched the whole procession, and we made sure none of the cursed coins touched us.

When the returning treasure finally came to a stop, I just stared at the overflowing chest, mesmerized.

The coins that had come back from the depths of the ocean had put another three or four inches on top of the pile – which delighted the golden dragon. It rose up out of the coins as if they were water, then dove back in, and continued to play like that for some time.

I turned to Sapientia. The phoenix looked very sad. "I suppose you're going to leave now," it said in a small voice.

"You were trying to keep us here as long as you could, weren't you?" I asked.

"Maybe."

I took a deep breath. "Is that all of the coins?"

It nodded.

"There are no more anywhere else? Not in the waters or anywhere?"

"No." the bird answered.

"And the poison in the ocean waters?"

"Gone. It was a manifestation of the curse on the coins. When they were pulled back, the poison disappeared from the water."

"Good."

I rested my back against the wall.

Sapientia didn't move.

I thought of something.

"Sapientia, what did you mean when you said, 'that's no dragon?"

"I meant, that's not a dragon."

I sighed. "Okay, but ... it looks like a dragon."

Sapientia nodded.

"But it's not a dragon?"

"No."

"Then what is it?"

"It's the spirit of the coins."

I blinked and looked at the little golden dragon, or whatever it was, playing in the gold treasure.

"Are you kidding me?" I asked.

"No. Yes."

"Sapientia, you know what I would like? I would really like a straight answer from you." I said.

The phoenix squawked repeatedly and ...

Hmmm ...

"I think it's laughing, Charlotte," Kym said, walking up to us and sitting down next to me.

I tried again. "Sapientia, is that a dragon or isn't it?"

The bird remained silent.

Jim walked up to the treasure chest. "Dragon, come tell her," and held out his arm.

The golden dragon jumped from the coins to Jim's arm, and he carried it over to me.

I watched the dragon as he approached with it.

The creature began to fade as Jim came closer to me, or, I actually realized, as he drew away from the treasure chest and the gold coins of the treasure of El Dorado.

Jim stopped before me, and the little dragon was almost transparent. It looked at me sadly and chirped, then hiccoughed, and a small spark of fire shot from its mouth.

I looked at Jim. "Put him back. He's sad this far from it."

Jim nodded and took the dragon back to its coin pile. He extended his arm, and the dragon leaped back onto the treasure, and curled up on the top, putting its head on its folded paws.

So much is so new to me.

I turned back to the phoenix.

"Sapientia?"

The bird looked at me.

"Were you just putting me on when you said you knew why I had come and that it wasn't about getting the coins out of the ocean?"

"No."

"You were not putting me on?"

"No, I was not."

"So, what did you mean then?"

"I meant that you came up to the top of this mountain for the treasure, but not this treasure." It gestured with its beak at the coins overflowing in the chest.

"The treasure of El Dorado? It's cursed. And before I knew it was cursed, I thought it was poisoned. I never wanted to take this treasure," I said.

"No, you didn't."

I sighed.

I felt the phoenix's feathery wing tap my cheek. "Hey," Sapientia said.

"What?" I asked.

"It's not that hard. You just don't know your own heart." *This bird speaks in riddles.*

"Okay, what treasure did I come here for, then?" I asked.

"You came for your heart's desire."

Chapter Thirty-Two
The Gift of the Phoenix

The coins had been removed from the ocean. So, I led my troupe back down the staircase, down the winding tower, down the wider staircase, and out the vault door, which had reappeared, where we met the sphinx again.

"Find it?" she asked.

"Yes."

"Coins out of the ocean?"

"Yes."

"Then why the long face?"

I turned to the sphinx and looked into the old woman's face. "That phoenix was a trickster. I'm not sure we can trust it."

"Sapientia? Yes, that bird's nature is to try to fool you," the sphinx said.

"So how can we be sure the coins are all out of the ocean?" I asked.

The sphinx thought for a moment. "Well, I don't think he lies, he's just a trickster. A joker."

I nodded, still unsure.

"Did you leave it up in the tower treasure room?" the sphinx asked.

"Yes. I didn't know what else to do."

"I think it's lonely up there. I know it's lonely here in my corridor."

I nodded.

"Being powerful magical creatures does not make us immune to loneliness," the sphinx said sadly.

"I would like to help you both, but I don't know what I can do," I said.

The sphinx rose to all fours and stretched, arching her back. Her leonine tail shivered in the air. She sat back down.

"Why don't I walk you all out?" the sphinx said.

"Can you fit?" Caroline asked next to me.

Kym lay her head on the sphinx's side and closed her eyes.

"I can fit anywhere," the sphinx said.

"Can the phoenix come, too?" Khepri asked.

"I don't see why not," the sphinx said.

Jim ran back through the doorway and up the staircase. We waited.

About ten minutes later, he came back down, and flying after him was the phoenix.

"Sapientia!" Christianne smiled.

"Sphinx," said Sapientia. "I was told you said I could come down?"

"Yes, Sapientia," said the sphinx. "We are going to walk these adventurers back down through the sanctuary and out to the lake of lava."

Caroline sat up. "The Anchorites tried to mug Khepri! OH!"

The sphinx turned to her, "Did they, now? They might have been trying to keep you from getting to me, you know."

"What do you mean?" Khepri asked.

"Nothing," the sphinx said, a small smile on her face.

The troupe, the sphinx, and the phoenix all followed me out of the passageway and into the sanctuary. The sphinx had somehow shrunk down and fit into the passageway; how, I wasn't sure. But fit she did.

If Jim and Kym can grow and shrink at will, I suppose the sphinx is able to as well. I envy these magical creatures. Well, sometimes.

We emerged into the sanctuary and looked around.

"Hello?" I called out.

No one answered.

"Maybe they're hiding?" Christianne said.

This was weird.

We visited the gathering room where we'd all eaten, then the rooms we had slept in. The Anchorites were nowhere to be seen.

"Where do you think they went?"

"Do you think they're hiding?

"Maybe they fled?"

"No idea."

"This is weird."

"Oh, well."

We all walked through the massive front doors and onto the stone path.

It was afternoon still, the sun was barely descending in the sky.

We walked out to the lava lake and stopped.

I turned to the phoenix and the sphinx. "Can you come all the way down the mountain?"

"We could, but I think we might just remain here," the sphinx said, sitting back on her haunches and lifting her face to the cool breeze that blew passed.

The phoenix, perched on her back, lifted and spread its wings, then stretched its head down low, and squawked.

The sphinx opened her eyes.

"Sapientia?"

The phoenix folded his wings back into place and lifted its head high. "Yes?"

"Did you make their wish come true?" the sphinx asked.

"Not yet," the bird answered.

My eyes widened in alarm. "What?!"

"Well," Sapientia said, "I got the coins back. I just didn't give you what you came for."

"Phoenix master, why do you tease them?" the sphinx asked.

"Because it's in my nature."

"That's a poor reason, if you think about it."

"I don't care. It amuses me."

"Think how amusing it will be when you finish the task."

The bird sighed. "I guess so." It turned to face me. "Charlotte."

"Yes?" I asked, bewildered.

"What does your troupe desire most?" Sapientia asked.

"Oh, stop it. Even I grow weary of your sidestepping word games, bird," the sphinx said, her eyes still closed, her face turned up to the sun. "Goodness, I forgot how wonderful the sun was."

"What are you talking about?" I asked.

Sapientia turned to me. "You all want something. It's the same in all of you. I can sense it, and, as the guardian of the cursed treasure of El Dorado, I have the power to grant this desire. But I can't tell you what it is."

The sphinx sighed loudly.

"It would be so much less fun!" The phoenix protested.

"Whatever," said the sphinx. "Just get on with it. The day grows long, and we must be returning."

"Very well." Sapientia turned to us.

"Your heart's desire changed as you came up the mountain, you know," the phoenix flapped its wings. "It's as obvious as the nose on your face."

"Huh?" Khepri said.

Jim slowly started smiling, "Ohhhh ..."

"Shhhh, djinn, don't give it away," Sapientia said.

Jim opened his eyes wide and gave the phoenix an inscrutable look.

We just looked at the phoenix, and then saw the sphinx was shaking her head.

The phoenix continued: "It is a far, far journey back to your ship. It is long and arduous. There is the ice wall, and the cyclops is still hunting. I can carry great weights. I can carry you back to your ship. Would you like that?"

"Oh, my God, yes."

"Yes, please."

"YES."

"Let's go!"

"How will you carry us all?"

"When do we leave?"

Sapientia made a bird-like sound like a chuckle, and spread his wings.

"Come close," the bird said.

We all came close.

"Now, hold hands. Hold tight," the phoenix instructed.

"Is there magic involved?" Khepri asked.

"Well of course there's magic involved," said Sapientia. "Just hold on tight."

We waited, my hands clasped tightly with Caroline on one side, and Christianne on the other. At the front of the line, Kym held Jim's hand, and he held his hand up, waiting for the phoenix.

"Now," said Sapientia. "Think of the treasure you desire ..."

What? The treasure was cursed. We didn't want it ...

Sapientia spoke again, "Think of what you treasure, think of your heart's desire ... think ... "

I heard feathers beating against the air.

"... Keep your eyes tightly shut ..."

I scrunched my eyes tight.

I felt myself lifted off the ground.

OH!

The sensation was ethereal. I did not feel the weight of Christianne tugging on my hand, but I felt my hand tightly gripping hers. It was enchanting! I felt us rise, and rise farther, up and up into the air, then the motion changed and we were moving forward ...

I opened my eyes.

The phoenix was far above me, above Jim and Caroline and Kym. I looked down and saw Christianne and, below her, Khepri. The sun was shining and there should have been no shadows, but I looked and saw something hanging from Khepri's grip.

Her eyes were tightly shut, I could see. And whatever was hanging from her grip was in complete shadow ...

We flew through the air and, although I thought it should have taken a very long time, we were drawing near the ship within minutes.

I could see the sailors below us, they ran about, scrambling to clear a large space for the phoenix to land.

The large bird descended onto the deck, and I felt my feet touch the wood.

It had been strangely easy, yet as difficult as anything I'd ever been through.

Sailors crowded around us, greeting us with smiles.

"Charlotte!"

"AHHHH!"

The phoenix squawked and squawked in a kind of bird laughter.

I looked up at it in all the chaos, and I could have sworn it winked at me.

'Think of your heart's desire ...'

"TAM!" Tears ran down my face as I ran through the others and into his arms.

"OOF!" He said as I almost knocked him off balance. "There now, Princess," he said, a gentle smile on his face.

"Tam! I saw you ... I mean, we all thought ... Oh, God! It's good to see you!" I burst into tears.

Khepri walked up then and begin to examine Tam. "Hmmm, let me check ... now that's interesting ... yes ..."

Greta jumped onto Caroline. "Mama!"

"Oh, child, I missed you!"

I laughed in happiness as tears ran down my face.

Tam took me aside, and held me, hugging me tightly. Then he pulled away enough to look into my face. Tears glistened in his eyes. "I thought I'd lost you forever," he said.

"You thought? I thought *I* had lost you! I had terrible nightmares and ..."

"I tried to reach you," he whispered, and nuzzled my cheek.

"Oh, Tam, I knew that was you!" I began to cry again.

"Hey now," he said, wiping my eyes with a handkerchief. "It's all right, lass. It's going to be all right. Shhhh."

I could not stop crying.

Finally, Tam just held me to his chest and gently rocked back and forth.

After a short while, I lifted my head and looked for Sapientia. Kym was holding the phoenix and stroking its feathers, and the bird had an absolutely ecstatic look on its face.

I walked over to them.

"Thank you, Sapientia," I whispered, hugging the bird, as Tam stood behind me, his arms around my waist. He had not let go since that first embrace.

"Oh, my goodness, I feel pampered. I may never leave this ship," the phoenix squawked in laughter.

The clear sky thundered resoundingly, the rolling sound carrying on for over a minute in the deep blue expanse.

"Okay, okay, I'm coming." Sapientia nuzzled Kym and fluttered its wings, then rose slowly into the sky and flew away.

We watched the magnificent phoenix fly back toward the mountain, then I turned to Tam and did something I had been dreaming about for the last year.

I stepped close to him, and kissed him.

We slowly walked back to my cabin, arm in arm. I wasn't willing to ever let go of him again.

I turned my head and smiled as I heard Greta's voice exclaim in delight, "YOU HAVE WINGS?! HA HA HA HA HA!"

Dear reader~

I'm so glad you read The Lost Treasure and I hope you loved it. I do hope you'll consider leaving a review. It means so very much to hear what you think.

Get book 4 of the series!

The Pirate Prince
On sale September 1st 2019!

Here ends The Lost Treasure, the third book of The Paladin Princess series. The fourth book will be called The Pirate Prince.

ABOUT THE AUTHOR

Samaire Wynne grew up in a lot of different places, and now happily resides on the East Coast, laboring away at writing stories every day. She is an animal lover with far too many pets, yet she still muses how she'd like to add even more. A lover of all things night and gothic, she also loves to read and reread her favorite books. Owned by a cat named Tyrion, she can be found haunting the shadows and mists that hang low over the hills of southern Virginia.

www.ingramcontent.com/pod-product-compliance
Lightning Source LLC
Chambersburg PA
CBHW020636020726
47494CB00001B/219